First published 2001 by Prowler Books,
part of the Millivres Prowler Group,
116-134 Bayham Street, London NW1 0BA

For more information: www.zipper.co.uk

A catalogue record for this book is available from the British Library

ISBN 1 902644 44 1

Printed and bound in Finland by WS Bookwell

BOYCAM

Sam Stevens

PROWLER BOOKS

The Idea

The television phenomenon that was Boycam started in a small office, in the heart of the Central London district called Soho. The sounds of traffic permeated the poster-covered walls but were studiously ignored by the room's occupants. In fact they had become so accustomed to the noises from the world outside that they had ceased to make any impression on their acute hearing faculties. Seven men sat around a large glass-topped table drinking coffee, dense, creamy mocha-chinos, flicking through a variety of glossy magazines, their chattering voices commenting on the new hairstyles of the rich and famous, jealously admiring the décor of their fashionable residences, looking for a picture or a comment that would provoke a fresh idea.

Matt Tavistock, the manager of the production company, MEN4U TV, sat watching the other six, all highly experienced in the world of television, and all desperate for a success, something to really get the new gay TV channel, 'Gay-Per-View', off to a flying start. MEN4U TV was Matt's baby. He had started it up two years ago and watched it grow and flourish with the innate pride of a doting father. It was a success story in the heady and fickle world of television production. But it now needed something highly individual and exciting to herald the launch of the new hardcore pay channel. He glanced up at the mirrored wall he faced, and ran a hand through his luxuriant hair, smiled at himself with the confidence of an attractive man and waited. He waited for one of his team to speak – to produce that vital spark of an idea. The idea that would catapult this company into the stratosphere of television triumph and make them all exceedingly wealthy.

'How about a docu-soap?' Christopher Klein asked the room. The only answer was a sea of raised eyebrows. 'No, I'm serious. We could follow some single gay guys living their lives, watching them work and play, and see how they behave out cruising.'

Chewing languidly on the end of his pen, Matt gave a wan smile. 'I don't think so. The public is fed up with this kind of reality TV programme. With cameras intruding into private lives, watching every move, analysing everything...giving simple actions greater significance for the sake of some cheap TV. Do we really want more programmes full of airport offices peopled by screaming non-entities, or watching some daft old biddy learning to drive? I think not.'

A chorus of nodding heads showed their agreement.

'Er...could I make a suggestion?' Dick Griffiths cleared his throat and waited for the complete attention of the others. 'We could go for broke and do the ultimate in reality TV.'

Matt cocked his head. He knew he could rely on Dick. Ever since he had joined the production company, his razor-sharp brain had provided some brilliant programme ideas. His wit and good humour had endeared him to all and he hadn't let the company down in any way. A real asset, and here was another idea.

'What do you mean by ultimate?' Matt asked.

Aware that the rest of the room was hanging on his every word, Dick spoke slowly and assuredly, instantly forming creative mental notions and speaking them out loud as he went.

'The ultimate real life show. We get a bunch of strangers, say eight or ten of them...gay men, who have no previous knowledge of each other, and put them together for an extended period in some unreal situation...like a big house, and watch them for twenty-four hours a day.' He paused, scratching his nose thoughtfully.

'Yes...go on...' Matt was intrigued.

'We have cameras all around the place, so there's no privacy. We watch their attempts at interaction, how they get on with each other, and at the end of every week they vote one of the group out of the house, until eventually we have one left, who'll win some money...I don't know...ten grand, for example. We could advertise in the gay press for participants, pick eight or ten really fascinating guys, a good cross-section of the gay community. Each one could send us a video diary of himself, describing his life and loves, including telling us all about his sex life...there could be a list of stuff they'd have to tell us, 'cause we'd need guys who weren't prudes, then we could just sit back and watch the fireworks.'

An excited babble broke out amongst the seven executives, all clamouring for more information or to add their slant on the project.

'Calm down. This needs some thinking about.' Throwing down his pen decisively, Matt gave Dick a huge smile of encouragement. He could picture it already. Hidden camera footage of hunky guys, living in an extreme situation, and with luck they'd end up becoming close friends and even lovers. The ratings would soar. He liked the idea. No...he loved it.

He grinned at Dick. 'Can you get together a plan? Rough budget particulars, location ideas, fill out the details for me? This is very interesting. We'll meet up again on Monday, and see what you've come up with. If all goes well, this sounds like what we've been after. It could be a ratings winner, and could be fucking horny too!'

VIDEO APPLICATIONS

Colin Crisswell

'Hi! My name's Colin Crisswell. I'll try to answer all these questions on the list as best as I can, so here goes. Well...I am twenty-four and live in London – in Walthamstow, actually. I work as a clerk at a firm of accountants in the City. The job is OK, I guess, a bit boring at times. I was born in Birmingham, but have been living in London since I left college. What next? Oh yes, you want me to describe myself. Well, as you can see I'm quite tall, fair haired. I work out a bit so I'm quite muscular. I think I'm quite good looking, and others have told me they think so too. Although I'd quite like to be a bit leaner...not so chunky, if you know what I mean. Although I know that there are plenty of guys out there who like their men to have a bit of meat on their bones. Now where is that list of questions? Here we are...

'What are your hobbies? Hobbies...well, I love going to the cinema. I'd go every night if I could afford it. I love Tom Cruise...he's fucking gorgeous. Sorry, am I allowed to swear? Anyway, I'd give him one any day. I like science fiction. I'm a great Star Trek fan. I go out clubbing every weekend, usually into Central London, trying different bars and clubs until I find one I feel comfortable in. I do usually get off with someone...although I'm not a slapper...cross my heart and hope to die. But I do love sex. I'm versatile really, although I'm probably more a top than a bottom, and love being sucked, but then who doesn't?

'What do you dream about in your quiet moments? Wow, that's a tough one. I suppose I'd like more money, to be able to live comfortably, without worrying about bills, and to have enough to treat myself to little luxuries. I am on the lookout for Mr Right, but then isn't everybody? I like having someone about, you know. Someone to chat to about the day's goings on. I still haven't found him yet though.

'What aspects of your life do you find frustrating? Hmm, well, I hate having to go the launderette. It is so depressing sitting there, watching your knickers going round in the wash, surrounded by old ladies who smell of pee. I hate travelling on the Tube. And I wish the working day started later, because I'm really a night owl. I just can't stand having to get up at the crack of dawn every day.

'What else do you want to know? Describe your most memorable sex. Gosh, that's a tough one. I've had lots of good sex, so it's hard to pick out one that was memorable. Wait a minute though…going back to travelling on the Tube…you won't believe this, but I did once have sex on the Underground. Absolutely true, I swear to God. I was on my way home from work one night, and the Tube was packed as it always is at rush hour. I got on the very front carriage. The Tube arrived, jampacked and so I squeezed on. I was crushed up against all kinds of people, and so I just held on to the handrail and tried to count the minutes until I got home. During the next few stops I got pushed down towards the front of the carriage where there are two rows of seats facing each other and the wall with the door to the driver's compartment. So I'm standing there, facing the full length of the carriage, when a hand starts to feel my arse. I couldn't believe it! I tried to look round and see who it was, but the crush was so immense I couldn't move. It had to be the person on the very last seat by the driver's door.

'I thought I must have imagined it, but then it happened again – a good, long feel of my arse cheeks from behind. As we reach the next stop, I manage to turn around and get a look at who it is, and I see a nice-looking guy, in a suit, like me, who looks up and winks at me. I smile back because he's actually quite cute. We seem to mentally acknowledge that what he is doing is all right, and as the train sets off he starts fondling me again, running his hands up and down my thighs. Now this is all quite unnerving really, because I'm pressed against this fat woman who is carrying bags of shopping, and I don't want to cause a scene. Now as we set off, the train lurches to a halt and I'm thrown back, falling against the guy, who reaches out and grabs my cock through my trousers, and it immediately starts to get hard. I say sorry and stand up again, moving in closer to him so that my crotch is right next to his face. Then he starts again, feeling and squeezing my cock, one hand moving round to the back again on my arse. I'm petrified that someone will see, but the carriage is so crowded that no one notices. I start to get a hard-on and so shuffle around a bit so that it doesn't bash into the fat woman next to me. I spread my legs a bit more and I feel his hand slip casually inside my zip. At the next station even more people get on, and so the whole thing is starting to get quite claustrophobic.

'Deciding to go for it, I manage to turn round so that my crotch is facing him. I look down and can see his eyes staring up at me, and he has a mischievous twinkle in them. Leaning his head forward, he starts to nuzzle into my cock, his hands massaging it and gripping it tightly. Then I gasp as he starts to suck me! It was unbelievable. He took me in his mouth right there, with all those people around. No one seemed to notice, so he really went for it, taking me right down to the back of his throat, and I'm not small, let me tell you...

'His other hand is playing with my bollocks, pulling on them, and I let out a moan of appreciation, which I have to turn into a staged fake cough, so as not to give the game away. My heart is beating in my ears, and I'm really sweating, my shirt sticking to my back by now. This is so fucking erotic. I just let him do me...sucking hard, licking around my cock-head, then swallowing the whole thing down. I actually think it was one of the best blow jobs I've ever had. I feel like

I'm going to shoot, and so I try to pull back. He doesn't let me...and carries on sucking even harder. With a huge effort not to show any reaction, I shoot down his throat, and can feel him sucking it down, swallowing every drop. I close my eyes and try to stay standing. I really want to collapse in an exhausted heap. Then very quickly, he stuffs my cock back in my trousers...it's getting rapidly softer, and sits back in his seat, wiping his mouth with the back of his hand. I'm not sure, but I think the guy sitting next to him must have seen everything because he kept his copy of his newspaper across his lap, and had a huge smile on his face, giving me a wink as he stood to get off at the next station.

'I always tried to get on the same-time train and be in the same position, but I never saw him again. Pity really, as that was such a horny experience. I can't think of anything else to say, so I hope that's enough for you, and hope you'll pick me to be on the programme. Bye.'

Peter Laurence

'Is this working? Right then...my name is Peter. I'm thirty years old. I'm a Leo, and I am a fun guy. What else? Oh, yes...I'm one of twins; my brother emigrated to Australia years ago. I'm honest and hard-working, and have never been in trouble with the law. My parents sort of disowned me when I came out to them, so we don't really speak anymore. At least my brother married and had kids, so they have their grandchildren and that took the pressure off me. I studied languages at university, and now have my own business, running a bookshop. That is really as dull as it sounds. That's really the reason I'm applying to be part of the show. My life needs some excitement. I don't have a boyfriend. In fact I've never really had a long-term relationship. That's not for want of trying. I think I'm a nice guy, but no one has really wanted to be with me for longer than a couple of months. Perhaps I'm too picky? I don't know. I do sometimes have a bit of a temper and can be quite possessive. Any guy that I've been with gets the third de-gree from me whenever he's been out. I can't help it. I just need to know that he is being faithful. I do have one-night stands, and I'm not ashamed of that, and I think I'm quite good at sex. I've always as-sumed it was my relatively sharp personality and my jealousy that has put potential boyfriends off, rather than any lack of ability to suck cock, which I do quite well incidentally...I've had quite a few flattering comments on my oral talents. I guess being jealous is one of my worst traits...and will probably need working on. Anyway, I'm fairly easy going sex-wise, and will try anything once.

'My dad is British, but my mum is from Greece, which accounts for my darker skin tones. I am octo-lingual, if such a word exists...speaking eight languages. My mum insisted I learnt to speak English and Greek from an early age. That gave me an interest in languages and so I found I had a natural skill at learning them. I also speak Italian, German, French, Spanish, Dutch and Russian, and that was a difficult one, believe me!

'I now live just outside London in Watford, which is really dull, with little or no gay scene. If I want some action then I have a weekend away in London or Amsterdam. I love going to the Netherlands, because they have such an open attitude to sex. You can go to bars and clubs there, and have sex. Many of the places have darkrooms, some with slings and such, or there are saunas and jerk-off parties...it is fantastic. That leads on to the most memorable sex I ever had. It was so good it has been burned into my memory. That was in Amsterdam, in a club called The Argos. I was there one weekend, and had decided on this particular club, even though the heavy leather scene isn't really my thing. It was dark and sleazy and full of big guys, some bears, some in leather and rubber, and the bar was hung with big chains, and boots and huge dildos and stuff. If you weren't prepared for it, the place could be quite intimidating. I ordered a drink at the bar and climbed the few steps up to the upper level where many attractive, and some not so attractive men stood around watching and cruising. There was a hardcore porn movie showing on several television screens around the place, which started to get me going. They had scenes of this young guy being tied up and used by this gang of bikers.

'Along one wall were some shaded doorways, and one I discovered was a stairway down to a lower level. I went down the narrow stairs and found a warren of darkened nooks, with some private lockable cubicles, as well as one larger cubicle containing a sling, which hung from the ceiling. As I looked in the cubicle, someone pushed me from behind and shoved me forward. I fell over and grazed my hand. The door shut and suddenly the room was very dark. It was so hot, that I was pouring with sweat. The bottle of beer I was carrying dropped from my hand and rolled into a dark corner. I was roughly pulled to my feet, and through the darkness I could make out three other figures. One was quite tall and muscular, the others both a bit stocky, and one of them was shaven headed. They all seemed to be wearing leather. I was held by my arms and I was stripped naked and my clothes thrown in a heap in the corner. I could have resisted, I suppose, but part of me was really getting turned on by the whole thing. I think that deep down I have a desire to be dominated, and here was a chance to experience that.

'I let them do what they wanted. I felt myself being lifted into the sling, my legs fastened to the chains with buckled straps, so my arse was exposed. My hands were also fastened, so I lay there helpless. The other guys started to strip until they were also naked. Even through the gloom I could make out that they had very big cocks. My arsehole was slathered in something cold and slippery and then one by one they started to fuck me. I couldn't help screaming out, as each cock seemed bigger than the last, and each penetration seemed more painful. In fact when I groaned, they fucked me harder. I guess my discomfort was turning them on. I knew it was safe because they did all put condoms on. Then one of the guys pulled the cubicle door open and let everyone outside watch what was going on. I should have felt embarrassed or humiliated, I suppose, but the thrill of being used with so many handsome guys watching and wanking off was the biggest thrill of my life. I seemed to lose all my inhibitions, possibly because I was a stranger in a foreign land where no one knew me and therefore it didn't embarrass me. Perhaps I am a secret exhibitionist... I hadn't really thought about that until just now. There you are, then. I would be a good addition to the programme because I'm not afraid of showing myself up.

'Anyway these guys were fucking away, getting harder and faster, and I so longed to jackoff, but with my hands and legs secured, I couldn't. It was as if they were reading my mind, because once they changed positions, each one moved round and began sucking my cock. They were expert at it, too! Each one of them had a different technique. One of them licked at my cock, around the head and then up and down its length, not really sucking it in his mouth too much. Another one really sucked hard, like a vacuum pump, pulling it deep inside him, while the third seemed to like nibbling around, and sucking on my bollocks. The whole thing was mind-blowing, being sucked and fucked at the same time. With the attention I was getting, it wasn't long before I shot my load, screaming out as I came. The guys also quickly jerked off over my stomach, then unbuckled my hands and legs and vanished. All I could then do was wipe up, get dressed, and leave the bar, absolutely exhausted. I got lots of admiring glances as I made my way through the crowd, I can tell you.

'I hope that is the sort of thing you wanted to hear. I've never told anyone that before! Anyway, I can't think of anything else to say, so I'll stop now and I hope I get picked for the show, as I do think I'd be a great asset.'

Simon Ho

'Hello, I would like to apply to be selected to appear on your programme. My name is Simon Ho, and as you can probably see, I'm of Chinese descent, although my father is American, so I have dual nationality. I am twenty-eight and was born in New York and my family moved over here soon after. I am an only child. I live in Brighton on the South Coast at the moment, working at a gay café. I love it there because I get to meet all kinds of guys, some of whom I do try to sleep with! Although I would hasten to add that I'm not a slut! The word everyone uses to describe me is 'feisty'. I don't know what they mean by that...probably that I'm quite a character, outgoing, opinionated and with a no-nonsense attitude. I am bright and intelligent, with ten 'O' levels and three 'A' levels. I suppose I could have gone into a better job, but I just love the fact that I can go to work, do the job and then go home and forget about it. Plus it's a friendly place, and there's always fun to be had.

'I think life at the moment is OK. I'm generally happy with my lot, but I'm always on the look-out for something special and exciting, which your programme sounds like being. I love people-watching and am somewhat of an amateur psychologist. I am always being called 'Jackie' by the customers, because people think I look like a younger, more handsome version of Jackie Chan, the martial arts film star. I don't mind that, as guys seem to think he's quite attractive. My favourite music is pop, really. I love Madonna, Kylie, Cher, Kate Bush, Annie Lennox, Shania Twain...all sorts. I have just finished a relationship that lasted six months, which is quite good for me. His name was Paul, and he was a budding musician, but I couldn't cope with his extreme tempers, and so I ended it.

'I admire all sorts of people, mostly like Nelson Mandela, for all that he did for his country, and do have a sneaking regard for Mrs Thatcher. I know she did bad things, but I have to admire her strength of mind. I'm not a political animal though, far from it...as long as I have money to spend, I don't care who runs the country. Mind you, I am quite worried about the George Bush Junior administration...I reckon having him in office could mean the world is a dangerous place.

I'm quite experimental, sexually, and have had my nipples and cock pierced, and now really love the 'Prince Albert' down there! My mother doesn't approve of piercings, but has finally realised that it's my life and I can do what I want with it. I think my cock looks wonderful now, and my sex life seems to have greatly improved.

'Er...what else? What would I like to change in my life? I don't know. Perhaps more sex. My sex life with Paul was quite basic. He was the kind of guy who would lie back for a quick blow job and then roll over and go to sleep. I have an active libido and would do sex all day long if I could. Now, the most memorable sex...that's easy...although it wasn't great, just memorable. I was in the café, one evening, at closing time. This guy came in for a takeaway coffee. He was very cute. Lean, blond, handsome, and obviously interested in me. So we got chatting. He was a tourist down for a few days, and was staying in a seafront hotel. We went back there and had sex. Now I'm not kidding when I say I've never seen such a big cock! It was huge, and I couldn't get my hand round it. The head was like a cricket ball. I couldn't even get it in my mouth, and believe me, I tried. He wanted to fuck me, but I just had to say no. There was no way he was going to put that whopper inside me. I'd have been ripped to pieces. I had to let him suck me off, which he was very good at. Incidentally, he loved my piercing, and wanked himself off playing with my cock and tits.

'I don't know if that's the sort of thing you want to know. I could go on for hours about the different guys I've had, some good, some bad. But then perhaps if I get on the show I'll tell you more...'

Jost Van Dijk

'Hi there, my name is Jost Van Dijk, and as you'll probably have guessed, I originally come from Holland – a little village near Edam, actually. I was raised and educated over there, but got out from it as soon as I could. There was a suffocating village mentality that drove me mad. I moved to the UK as soon as I could. I'm now twenty-five years of age. I am unemployed at the moment, but recently worked in a telephone call-centre, selling insurance. I couldn't stand the job, so gave up and left when my contract expired. I have also worked as a waiter, an in-store demonstrator and a mystery shopper. That's someone who goes round shops secretly checking up on their standards.

'I saw your programme advertised in the gay press and thought I would apply to be one of the participants. The chance to appear on television and even to win some money at the end is extremely appealing. I could do with a windfall. I hate being poor, not having the money to do what you want. To be able to go to the theatre, or eat out whenever it takes your fancy.

'I have travelled a lot in my life so far, having spent time on a kibbutz in Israel, and on a commune in India, so I can honestly say that I am well prepared for living in such close proximity with the other contestants. I would describe myself as a spiritual person, with deep interests in yoga and meditation. I can read tarot cards and sometimes have been known to exhibit psychic abilities. I don't really have any fixed ambitions, just to be happy and successful. Does that sound trite? I hope not.

'I do have an on/off boyfriend, a beautiful sexy man called Phillipe, who shares my flat, who I love dearly, mostly as a friend...you know...a fuck-buddy, I think they call it these days. He doesn't really approve of my applying for this show. He thinks I should be content with my lot, doing menial, insignificant jobs and earning a pittance, as long as I am home in the evenings to cook his supper. I am a vegetarian, and won't eat red meat or white meat, just the occasional piece of fish, and no, I'm not a hypocrite...I just think that fish don't suffer as cows or sheep do when killed. Plus with recent scares about Mad Cow Disease and the Foot and Mouth epidemics, I'd rather stick to a good meal of vegetables.

'What would be your motto for life? Let me think... Probably, "You are in control of your own destiny". I do believe that. Whatever you do, you have to take control of your own life and make success happen. This is why I applied for the show. I'm taking a chance, and going for it.

'My favourite song is "Don't Cry Out Loud" by Elkie Brooks. It makes me fill up whenever I hear it. It moves me utterly. Thinking about all those times when I've been lonely and depressed, but have just got on with things and kept all my hurt inside.

'And my most memorable sex? I have to think about that for a moment... I do practise Tantric sex, like Sting and many others. I have tried to model myself on him and some say we are similar in looks. I think so anyway, especially now that I've had my hair dyed the same colour. Mind you, I'd love to have his money. I was introduced to Tantric sex by a next-door neighbour when I first moved into my current flat three years ago. I had been in the place just a couple of days, and it was a mess, packing cases all over, bags of clothes here and there. He knocked to introduce himself, said he lived across the landing, and asked if there was anything I needed. I have to admit, I was quite embarrassed because I was in the middle of...well, I was playing with myself, and I was only wearing some jogging bottoms that I had slipped on when I heard the knock on the door. He was in his mid-forties, quite tall, taller than me...so about six foot, with jet-black hair and a scar that ran down his right cheek. He was lean and very fit. I do not tend to go for older men, but he was very attractive. He was in extremely tight jeans and a white T-shirt, plain but appealing. I saw that he was giving me the once over, his eyes wandering from my head down to my feet, lingering over my crotch area, where the remnants of my erection was still obvious.

'I tried to arrange myself, uncomfortable with his intense scrutiny. I offered him a cup of coffee and we went through to the kitchen. As I was making the coffee, he noticed that I had a dripping tap and offered to fix it, as he said he was a plumber by trade. I tried to say "no thanks" but he ignored me, got up and returned with some tools. He did fix the tap, but stupidly got soaked from a jet of water. We both knew what this was a lead-up to, because he took off his sopping T-shirt and sat there with his lovely chest bare. Then he started telling me about the delights of Tantric sex and asked if I'd ever done it. I said no. Apparently it is all about taking your time, and not going straight for a climax as soon as possible. He said that he would be happy to demonstrate to me the full Tantric experience, and I accepted.

'We went into my bedroom, which was still bare except for the bed and a chair. He asked if I had any candles and I fetched and lit some. He left for a few moments and came back with some massage oils, ylang ylang and lavender, he said. He told me that he did a massage course several years ago and so knew what he was doing. I stripped down to my undies and lay face down on the bed, and he started. He said that Western-style massage tends to avoid making contact with certain erogenous areas, but Tantric massage is less stuffy. He massaged me with his fingers and palms, which felt great, and soon he was also using his mouth, lips and teeth, biting and licking, sucking and stroking. I can't describe the feeling of elation at his touch. Every time he touched me it felt like I was floating. Every lick and suck was a protracted act which seemed to get me boiling up. I so desperately wanted to come, but he didn't let me. He was now squatting with his knees either side of my thighs, and I realised that he was naked, because I could feel the telltale heaviness of his bollocks resting against my arse. I started to squirm, loving the sensations.

'He then got me to turn over, and he slipped my boxers down, my erection now substantial, and he started playing with it, making very complimentary comments about it. I do have a nice cock, by the way, I don't know if that's something that will count in my favour during selection. I looked down and saw that his was also sizeable, and now rock-hard. He asked if I wanted to suck him. I let him move up my body, until he was hovering over me, his cock just inches from my mouth, and slowly he let it slide in. I started sucking him, attempting to do what he had done to me, taking it at a measured pace, teasing the blow job out, and trying to make it special. I could tell I was succeeding from the noises he was making. I felt like I was now choking on it, as the cock filled my throat. I didn't know how long we were like this, but then he suddenly stopped and pulled away, moving back down and sucking me. His stubbly chin grazed the skin on my thighs as he went into action. The next thing I knew was that he'd flipped me over again, and I could hear him rubbering up, and then slathering my arse with lube. Again, I cannot describe the utter bliss when he started to fuck me; I was completely euphoric. It seemed as if his whole self was being pushed up inside me, stretching and pounding, while his hands continued to massage and probe my body. Every time I thought I was going to explode, he slowed down, bringing me to the point of no return, and then backing off. It was unbelievably exciting, and I can honestly say I've never had a fuck like it. He must have fucked me half a dozen times, always breaking off and sliding out, going back to sucking and licking me all over, then resuming the fuck. There were times when I was so desperate to come that I would grab my cock and start to wank, but he'd gently take my hand away, and if I tried again he'd just hold my hands tightly by side so I couldn't move.

'I lost track of all time, until after what seemed like hours, he finally allowed me to ejaculate, as he did too, shooting inside me, as I jerked off on the bed. The whole thing was so erotic, and I vowed to try and make each sex session I have in the future as wonderful as that one. He taught me many things over the next few months, things which I've never forgotten. He moved out the following summer and we lost touch. Pity, really. Still, that's life. I've been on the lookout ever since for someone who is as imaginative as he was. Phillipe is quite good at sex, but tends to finish quickly and doesn't have my staying power.

'I'm not sure what else to say really. I think I'd be a good member of the team, mixing well with whoever you choose, and could offer a relaxing massage to anyone if they got too stressed out by the entire thing. Thanks and I hope to hear back from you soon.'

William Blake-Harper

'Hello there. Firstly, I suppose I should introduce myself to you all. You'll have to bear with me, as I'm not particularly 'au fait' with video recording equipment...

'Right, there we go...so, my name is Will, William actually, William Blake-Harper, which is a bit of a mouthful. And there's nothing wrong with a good mouthful! Ha! Sorry...I do have quite a lewd sense of humour.

'Born in Cambridge, educated at Eton, and now I'm a reasonably successful stockbroker in the City. I have just celebrated my thirtieth birthday. I suppose you could say I was quite well off, if you were to be vulgar and ask what I earn, although the figures are a secret between my accountant, the Inland Revenue and myself.

'I have a rather comfy apartment in Chelsea Harbour, overlooking the Thames, which is full of plants, books and cats. I adore my little pussies... Patsy, Edina and Saffy, named after those astonishing characters in my favourite television programme ever... *Absolutely Fabulous*. I am quite house-proud, and cannot abide filth and squalor. That's the only thing that I would have to insist upon if you were to select me for this show, absolute hygiene at all times from my fellow compatriots... anything less would be too disgusting.

'What are my best qualities? Well, I should say that I am definitely forthright; I speak my mind. I won't suffer fools gladly, and get very angry at ineptitude. If I can do my job well, then I expect others to do the same. I am punctual, and I should say I am honest. I do have a wide circle of friends who'll back me up on this. I reckon I have a sense of humour, and love a laugh over a good bottle of wine...I cannot stand cheap supermarket plonk. I like my appearance, although have wished in the past for tidier hair. I hate the way it looks as if it has fought a losing battle with a comb. One of these days I'm going to have it all cut short, that might be quite smart, actually...you know...one of those severe military cuts. I'd probably look an absolute arsehole, but it would be worth it for the change of image. Incidentally, if anyone makes the mistake of saying I look like that prize numbskull Hugh Grant they'll end up with a bunch of fives. Just because I have the same kind of persona as he did in that bloody stupid film about the weddings...well, that's no reason to compare me with him. I am quite happy with my facial looks too, square jawed is good as far as I am concerned, and I have deep, dark eyes, which I think are exceedingly attractive. I think that well developed, self-assuredness is something that men go for. Although precious few have wanted to go for it lately. I do the occasional sit-up, and now and again go for a jog around the local park, but no way could I be described as a fitness fanatic. My body is in quite good shape, though.

'What do you dream about in your quieter moments? Ah, good question. Probably settling down with the right man, finding someone handsome and virile to love me, and make love to me every night. Wouldn't that be heaven? Perhaps a spell of celebrity might help that...that is, if I get selected for the show. I have had my fair share of short relationships...I don't really approve of one-night stands, they are so cheapening on the soul, don't you find? Or sex without love. One of those kind of men broke my heart once, many moons ago. I was just out of college and full of romance, having doused myself in Byron and Shelley, and gone wandering around Europe. I met a tall, dark gorgeous chap called Guido on the Spanish Steps in Rome and we had a tempestuous affair for three months, with constant sex, and what I thought was love, turned out to be merely lust on his part. He just didn't turn up one evening for our date, and I saw him the next day with some vapid queen, to whom he had attached himself. I still think fondly of him though, and hope that he's happy. He certainly gave me a great deal of happiness, even though it was short-lived.

'What else? I realised I was homosexual at an early age, and made the most of it at Eton, I can tell you. There was so much repression there that getting sex was a total doddle, if you'll allow me to use that slang expression. I was the 'fag' of a boy in my house, Rogerson his name was; he must have been about eighteen. He was a real slut and seemed to delight in having sex whenever he could, and with whomever he could. Once, when I was sixteen, I walked in on him actually being sucked off by this temporary English professor, who was quite young himself. I didn't know what to do or say and was rooted to the spot in total fascination. Rogerson just smiled and invited me in and asked if I wanted to join them. I recall the professor going red with embarrassment, and buttoning up his trousers. I do remember vividly that his cock was quite small, certainly compared to Rogerson, who had an absolute whopper between his legs. I was always fascinated by it, whenever I went to his room and found him lounging around naked. Anyway, he got the professor to carry on, and he did, keeping one eye on me, as he sucked. I just sat on a chair, glued to the scene, deliriously learning what men did to each other, but too frightened to do anything about it. I can still get that terrible pounding of my heart when I think back, the nervous rush of adrenaline, at the thought of what I was seeing. It took me a few years to completely overcome my fear of bodily contact, but once I did I became an absolute slut.

'I think that is actually all I have to say about myself. I don't like to be accused of blowing my own trumpet...although that's a good trick if you can do it! I believe I would be someone that your show would benefit from having on board. My sense of values and my forthright nature would be a good thing for the project. Besides, you should have people from different social backgrounds if the experiment is to prove in any way realistic. I look forward to hearing from you.'

Rhys Llewellyn

'Hello everyone there. This is my video to show you all about myself and to hopefully win me a place on your programme...which sounds like a brilliant idea, actually!

'My name is Rhys David Robert Llewellyn, and as you'll probably have guessed by now, I'm from Wales. I live in a small town called Tredegar in Gwent, where I was born and bred, and still live here with my parents. I came out to them when I was sixteen, which was four years ago, and they were fine about it, probably because as the youngest of five boys they knew they would be having grandchildren with the others anyway, and so having a poof in the family was no big deal. And thank God for that, as I'm no good at confrontations. I don't know what I'd have done if there'd been a big scene. Thankfully they just said it didn't matter what I was, as long as I was happy, and I'll always love them for that. As I said, I have four older brothers – Thomas, Lloyd, Huw and Aldwyn, who are all pretty good blokes. They all accepted I was gay, and say they knew even before I did. They do kid me about it, but I know they are just joking. Sometimes they would try and get me to admit my sexuality by prancing around in their underwear, rubbing themselves and trying to turn me on, but it didn't work. Not that my brothers aren't horny, because they are, all of them are lookers. Although I seem to have ended up with the baby looks in the family, you know, these big brown eyes and hair, and soft skin and rounded features. Well, you can see them for yourselves, can't you?

'Right then, let's answer some of your questions...my favourite song is "Smalltown Boy" by Bronski Beat. It is just such a brilliant song and so poignant. I was lucky in that I never had to run away from home because of my sexuality, but there are so many poor boys who do. My favourite book...well, I love all the vampire books of Anne Rice; they are so erotic, and I love the character of Lestat...I'd love a tall handsome blond to sweep me off my feet and make me his forever, although I'm still looking for him at the moment. My favourite film is *The Wizard of Oz*. It is so magical, and I cry every time Judy sings Over the Rainbow. Anyone who isn't moved by that can't have a heart.

'What do you dream about? I don't tend to remember my dreams. I'm a really heavy sleeper, but I do have daydreams about being successful. I work in a local bowling alley, and I would love to get away from all that...handling other people's shoes and mopping up spilt drinks and vomit is so horrible. If I could, I'd move to a big city like Manchester or Liverpool and open up a gay disco, somewhere with no attitude, where every guy is welcome whether he's fat or thin, young or old, and it'd be wonderful. I don't have that much experience of going to clubs, though, as I just don't like to. I'd end up being questioned by my mam. You know the kind of thing..."Where are you going? What time will you be back? Who are you seeing? Where've you been?" All that kind of stuff. It's much easier to keep to myself rather than make my life awkward. Besides, if my brothers thought I was up to anything a bit naughty, they'd start wanting to know all the details too and would want to probably beat up anyone who I was intimate with. They do love me, and that's nice, but they are over-protective sometimes.

'I can't really tell you about any memorable sex because I haven't done it much. I'm twenty now, and as I said it's difficult living in such a small place and doing anything sexual without the whole town finding out. That would be too awful, not just for me but for Mam and Dad too. I'd just die of shame if they knew I'd done anything bad. They'd just think less of me and that would break my heart.

'I could tell you about my first time though, if you'd like.

'OK...well, it only happened about eight months or so ago. I was working at the bowling alley, on cleaning detail, mopping up the tables and throwing away litter. At one point I had to go and swab out the gent's toilets, which do get quite horrid after a while. What I did was stand the big 'closed' sign in front of the door to stop anyone coming in. I went inside and there was this guy standing at the urinals, and he was there rather a long time. I asked him to hurry up, as I had to clean the place. He smiled at me and then it was really clear what he was doing. He moved away from the urinal a bit and I saw he had a hard-on. God, I had dreamt of men for a long time. I used to wonder what I would do if a real man were to show interest in me. I had a stolen copy of a women's magazine hidden under my mattress which had naked men in it, which I used to wank over all the time.

'So there I was, half nervous and half excited. He just stood there with it sticking out of his flies, big and hard. I froze, and my heart was beating like the clappers. He walked across to me and started to fondle my chest through my red striped work-shirt. He unbuttoned it and put his hand inside, feeling my nipples. Now this really got me going and I got an immediate hard-on. I've discovered that they are one of my weak spots. He then helped me off with my shirt and began to bite and lick me around my chest, and armpits. By this stage I was so completely in his spell that I let him do anything he wanted.

'Then he started unbuckling my trousers and I could feel my hard-on straining at the leash, and my stomach was turning somersaults. I was completely terrified that someone would come in. If I had been caught, I would've lost my job. I smelt his aftershave when he started to kiss me. Then he knelt down and began to do things down there, the stubble on his chin grazing the skin around my thighs. He began to nuzzle at my hard-on through my Y-fronts, and I thought I was in heaven. He started sucking me, and doing weird things like putting his tongue in the hole. It felt amazing. I gripped his shoulders and started pumping his mouth, which seemed to turn him on, as he made grunting and moaning noises. I told him to be quiet, as I didn't want anyone to hear us. Then he started on my balls, sucking them into his mouth, and that felt even better. My legs were trembling and I found it hard to stand up, as if they would buckle under me.

'He did this for a bit, which was great, but then he led me, shuffling along with my trousers round my ankles to one of the cubicles. Then he pushed me down onto the seat and locked the door. He unzipped himself and pulled out his cock, which was so big! Much bigger than mine, and I'm quite happy with the size of that. My brothers' cocks are bigger than mine but they are bigger and taller than me, too.

'I closed my eyes in dread anticipation, until I felt something bumping against my lips, and just for a second I didn't know what it was. I opened my eyes and was looking straight at the end of it, hovering near my mouth. It wasn't circumcised, and so he pulled the foreskin back, letting the head pop out, big and purple. I gulped and knew I had to do it for my first time. I opened my lips and let him put it in my mouth. It filled me and really stretched my jaw wide. It tasted salty, but not unpleasantly so, and so I started to suck, doing what I thought was my best, as I'd had no experience of what to do. Like just letting it slide in and out, filling me, then after a while doing a bit more, like sucking and licking. He seemed to be enjoying it, as he was groaning again, and saying things like "Yeah, that's it...suck my cock...yeah, eat my dick, you little cocksucker.' Stuff that sounded so rude that it was incredibly horny.

'Anyway, I guess I'm giving him a good time because he starts to come, suddenly and without warning. He pulls out of my mouth and shoots over my face. I had a go at licking some of it, and it tasted strange, not unpleasant, slightly creamy and musky. He ruffled my hair and zipped up quickly, then bolted from the cubicle, leaving me covered in his spunk. I had to clean myself up sharpish and finish my mopping up, and the most difficult thing was going back to work, and acting like nothing had happened, even though I was bursting to tell someone 'I just sucked a cock!'

'I felt wonderful.

'So that's that, really. I haven't done a lot else, although I get so frustrated and horny that at times it's unbearable. We have no gay places where I live, so I go into Swansea or Cardiff sometimes, but that's quite rare, and unfortunately I never have any luck there either. Perhaps guys can tell I'm someone with no experience and they don't want that. I'd have thought a fresh-faced young lad like me would have had better luck. Hopefully if I win the money, I'll be able to move away and start afresh somewhere else, and my love life might improve. That's all I've got to say, I think, so I'll say cheerio and hope I get picked. Oh, and you can contact me at my parents' number because I've told them I'm entering for your show...bye, then. And thanks.'

Skye Blue

'Right then. This is my video application to appear on your pro-gramme. I have your list of questions which do seem a bit predictable, really, so if you have no objections I'll just talk about myself.

'My name is Skye Blue. Well, it's not actually, but it's the name I've adopted since I started working in the porn industry. I think I'd prefer to keep my real name secret for the moment. Not that I'm ashamed of what I do, it's just that it would confuse things and I'm happier being Skye than my real self. He is so much more exciting and outgoing, and has the chance to live life to the full. I live in London, obviously, as that is where the bulk of my work is. But I have done some porn videos abroad in Spain and Holland. I also do modelling for magazines and calendars and the like. I am twenty-six now and have been doing it for the last four years.

'I guess you are all asking why. Well, I come from a dull, middle-class family who are totally undistinguished. I knew from an early age that I was gay, and found out that I was good at sex. I used to hang around my local cottage a lot, and soon realised that I had a bigger cock than most. Some of the older men who came in would totally drool over my knob, desperate for it. I learned that I had power over people because of what I had down there. It was when I saw a copy of a gay magazine which had this advert for models that I applied. The photographer said he'd rarely seen such a beautiful cock and that with my good looks I could make some serious money...you know this blue-eyed, blond, boy-next-door thing that I've got going. Do you want a look at my cock? Just a second... there it is...nice, eh?

'I started in the business slow and did the odd magazine spread, getting a boner for the photographer wasn't hard, in fact I loved the exhibitionistic side of the deal, knowing that guys would soon be whacking off over pictures of me and my dick.

'So I soon graduated onto hardcore porn videos. I had made some contacts through my modelling and was introduced to this guy who made this stuff, and he was really interested in using me. He'd seen some of my photo spreads and had this part in mind for me. The money seemed good and I said yes straight away. We filmed it in his house, which was old and rambling, and full of stuff like portraits and suits of armour. I played a young nobleman out in India during the Raj, who seduces all his staff, including the butler and the boot-boy and the punkah-wallah. The title was *A Back Passage to India*. Crass or what?! It was great fun actually, more fun than I thought it would be, and I got to have some fantastic sex with these other guys, all well hung and all fucking hot, plus I got paid for it.

'That lead onto more video work offers and I jumped at the chance. I even went abroad, doing some in Amsterdam and Barcelona. I admit that I do like to live the good life, so the money doesn't stay in my bank account very long. This is why I'd like to be on your show. I think I'd give it an edge. Someone who doesn't let life beat him down. Someone who goes out there and grabs whatever he can get. I'm not one of these moaning Marys who just make a song and dance out of life. I take what I can and enjoy it. What's the point in being dull? Who wants to live in a tower block, work in a bank, and come home to a microwave meal and watch the telly until it's time to go to bed? I certainly don't.

'I will tell you about the most memorable sex I ever had, as it was on a video shoot. It was a cowboy picture called *The Magnificent Seven*

Inches. Quite a good movie, actually. Have you seen it? Who cares. Anyway, shooting porn is a very unsexy business. You sit around for hours, then have to get a perfect hard-on and perform at a second's notice. I look on it as a good laugh, and generally have as enjoyable a time as I can. On this shoot, which was just outside Barcelona, I was the only English guy in the cast. The rest were all Spanish and German. When I arrived on set that morning, the star, a dark-skinned Catalan called Juan, was already wandering around sporting a huge stiffy, proud of it and showing it off to anyone who was interested. He seemed to make a bee-line for me and kept standing by my chair, waving his cock under my nose. I decided he was making a very tempting offer, so I went down on him. It was a gorgeous piece of meat, and I had a great time, then someone else came alongside and got their dick out, and so I went down on that too. I mean, wouldn't you?

'From then on the whole thing degenerated into an orgy, where guys were appearing out of the woodwork, both actors and crew. Even the director joined in, and he was probably the biggest stud there...a stunning guy called Santos, who had a massive cock and ended up fucking about five of us in turn, while we were sucking off five others standing before us in a line. The whole morning was just a riot of endless sex with the most fab guys. Now you tell me...why wouldn't a handsome gay guy want to get into porn? We didn't get a lot of filming done that day...

'What else? Well...I would say that I am a show-off...but that should be obvious to even the most stupid person. I enjoy being in front of a camera. But I also mix well with others. I have a friendly personality, and a genuine interest in what other people do. I see no point in being a stuck-up git...it gets you nowhere in this world. I think that's probably all I've got to say on this video, and so look forward to hearing back from you. I hope you do choose me...you won't be sorry.'

Jackson Leroux

'Hello, everybody. I'm Jackson Leroux, and this is my audition tape for your show. Erm...well, here goes. I was born in the West Indies, but my parents moved over here when I was just one year old... I'm now twenty. I'm black, as you can probably see...of course you can...I'm babbling now, sorry, nerves...

'I was brought up in Birmingham, but for the last year I've been working my way around Europe, seeing the world as it were, and I'm now living in a bedsit in London, Wimbledon actually, which suits me fine as it's very cheap. My landlady is this fat old woman who has arthritis and cannot get out of her room, and is surrounded by cats. I just leave my rent on the hall table and she collects it when she can. But you don't want to know that, do you?

'I would so love to be on your show, as I've discovered I desperately need some excitement in my life. It's all got a bit boring. Since travelling around, I have realised the world is a very small place, and to just exist, living out one's life is very dull. The whole concept of your show sounds brilliant! So different. The thought of being forced to live with these other guys, making friends and trying to exist in such strange circumstances is very appealing. I do think I'd be an ideal contestant because, as I said before, I have been to many interesting places, which has given me a unique insight into people. I know that I can get on easily with others, although I've been known to have a bit of a ruthless streak in me. If I want something I go and get it, sometimes not caring if I've trampled on anyone to get there.

'I have always been gay, even though it took me a while to admit it to myself. I didn't want to face up to the reality of being different. When my dad died last year, I decided to tell my mother, but just couldn't. Then she stupidly opened a letter I'd got from a guy I'd been seeing and she tackled me about it. I had to own up and tell her the truth. I was sorry she was upset by the news, but I couldn't carry on and live a lie. We don't speak very much these days, which is sad for me, but whenever we do, it's tricky and she inevitably starts crying and asks what she did wrong.

'I am working at a health club and swimming pool at the moment, as an attendant, you know, hanging round the pool watching people, telling them off if they break the rules. I don't do any of the diving in and saving drowning swimmers; I leave that to the trained guys. I guess it suits me fine at present, because I get paid for just watching half-naked men getting wet! I also have to mop the floors and swill out the showers and check on the changing rooms. I keep myself fit, doing fifty sit-ups every day, so I've quite a good physique. My body is well-defined and I am proud of my washboard stomach.

'What else can I tell you? Where are those questions you sent? Right, here goes...my favourite TV show is *Friends*. I really love the whole American humour thing, and in that show they've got it perfect. Plus, I think Matt Le Blanc is the horniest guy I've ever seen. My favourite song is...difficult...I love everything Madonna has ever done, and probably would say that "Vogue" is my favourite track. I don't really have hobbies, but I do like to go out every weekend clubbing. I can lose myself on the dance floor for hours, just getting into the beat of the music. There is not much I'd like to change in my life...things are kind of OK. I'd like to sort everything out with my mum – that'd be nice – and I'd like to be rich enough not to have to work, but doesn't everyone dream that?

'I don't know who would play me in the film of my life...probably Denzel Washington. He's got looks and a great body and can act. What annoys me about modern life? That's easy. I hate inconsiderate people. Those bastards who think they own you, or think they are superior, who waltz through doors when you hold them open and don't even say thank you. Those people who jump queues, or who park badly and take up two parking spaces. And those shop assistants who ignore you when you come into their shops. I hate people who talk in the cinema...if they wanted a fucking conversation, why not stay at home? You've got me started now! I hate mobile phones. One even went off at a funeral I was at last month. It was awful. Everyone diving for their pockets and the vicar had to stop his sermon. I especially hate these appalling teenage girls who haven't even reached double figures yet and have got a mobile phone. What must their parents be like? I hate to think. I hate condoms that are too small. I do have quite a big cock and so some brands are too tight. I have to be really careful what ones I buy these days. I hate guys who are lazy in bed...the ones who just lie there and expect you to do everything. Sex should be a two-way thing, with effort on both sides. If I end up sleeping with a guy who expects me to nosh him off and doesn't even react, then I kick him out of bed. Life's too short for boring sex.

'On the subject of sex, I should tell you about my most memorable. But a lot of my sexual encounters have been memorable, so that's a tough choice. I could tell you about my most recent one, which happened yesterday. It was at the pool, actually. I was in the attendant's office, which is next to the changing rooms. It has one of those big two-way mirrored windows, so we can watch them, but they can't see us. I can't tell you the times I've just sat and watched some spunk stripping off, and I've seen some fascinating cocks too, big, small, fat, thin, the lot! Anyway, I'm sitting in the office with a mug of tea and I'm reading *Hello* magazine, there are these pictures of

Michael Jackson looking like a corpse, but that's beside the point. The pool is fairly quiet, as it's about three in the afternoon. All the mothers and toddlers have gone and it's too early for the post-school crowd. This guy, probably mid-thirties or so, comes in and starts to take a shower. I can see right down the length of the changing rooms to the shower stalls from where I am sitting. He is very fit, muscles and a tan, and little clumps of hair around his tits. He starts soaping himself down, keeping his Speedos on, but I can tell that he is kind of hard, as there is a bulge in them. His eyes are closed and he doesn't think anyone is watching. I feel myself getting stiff, and so slip my tracksuit bottoms down to get my cock out. I needn't worry about anyone else coming into the office because the door is at the far end of the changing rooms and I'd have plenty of time to make myself decent.

'Suddenly he looks up and stares in my direction. For a moment I forget that he can't see me, and hide my stiffy. But then I remember the two-way glass. Even so, he is looking straight at me. He turns the shower off and walks slowly down the changing rooms to his locker, which is right next to the window. He opens the locker and begins towelling himself off, droplets of water splashing on the window. He seems to be spending a lot of time rubbing around his arse and cock, which I can see is getting bigger, and it's very nice. Not huge, just average, but it is a lovely shape, and curves up to a big head. He turns to face the window and lets his cock bump gently against the window as if he's trying to catch my attention. Believe me, he does! I get my cock out again and start wanking slowly, and he does the same. It's quite eerie though, as all he can see is his own reflection, while I can see every move he makes. I stand up and move closer, letting my cock rest against the glass like his so they're almost touching. As if he knows this, he starts rubbing his cock up and down the glass. I can see the veins bulging, and the skin sliding up and down. It's so horny. I do the same, and imagine we are actually making contact.

'I think I'm about to come, when he pulls away and spreads his arse cheeks. Now one of the most erotic sights for me is a spread arse, and that pink hole, ready for me to dive into, and so my eyes pop out of my head. He is fingering himself, and one wet finger slips inside, as if he's taunting me, inviting me inside. The temptation is almost too much. I so want to fuck that hole. But I know that if I get caught that I'd be fired straight away with no chance of explaining myself. My own cock is absolutely rigid by now, and aching for it. I start to wank, and I don't know if he hears me because he stands up and squints at his reflection in the glass. Then he grabs his dick and wanks himself too. Amazingly, we both come at exactly the same moment, shooting out over both sides of the window.

'That was pretty hot. And I can't believe I actually told you that! If it ever gets out, I'd be so embarrassed! Anyway, I hope you are interested in me...I am really interested in the show and hope that I get picked. Thanks and bye.'

WEEK ONE

Monday

The house was a large, Victorian mansion, set in its own rambling grounds on the outskirts of north London. It had been especially selected for its location. No other buildings intruded on it, and it had a lockable front gate and tall walls surrounding the gardens. Secrecy was definitely assured. The production company made sure that the eight contestants' contact with the outside world was completely curtailed by planting barbed wire along the top of the garden walls. Fifty tiny cameras were dotted around the house and gardens, along with as many hidden microphones, so that there was nowhere that the contestants could go to find privacy. Every waking and sleeping moment would be caught on film. There were no dissenters among the eight guys selected for the programme, as the lure of television fame and the prize money clouded their doubts over whether they should be seen in the shower and toilet. They all agreed to stay in the house for six weeks, under the ever-watchful cameras, to live their lives with each other, and to vote out one contestant a week, until two were left.

Every week they would be given tasks to perform and complete successfully for points. Of the two remaining contestants, the person with the most points would be declared the winner and scoop the prize money of ten thousand pounds.

There were four twin bedrooms, and the contestants would decide amongst themselves who would share. There were two bathrooms – an upstairs one with shower and bath and a smaller one downstairs, a large kitchen, dining room, living room and a games room with a pool table and loads of board games. In the garden was a vegetable patch and flower beds, and an old wooden swing attached to the branches of a decrepit oak tree. They would be able to go wherever they wanted as long as they didn't leave the compound. The only time they would be allowed out was on eviction day, when the nominated evictee would be escorted back to his normal life. There was a delivery box by the front gate, where the producers could leave messages or orders for the inmates, as well as details of their weekly group tasks.

The eight gay men selected to take part knew nothing about each other. Part of the learning process would be to discover all about the others and to try to establish friendships, a difficult thing to do in such a rarefied atmosphere. The producer had told them to do whatever they wanted to do. There was no limit to their behaviour. If they ended up having sex, then that would be great for the ratings. They should act as though the cameras weren't there, and just be themselves. It would probably take a few days to get used to the conditions of the house, but he was confident they soon would.

The introductions went well, all eight men shaking each other's hand, and finally sighing with relief that the big day had arrived and their fellow inmates seemed to be nice guys.

'Thank God, you all seem normal.' Jost Van Dijk smiled around him, slumping on one of the big sofas in the living room. 'I was so nervous...I imagined ending up with a bunch of wankers, and hating every minute.' Ever since he had received the call from the production office to come in for an informal interview, and had been told afterwards that he had been selected for the show, he had been on a high. His head had been buzzing with the thought of the journey he was about to embark on, and he couldn't wait for it all to start. Now that the great day had arrived, nerves had also arrived in the pit of his stomach from wondering whether he would have the guts to go through with it. Still, the others seemed OK at first glance. No one looked a complete shithead yet. This was going to be fun and he shook his head to clear any initial doubts away.

'Same here,' said Simon Ho, who sank down beside Jost. 'Christ, I could do with a drink.' His mouth was exceedingly dry, not that Simon was an alcoholic, he just felt the need for some kind of stimulant to help him get through this first awkward day. He had felt sure that he wanted to be involved with this project, his whole philosophy of life telling him to take risks and not be complacent. Life was nothing if it stood still. Whatever happened in the Boycam house was bound to be a positive experience. He just hoped that his new housemates would play by the rules and respect him as a person. One glance at them all indicated that they were an OK bunch.

Colin Criswell raised an eyebrow and said, 'I think I'll take recce around the kitchen. Perhaps there is some alcohol hidden somewhere.' The relief of actually being inside the house had taken its toll on him. He needed to get away from the others and take a few solitary moments to centre himself. He stood up and headed for the door.

'Could you cope with a little company?' Peter Laurence gave him a friendly grin, which was hard for Colin to resist. Perhaps he'd be able to have a few quiet minutes later. On their first day together it seemed appropriate to show some willingness and determination to get along.

'Sure.' With a gentle chuckle Peter joined Colin at the door and cheekily gave him a small pinch on the bottom, something that didn't go unnoticed by the others. 'Back shortly.' This guy Colin seemed nice and how better to get to know someone than to make the effort?

'I'd prefer coffee if you are in the kitchen.' Rhys Llewellyn perched himself on the arm of the sofa and gave the two lads a shy but encouraging grin. They looked like pleasant people, and Rhys was glad. Ever since the day he'd been told he would be included in the house, he had slept badly, the worry of whether he'd done the right thing tormenting his dreams. His brothers had been totally impressed by his announcement and had been incredibly supportive. No one they knew had ever been on the telly before. And although they didn't have the gay subscription channel, and wouldn't be able to watch their little 'bro' in action, they wanted him to do his best and succeed. Not forgetting that the money would come in very useful – all of them full of plans as to how they would spend it for him. He looked around the room and saw nothing but smiling, open faces. Perhaps every- thing would be all right. Nevertheless, he would be on his guard to begin with, having little or no experience of gay life, and didn't want to embarrass himself unduly so early on in the project.

'Sure thing. But I don't know how long it'll take us, not knowing our way around the place.' Colin grinned back and stalked from the room, Peter at his side.

'There's no rush. We aren't going anywhere,' called out Skye Blue at their disappearing backs. He looked at the other five all now seated in the spacious and comfortable living room, all totally unsure of their next moves. 'Well, I guess they will be sharing a room together. Any other thoughts on possible roomies?' Such things were on his mind, creature comforts being of the utmost importance to him.

Jackson Leroux looked from one guy to another. 'I reckon we should hang fire on that and decide later today. See who we get on with best.' Jackson was cautious by nature and he didn't want to make a rash move and end up sharing with a guy he didn't get along with. At first glance, the others all appeared friendly enough but any foibles wouldn't start showing themselves for a while yet. So far none of the guys struck him as good room-mate material. What he wanted was some nice hunk, who didn't snore and who wouldn't monopolise the room. He didn't think that his wish was going to come true.

'Good idea.' William Blake-Harper agreed with the handsome-look- ing black guy and winked conspiratorially. 'Let's see who is our best bet for a bit of "you know what" and then make our sleeping arrangements.'

The others groaned. Trust someone to lower the tone of the experiment so soon.

'That's a bit of a cynical thing to say,' said Simon.

'Well, it's true. Don't say you all haven't thought about it. The producers are desperate for us to be shagging like rabbits, and you know it. Even the tiniest glimpse of cock will help their ratings and make us celebrities. So I strongly advise you to mark out possible partners and get down to it as soon as possible.' William reached into his pocket and pulled out a packet of cigarettes, lighting one and taking a deep drag. He had leapt at the chance of appearing on television and was probably one of the only guys in the house to actually have a subscription to the Gay-Per-View channel that this programme was to be shown on. He wanted fame and fortune, even though he would happily describe himself as comfortably well off. He didn't need the money, but as with all guys of his type, he wasn't one to turn down the chance of making extra. This whole project would be a laugh, and if he got a shag out of it he would be delighted. There were a few good candidates for that already, and his eye had fallen on the stunning blond on the sofa. What had he called himself? Cloud. No, Skye. That was it. Fairly pretentious. But lovely to look at, and carrying a beautifully developed package beneath those tight trousers. His eye wandered across to the young Welsh lad. An obvious heartbreaker. One who would look at you with his deep eyes and just beg you to fall in love with him. Probably inexperienced in the ways of the world, and probably ripe for a good plucking. Then there was the young Dutch guy. William struggled to recall his name but gave up after a few moments of mental wrangling. He was certainly a delicious young thing, probably about mid-twenties, and definitely fit. He had an air of self-assuredness that was very attractive...a man who knows what turns him on and then goes for it. He might be an interesting companion, and should the opportunity arise, he'd try and get to know him better.

'I still think you are being overly cynical,' said Simon, bringing

William's mind back to the present. 'How do you know they don't want to film a social experiment, a chance to purely watch how people interact with each other?'

'Because we are living in an age of crass commercialism, dear boy. Ratings are all. Why would anyone want to watch eight men talking to each other, if they can be watching them shagging? It's human nature. Believe me, sweet one, the sooner you get your bits out for the cameras, the more they'll like you. I will...given half a chance.'

Skye sat intently watching everyone's reaction to this piece of homespun philosophy. 'I hate to admit it, but I think he's right.' He gestured nonchalantly towards William. 'William-boy here, has a point. Why else would they put eight shirtlifters together in close confinement, if they didn't want a little man-on-man action?'

Rhys raised a hand to speak. 'So what if we agree not to...I mean agree to stay celibate? I for one don't want to be a porn star.'

Uncrossing his legs and spreading them proudly, giving his widest smile, Skye stared straight at Rhys. 'It's not so bad, you know. I've made a good living out of it.'

Stunned, Rhys shut up, staring at the floor, scuffing the richly coloured carpet with the toe of his shoe. He already knew one man he didn't want to share with. His life so far hadn't prepared him for the close attentions of someone who fucked for a living. Deep down he was still a riot of nerves, his stomach roiling with apprehensions, although he was doing his best to appear unconcerned and normal, and when he spoke his voice was flat and somewhat distant. 'I wonder how long they'll be making that tea?'

Colin looked around the kitchen and was delighted by the vast expanse of gleaming chrome. Being someone who loved to cook, he could foresee many happy hours pottering around among this room's culinary adornments.

'Right, where's the kettle?' Peter scanned the worktops, and smiled as his eyes lit upon the shiny metallic object. 'You look for mugs and tea and coffee.' He squeezed past Colin, letting his buttocks graze the front of the young man's trousers, gently feeling the raised mound that lay dormant inside them. Of all the men he had just been introduced to, Colin seemed the most attractive, with a nice body, not too thin, but muscular and beefy, while that striking head of fair hair, beautifully cropped, was very masculine. He looked like he was a sexual athlete, one of those guys who knew how to make love, and how to satisfy another man, probably a great fuck...he had to stop his mind from dwelling on this exciting possibility as Peter found himself becoming aroused – and that would never do on their first day in the house. Still, it would be good to share a room with Colin, if he was up for it. He had decided to make the most of the next six weeks. Not many people got the chance to take part in such a show, and he was determined that this would be a life-changing experience. But of course, if he should happen to connect with a handsome guy in here, then that would be a wonderful bonus. He set his sights on Colin.

'Here's all the stuff.' Colin started to lay out mugs and fill the sugar bowl, one eye on his task, one on Peter, who he noticed seemed already interested. He wasn't bad looking. In fact he was very nice. His face was strong, and nicely surrounded by a mop of dark hair. He must have been slightly older than Colin, late twenties perhaps? He must have kept himself fit, as he had what looked like a good physique. It might be fun to get to grips with him. He was the nicest of the seven others he'd met this morning. Colin opened his mouth to speak, and his voice cracked as the words tumbled out. 'So why are you doing this thing?'

Peter watched the kettle intensely, hearing the faint bubbling sound of the water starting to boil. 'I suppose because my life is a bit ordinary, really. I wanted the chance to do something more exciting, and this is it. What about you?'

'The same sort of thing, I guess. My job is boring and my sex life kinda the same at the moment, and this seemed like a fun thing to do.'

'I can't believe that your sex life is boring. Surely an attractive man like yourself should be beating them off with a stick.'

Shrugging his shoulders, Colin crossed to the fridge and grabbed a carton of milk. Grasping it tightly, he turned back to face Peter across the wide expanse of kitchen floor. 'That's very nice of you to say so. Some guys say I'm attractive, and I guess I do see it, but most of the time I think I'm not what men want. I seem to frighten them off, or they go for the slimmer type of guys.'

'So you don't have a boyfriend?' Peter's lips were dry, all thoughts of tea and coffee and kettles vanished from his mind.

'No, and I haven't really had a steady relationship ever. What about you?'

'The same really. No one has ever been interested in me as a partner, just as someone for a quick one-night stand, fuck me and then fuck off.'

'I wouldn't do that.'

Peter shifted a little, his left leg had gone to sleep and he could feel the tingling, rushing onset of pins and needles. He started to rub his thigh, wincing as he did so.

'What's the matter?' A spasm of concern corrugated Colin's placid features. 'Are you all right?'

'Just pins and needles. It'll go in a few minutes if I keep rubbing my leg.'

Colin drew in a deep breath. This could be an important moment. This was the first day that the eight participants were together in the project, and would he look like a cheap slut if he were to make advances on one of his fellow contestants so soon? He looked up and tried to see where the hidden cameras were secreted around the kitchen, but the modern pinhead-sized lenses were impossible to spot. He had to assume that every move they made and every word they uttered were being watched and recorded by the production crew, and being beamed to the viewing public's television sets. Did he want to be seen as a slapper, a man of loose morals who would hit on another guy so soon? Or did it matter at all? He didn't know. All he knew was that here was a handsome guy, and the air was filled with that palpable sexual tension that existed between two attracted gay men.

'Let me help.' He crossed the room, and stood facing Peter, each one's eyes holding the stare of the other. He let his hand fall by his side and it tenderly brushed the soft corduroy of Peter's trousers before landing on his upper thigh and squeezing and massaging the hard slab of muscle. He looked away from Peter's strong gaze and saw that he was beginning to get an erection, a growing hill of hardening flesh becoming more apparent by the second. With his free hand, Colin felt his own crotch, squeezing his rapidly swelling cock with eager, trembling fingers.

'Should we be doing this?' Peter's voice was soft, almost too quiet for Colin to hear. He looked up and raised an eyebrow. Peter needed to see how far this guy was prepared to go. If he was up for it, then so was Peter. Even though they had only just met, and he had got a good fuck only two nights before, he wanted sex now.

'What?'

'I said...should we be doing this?'

'That is a very good question,' said Colin.

'And what is your answer?'

'Well...we've only just met, and those people watching us will think we are a couple of sluts. Besides, I don't actually think I want to be watched having sex. Do you?'

'It doesn't bother me. Actually, I think it's quite a turn on.'

Colin stared hard at his new friend. He transferred his hand from Peter's thigh to his crotch, watching with narrowed eyes as the darker guy gave a short exclamation at the tender touch. 'There is no sense in pretending that we don't want to have sex, because I know we do. I think we should just go for it.'

Peter stared back at this gorgeous young guy, and knew that he was absolutely right. He wanted to have sex with Colin badly. He had offered himself and now Peter knew he had succeeded.

Without another word, Colin crossed the kitchen and pushed a tall, metal stool up against the door. 'So we are not disturbed.' Then with one swift, practised motion, Colin unzipped Peter's trousers and let his hand delve inside, instantly making contact with the now rigid cock. He smiled as he realised that Peter wasn't wearing underpants. 'So you came prepared?' He chuckled softly, his hand kneading the swollen member, coaxing it, willing it to respond with a tell-tale jerk.

Peter tried to speak, but his throat was dry. Swirling some saliva around to lubricate his mouth, he put a hand on Colin's shoulder. 'Are you sure about this? Think about the cameras...'

'Ssssh, sod the cameras.' Colin started to remove his own shirt, pulling at the buttons of the white cotton garment, exposing the broad expanse of his sturdy, manly, hairy chest. His shirt off, he stood to remove his trousers, letting them fall to the floor and stepping out of them, perfectly at ease now, his cock bulging against the white net of his jockey shorts. Peter watched, breathless and full of nerves, unable to take his eyes off the man before him, his body well-defined, and unquestionably erotic. His pale, bright eyes shone in the gleam of the sparkling kitchen.

'Very nice. I can see you've got a lot to offer.' Peter spoke, eyeing Colin's underwear, and the straining monster beneath. 'But...you can still change your mind.' He gave a slight, imperceptible gesture with his eyes, upward and toward the corner of the room, indicating the presence of the ever-prying cameras.

Ignoring the implications, Colin moved toward Peter, his cock bouncing in his confining briefs at each step. The two men stood side by side, until Colin put his arms around Peter and drew him close, so that they faced each other, Colin's hard cock pressed against Peter's stomach, rubbing against the belt buckle on his trousers.

'Tell me what you want.' Colin's voice was husky, tremulous.

'Just hold me tight.'

'I am holding you.' Colin's face creased with an amused smile, but he pulled Peter tighter to him, their bodies melting into one sinuous entity. Leaning his head to one side, Peter let Colin kiss him, concentrating on the taste and feel of Colin's tongue inside his mouth. It was young and sweet, tender and attentive, like the gentle lapping of a puppy, his breath cool and fresh. The younger guy explored the insides of Peter's mouth, his long tongue flicking around, playing over the folds and crevices.

'Christ, you kiss well.' Peter pulled away and stared into Colin's big eyes, holding his face between his hands, the tiny scratching of his stubble grazing his palms. Then he slid his hands down the back of Colin's head, enjoying the silken fuzz of the hair at the nape of his neck, then let them fall in longer, heavier strokes down Colin's spine, until they came to rest at the elastic waistband of the other man's briefs. With trembling hands, he moved lower, lightly caressing the buttocks, which felt firm and warm, and beautifully complemented the well-exercised V-shape of Colin's muscular torso.

'Hmmm, that's nice,' Colin sighed.

'Good.' Peter spoke with a clear purpose now, the heat of the moment outweighing any uncertainty of doing this on camera. Here was a stunning man, who was up for sex, so why not go through with it? He pulled one hand back and let it cup the balls that nestled weightily in the soft white cotton. Colin groaned again, a sign of his approbation. Peter let his head bow down, until his tongue could make contact with Colin's chest, the large symmetrical nipples standing hard and proud, surrounded by the wide patches of darker skin. He began to lick and suck, taking the fleshy mounds into his moist mouth, sensing Colin's delight, feeling him squirming in his arms. His exploration of Colin's chest moved south, his tongue wandering down the valley between the muscular breasts, lingering over his stomach, until it met the soft elastic of the waistband. All caution thrown aside, Peter fell to his knees, his eyes now held level with the impressive bulge in the fresh-scented briefs.

'Go on...suck my cock,' Colin said.

Without pause and in one seemingly practised gesture, Peter slid his fingers into the waistband and yanked the briefs down to Colin's ankles, his eyes widening at the sight of the cock bouncing free, curving up, beautifully erect, circumcised, the head purple and proud. Perfect.

Colin gasped as he felt the length of his prick slide down Peter's throat, the tip nudging against the back, the tongue squirming beneath the shaft. With an intake of breath and determination, Peter began to give Colin the best blow job he could, sucking with a vigour and intensity he never knew he possessed, rubbing the balls in his hands, sliding back and forth, allowing the monster to ride in and out of his warm, moist mouth. His tongue slipped against the underside, occasionally flicking across the velvety head, sometimes holding back and blowing gentle puffs of cool air over the trembling glans, this simple action making Colin's knees buckle with delight. Leaving the balls, Peter slid his fingers up over Colin's stomach, feeling the muscular result of his physical exertions, marvelling at the extreme beauty of his form, then let his hands wander down to the buttocks, kneading and squeezing them, teasing apart the two fleshy mounds to reveal the pink hole.

It didn't take long. He sensed Colin's balls tightening, and with a grunt of satisfaction he came, hard and sharp, pulling his cock free from Peter's mouth and pumping his seed across the linoleum floor, in several great spurts. Peter leant forward and let the tip of his tongue sample the pearly drop that hung between the lobes of the cock.

'Hmmm. Nice. Very sweet, not salty or bitter at all.'

Colin grinned, his face lighting up with a reddened glow. 'Glad you approve. We aim to please.'

'Can we lie down somewhere and do this properly?' Peter's eyes were filled with the look of a man pleading for his life, desperate and intense. He had to have more of this gorgeous young man. 'Shall we go to one of the bedrooms?'

'That might be wise.' Colin jumped into his clothes and dressed quickly, before opening the door, and peering out cautiously. The coast was clear. They dashed down the hall, past the half-open living room door, and up the staircase. The first door they came to was wide open, and they bolted inside, quietly shutting the door, smiling at the sight of the two single beds on either side of the room. Colin took Peter's hand and led him to the bed furthest from the door, and lay down on the springy mattress.

'Where the hell have those two got to?' Skye turned his head toward the door, then let his eyes fall and scan the face of his chunky wrist-watch. 'They've been gone half an hour.'

Simon stood with a determined air and surveyed the other five in-mates. 'I think someone should go and find out. Anyone fancy coming with me? If they are shagging I shall want a fellow witness, or you might all decide not to believe me!'

Chuckling, Jackson got to his feet, his face wreathed in smiles. 'Sure. We might even get a look at what they're up to...and I haven't seen a good live sex show for ages!'

'I have.' Skye grinned at the room, talking to no one in particular, and watched them go as they headed toward the kitchen. He had noticed that people were being slightly wary of him, and at this stage in the show he needed allies, or he could find himself voted out sooner than he hoped. He gently slid down the arm of the sofa, sitting closely beside Rhys, who hadn't said very much since his arrival. Here was a young lad who was obviously wondering whether he had done the right thing. He needed cheering up and he also needed to see that he had no reason to be wary of Skye. Guessing that the kid from the Valleys had not a lot of experience of the world and life and pornography, Skye decided to take him in hand, teach him a few things, broaden his horizons and bring him out of his protective shell. It should be a fun experience. Here was his very own "Pygmalion" with Rhys as the naïve youngster and Skye as the knowledgeable and worldly-wise teacher. He rubbed his hands and put an arm around the lad's shoulders. He could feel the youngster flinch, but at the same time he was appreciative of the hard muscles that lay beneath his clothes.

'There's no point waiting around for tea that isn't going to arrive is there? What say we go and explore the house?' He stood and gave Rhys a stare, almost daring the lad to defy him.

Unable to think of a single reason not to, Rhys eased himself to his feet and meekly followed Skye from the room, and up the staircase.

'And then there were two.' William raised an eyebrow at Jost, who sat chewing the end of a fingernail. He eyed the middle-class Englishman carefully. What was he suggesting? Of all the men in the house together, Jost was the least sure of William. He had a superior air about him, a desire to be the top dog, to somehow control the situation. It wasn't a character trait that Jost particularly admired. Still, he should be given a chance. It was only their first day, and one shouldn't judge by appearances. Get to know him. You may have to spend the next six weeks with him.

'Indeed.' Jost stood and crossed to the large bay window at the rear of the sitting room. 'The garden looks lovely. Fancy a stroll? You can tell me all about yourself…if you like.'

'Champion idea…if you'll do the same.' William leapt to his feet and held the door open with the affectation of a society gallant. 'After you, sir.' He bowed low, not seeing the raised eyebrows and pained expression that momentarily crossed Jost's features, and followed the Dutchman out into the hallway and through the front door toward the lush greenery beyond.

The garden had been well tended with a number of pleasant-looking flowerbeds and an expansive lawn with lots of room for ball games, or sunbathing.

'This is nice,' said William, realising the lameness of the comment.

'Yes.' It was all Jost could think of to say. He furrowed his brow and made an effort to get the conversation going. 'So, what are you doing in here?'

William stopped and turned to the young guy at his side. He seemed to be trying to chat, so he would do his best to answer. 'Oh, like everyone else, I suppose. Wanting something different from life, the chance to be a bit daring, to be one of the chosen few, and I suppose to earn a little notoriety.'

'But is notoriety the right motive for taking part in a show like this?' Jost had stopped too and was now facing William, hands deep in his pockets.

'It's as good a reason as any. Besides, surely we are all here wanting to win that money, aren't we?'

'It would be nice, but that shouldn't be our only reason for being here.'

The insufferable attitude that Jost was now full of had started to annoy William intensely. This guy was handsome, and probably a good fuck, but come on. William decided to change the subject.

'So…have you seen anyone you like the look of yet?'

Jost answered with a swift nod. 'Oh, yes. Skye is a fascinating character, full of angst and superiority…'

'And what looks like a very big dick.' This was the thing to give this guy, see what his response would be.

Without flinching, Jost countered this attack. 'Probably, but cock isn't everything, is it?'

'It is with me,' grinned William as he sauntered up to the tree, and sat down on the creaking rope swing. 'What's wrong with a nice bit of cock?'

'Nothing at all, in the right circumstances.'

The conversation now had William in its grip. He wanted to know more. 'And what might they be?' His hand had dropped to his crotch and had landed innocently upon what lay slumbering beneath. He hadn't had any sex for a while, and the juices had started to flow.

'A romantic setting, with a guy you love. Candles and soft music, and then who knows?'

'Sounds lovely,' said William, giving his cock a surreptitious squeeze. He saw that Jost had noted this and shuffled uncomfortably from foot to foot.

'I know what you are after,' he said darkly. 'And it won't work.'

'Really? I don't think I believe you.' With another, more sensuous squeeze, William could feel his cock getting harder, and his erection was now obvious in his trousers. He could see that Jost was troubled, in two minds. He had principles, yes, but would he pass up the opportunity to give a guy a blow job when it was offered?

'I think you would do anything anywhere.' William smiled, unzipping himself, and heaving his cock free, sighing slightly as the breeze wafted across his tender skin.

Jost licked his lips and swallowed. This wasn't how this first day was supposed to be. He didn't want to fall to his knees and suck on this stranger's cock. He had to get to know someone better first.

'I don't think so.' He turned and headed for the house, determinedly keeping his eyes straight ahead.

William stuffed his cock back inside and zipped up. 'Pity,' he muttered to himself. 'Some people are so picky.'

Wednesday

The last two days since their arrival had been something of a revelation for the eight participants. None of them had been prepared for the strain of living in such close proximity to a varied bunch of gay men, all with neuroses, foibles and needs. All wanting attention in some way or another, all determined to be the last surviving member of the house and the lucky man to walk away with the money.

That first day, the eight of them had naturally paired off and the bedrooms had been filled by the four couples – Colin and Peter, Jackson and Simon, Skye and Rhys and lastly Jost and William. It was completely obvious to the others that Colin and Peter were already 'getting it on,' as Skye called it jokingly over breakfast Tuesday morning, when the two offenders had straggled down late, looking the worse for wear, through lack of sleep. Then had followed a day of becoming accustomed to living in the extreme atmosphere of the show, knowing that every conversation, each trip to the toilet or shower was being scrutinised thoroughly, and their motives deciphered by a panel of unknown experts. On the surface though, each of the guys seemed relaxed and ready to make a go of the next seven-week stretch. Nothing much had actually been done, with the guys spending time talking to each other, weighing the each other up, trying to make an early decision about who they liked and who they didn't, knowing that in five days, on Sunday evening, they would be having the premier vote, expelling the first of the eight from the house.

That day had passed relatively easily, Jost had offered to cook their evening meal, which turned out to be a tofu salad with new potatoes and red cabbage. This vegetarian repast did cause a few raised eyebrows around the dinner table as the meat eaters tucked into the soya bean curd, trying to look as if they were enjoying the sloppy white mush. After they had eaten, Jost attempted to build bridges with those who had patently hated their food and offered a relaxing massage to any of the inmates. Simon and William put their hands up straight away, and after the session both said they hadn't felt so blissful and relaxed in ages.

Wednesday morning brought the first of the challenges. Jackson had gone outside for a walk round the garden, and on opening the front door found a large cardboard box sitting on the doorstep.

'Look what I've found,' he called out to the others who were sitting and standing around the kitchen in pyjamas, T-shirts and boxer shorts. 'A communication from our lords and masters.' He dumped the box on one of the worktops and started to open it, his eyes widening with glee at the assorted contents.

'Boycam house!' A voice boomed out from nowhere, making the guys jump, and Rhys to spit out a mouthful of coffee which he was just about to swallow. 'This is Matt speaking.'

The voice of the show's producer echoed around the kitchen, bouncing off the walls with an eerie electronic crackle. 'I hope you are all settled into life inside the Boycam house. So far some of your exploits have made for some very interesting television.' Peter and Colin tried to look nonchalant, aware that he was probably talking about their nights of unstoppable sex. 'You have all had two days to acclimatise yourselves, but now it is time for you all to start the first of your weekly tasks...a challenge that should give you something fun and stimulating to experience. Remember to do your best because you will be given marks which will add up, being a vital component of who actually wins at the end. Also, remember that the first voting session will be at 6pm on Sunday evening, so be aware of your fellow competitors, one of them will be forced to leave, and it will be down to your votes. You have until midday on Saturday to complete your task. Have fun!' The voice vanished and the eight men looked around at each other, all wondering who they would vote off. No one had really done anything to annoy the others yet, and conversely they didn't really know any of the others well enough to judge who'd be fun to live with, and so the choice was difficult.

Delving deep into the box, Jackson pulled out a sheet of typewritten paper and began to read aloud, his deep, soothing voice giving emphasis to the words. 'Housemates. In this box you will find eight small packages. Each contains a "Penis Moulding Kit". You are to pair off and create a mould of your compatriot's penis, in any state you choose. From this mould you will make a rubber version of that penis...it can be painted and decorated, or left "au naturel". The most imaginative and life-like member will win the most points. You will draw the name of your model from a hat, so there will be no favouritism. Have fun!'

Jackson burst out into a peal of dark laughter. 'Fucking hell...what a laugh!'

The laughter assumed an infectious air and soon everyone was joining in.

'So shall we draw names now, and see who we've got?' Skye leapt to his feet and padded into the sitting room, where he found some sheets of paper and a pen and, settling down by one of the counters, started to write everyone's name, then put the separate pieces in the now-empty cardboard box.

'OK, so who wants have the first pull?' he asked with a raised eyebrow, the intention of the double entendre lost on none of the others.

'I will.' William stepped forward and dipped his hand in the box pulling out a scrap of the paper and reading aloud. 'Peter.'

Peter looked suitably disappointed not to be paired with Colin but he bore the news with a stoic smile and shrugged his shoulders.

The rest of the pairing was equally unsettling, but giving each of the eight the chance to improve their relationship with another guy. Colin was paired with Jackson, Jost with Simon, and almost inevitably Rhys with Skye. The young porn actor chuckled to himself, and gave silent thanks to the fates that he had been twinned with his protégé. Rhys looked glumly at the floor, already ruing the moment when Skye had attached himself, his brand of forthright humour and worldly knowledge still very daunting for the timid Welshman.

Simon turned to the hand-written chart on the side of the fridge and read from their carefully worked out rota. 'My turn to do the washing up, so bugger off you lot and let me get on with it.' With a general murmur, the others disappeared.

It was noted that some of the housemates threw themselves into the task with gusto, while some exhibited signs of reticence. Almost immediately Colin and Jackson vanished into one of the bathrooms giggling like naughty schoolchildren, with the plastic bag containing the soft moulding plaster into which the appropriate phallus would eventually be pushed.

William and Peter spent the day in a huddle, discussing designs and colour schemes, whilst Jost and Simon studiously avoided each other until tea-time when they met in the garden for a 'getting to know you' session before the probable embarrassment of handling each other's genitalia. Skye kept close to Rhys, dogging his footsteps all day, until he eventually gave in and allowed himself to be taken up to their bedroom to start the task.

'It'll be fun...trust me.'

Rhys stared at Skye, still not understanding the man's motives. For some reason he had latched onto him and seemed fascinated by all he did and said. Nothing the Welsh lad did would shake Skye off. And now here they were together having to become intimately acquainted with the other's privates. Rhys blushed a deep crimson at the thought of it and sank down on his bed, unsure of what to do or say next.

'Right then, let's get started. We'll need some warm water for the putty, and a flannel and towel to clean off afterwards. Who wants to go first? Me, I think.' He began to strip off, his back to the lad and out of the corner of his eye saw that Rhys was slyly watching his every move. Perhaps there was a flicker of interest in the lad's loins. Perhaps he had a secret longing to get to grips with his cock. He wouldn't be the first, and certainly wouldn't be the last. Even if Skye won the prize money he had decided to still make porn, as the thrill was immense and the satisfaction undeniable.

Slowly peeling off his T-shirt, he flexed his arms, stretching them over his head, showing off his admirable torso. He could feel Rhys' eyes on his back, boring into him, scouring every inch of his smooth skin with his piercing gaze. He turned back to stare at Rhys, the lad's eyes darting away towards the floor. Surely this attractive young guy couldn't be as bashful as he seemed? Skye was of the opinion that any young gay lad who wasn't out enjoying his sexuality was definitely missing out. Somewhere deep inside his stomach Skye felt a pang, an intense spasm which he hadn't experienced in many years. He looked away and stared out of the window for a moment trying to compose himself. Was he having butterflies? Was he actually nervous about stripping off in front of this charming and unassuming young beauty? Yes he was, and he didn't know why. He turned back, catching Rhys' shy gaze, and decided to take the bull by the horns. Now was as good a time as any to really get to know the lad.

'Have you ever been in love?' He was stunned by the forthright nature of the question, as was Rhys, who seemed to shrink into a ball, hugging himself close.

'No.'

'Never?'

'Never.'

Skye sat beside the lad and took a deep, calming breath. 'Have you ever wanted to be?'

No answer came from Rhys, who sat, still as a statue, chewing over the question and slowly formulating his reply. 'All the time. I just never met anyone I ever felt that way about. I've loved people of course, but never been in love...there's a world of difference, you know.'

'I know.'

The flood gates had opened and Skye sat and listened as Rhys spoke, the heartfelt nature of his words totally sincere. 'Ever since I knew I was not normal, I was aware of guys in my town, school-friends, people at work, customers at the bowling alley, guys who were so beautiful that I felt an ache in my insides. I desperately wanted to know them and to be with them, to be held by them and made love to. But it never happened. I was too scared, I guess. If I'm honest, I have to admit that men scare me. I wish it wasn't so, but it is. The whole 'gay' thing is not the norm in life and I suppose I was and still am scared of being ridiculed. My family all know and accept me, but deep down I have a hard time with the truth of it.' He stopped and waited, his fingers aimlessly tracing the pattern on the bedspread.

Skye exhaled. 'Phew. I don't know what to say to all that. Except I think you need some gay friends. You need to see that being gay is as normal as any other life style. And this is the perfect opportunity to make those friends. You've already got one.'

'Have I?' Rhys stared deep into Skye's eyes, puzzled and questioning.

'Of course, you daft bastard, me.' He put his arms around Rhys and squeezed affectionately, surprised at the speed at which the lad responded, throwing his arms wide and taking Skye in a tight hug, breathing in as he did so, enjoying the smell of his body, clean and fresh.

Slightly embarrassed by this display of emotion, Skye gently pulled back and put a finger under Rhys's chin, lifting his face and smiling. 'So shall we start our challenge, then?'

Rhys grinned back, blinking back a tear which threatened to press itself out from the corner of his eye. 'Why not? Get your clothes off, then!'

Skye didn't need to be asked twice. He shucked his shoes, socks and trousers and stood at Rhys' side in just a pair of plain white briefs, tightly hugging his sizeable package. He saw that the lad's eyes were irresistibly drawn to it, and he smiled inwardly. If he had had little experience of men and their cocks, then he was in for a big surprise. Skye hadn't gone into the porn industry purely because of his good looks. He had something else in his favour, and he was very proud of it. Grasping the elastic waist of his briefs, he gently pulled them down, slowly, easing them lower, watching Rhys' eyes widen as first the soft bush of pubes was revealed and then the meaty base of his cock. Inch by inch he slid the briefs down the meaty length, until he stepped out of them and stood, naked and unashamed before the lad.

'All right?'

Rhys was speechless. In all the days and nights that he had dreamed of men, dreams full of lusty images of handsome guys, unclothed and ready for him, he had never conceived of such a perfect specimen as Skye. His chest and stomach were the creation of some higher power, stunningly shaped as they were, with firm, rounded breasts, and a stomach that had such line and definition that its owner must obviously perform innumerable daily sit-ups. The legs were sturdy and virtually hairless, the thighs strong and sensual, while the object of Rhys' unblinking gaze hung magnificently between his legs, thick and luscious, the bulbous head gently resting against a bronzed thigh, the balls heavy, hanging low in a stretched sac of skin.

'You are beautiful.' There was nothing else that Rhys could say. He had never thought that one day he would be privileged to gaze upon utter perfection. It was the kind of body that inspired worship, that would cause supplicants to fall on their knees and adore, the kind of body that had been immortalised in the genius of such creators as Da Vinci and Michelangelo, and here it was in front of a simple and inexperienced lad from a simple and inexperienced background.

'So let's do it then. Where's the stuff?' Sensing the electricity in the air and wanting to break the tension, Skye span on his heels and picked up the moulding kit from the bed. 'The question is...up or down? Shall I be hard or soft? What do you think?' He looked down at Rhys and paused.

'Hard.'

'OK, so we should mix up the putty and get on with it then.' He poured a small amount of water from a glass by his bed into a small bowl and began to stir in the grey powder, until it coagulated into a malleable putty. 'I'll need to get hard now...any suggestions?'

Skye moved closer to the bed, his groin only inches from Rhys' face. The head of the cock swung gently, slapping between the thighs as he moved. Rhys inhaled, again smelling the just-washed scent of the man before him, an odour of strength and manliness, the musky smell of a sexually active man. He was so overpowered with lust and fear that he closed his eyes for a brief moment, before staring ahead at the prize. Gently he put out his tongue. As he did so, Skye placed a guiding hand on his shoulder, a gesture of encouragement and concern.

'It's all right. Go for it.'

The tongue licked across the purple head, leaving a shining trail of saliva, and forcing Skye's hand to tighten and grip Rhys' shoulder more intensely. Rhys shuffled himself forward on the bed, and once comfortable, opened wide, letting the head in, sucking it into the warm cavity of his mouth. Skye gasped, and threw his head back. It only took a moment for the cock to harden and grow, filling Rhys' mouth and throat, growing rapidly, filling with a surge of excited blood. Breathing quickly through his nose, Rhys became accustomed to the sensation of such a big object in him, and relaxed slightly so the monster could slide out from between his lips. He noticed the groan Skye gave as this happened and so let it ease back down his throat and repeated the action. This was nothing like that first blow job he'd given to the stranger in the bowling alley toilets. That was all done so quickly and without passion and desire, but this felt different. Better. Nicer.

Skye stood stock still, letting Rhys have his moment. He could feel the lad's tongue all over his cock, in quick succession from the tip to the base as it lay deep in his mouth. He felt the tongue flick at the slit, licking up the droplet that oozed there. The mouth was wet and warm, confining and comforting, sucking him deeper and deeper into the boy's very being. He had difficulty in believing that Rhys was so inexperienced; perhaps he was waiting for the right cock to practise on. Skye wanted to know what the boy was thinking, and he hoped he was enjoying himself.

Rhys had never known anything like it. His mouth was totally full of cock, and he wanted to savour the moment forever. With his eyes tightly shut, he concentrated his efforts on the blow job, engulfing it and working his tongue around the head, and easing back as he felt Skye start up a fucking motion, back and forth, pulling out and then forcing himself back inside, stretching the mouth with increasing strokes. Rhys placed his hands on the bed behind Skye's arse for support and doubled his speed, soon his head was a blur of sucking action, the saliva from his mouth spilling out and pouring down his chin, slathering along the cock's shaft. With a look of utter amazement on his face, Skye was caught unawares by the ferocity of his climax. It happened without any warning and he shot a load of come out and down Rhys' throat. The lad licked it dry and held onto the cock in his mouth until he felt he couldn't any longer. With his wide, blue eyes he stared up at Skye, almost as if he couldn't believe what he'd just done.

A moral pang shot across Skye's mind, and he tried to concentrate on the challenge. 'Er...thanks Rhys, that was very nice, but let's get on with our task.' He pulled away from the lad, still rock hard, his cock slippery and trembling, a ring of saliva around Rhys' lips testament to their actions. 'So can you slop the putty over me?' He stood with his hands on his hips, waiting.

Rhys shuffled forward on his knees, and grabbed up the mixing bowl and quickly shoved his hands into the accompanying rubber gloves, delved into the mixture and slapped a handful on the towering dick, smearing it all over, covering it with further handfuls until it stood grey and rather comical.

'How long do we wait?' He stared up at the blond Adonis, drawn into his dazzling blue eyes.

'About five minutes. This stuff will get hard quickly.'

'How does it feel?'

'Strange, but quite horny. I can feel the stuff hardening and getting tight. It is sort of clamping around my cock, kind of squeezing it, like a hand job, sort of. Still, you'll find out soon enough.'

Saturday

By the group's sixth day in the house, all barriers had started to break down. The guys were becoming more relaxed in each other's company. The pairings that had started the week had dissipated and they had melded into a tight, mostly friendly octet. There had been some friction, but generally only over the smallest of complaint, and the arguments were soon resolved.

'Game of cards anyone?' Jost called out. It was eleven o'clock in the morning, and most of the guys were either still in bed or putting the finishing touches to their penis sculptures. Jost was sitting in the kitchen, bored. He and Simon had finished theirs quickly, and Simon had decided to decorate the moulding of Jost's cock, to make a distinct impression on the judges. It was a rubber moulding of the Dutchman's semi-hard member, with integral bollocks where Simon had been very liberal with the putty. His own moulding was a definite hard one; Jost had been impressed with the shape, size and the Prince Albert piercing which graced it. Jost had made his mind up that the whole challenge was a bit silly and superficial, and once he had tied a red ribbon around the base of Simon's moulding, left it in a natural state.

'Are you just going to leave it like this?' Simon strode into the kitchen brandishing his rubber willy, the red ribbon flopping lifelessly around the bottom of it.

'Yeah.' Jost didn't even look, up, his attention directed at the pack of cards he was shuffling out in the shape of a clock face, ready for a game of Patience.

'Aren't you going to do anything more to it?' There was a tone to Simon's voice that made the Dutchman look up.

'We don't have to, you know. We were told we could leave them in any state we want.'

'I know that, but extra effort will earn extra marks, and as it's my dick you've done, I feel a bit proprietorial about it.'

Jost turned back to the kitchen counter and turned over an ace, placing it in position and turning over another card. 'Well don't. It's my decision not to do anything with it, so just mind your own business. Why don't I take you upstairs and give you a good hard...massage?'

'Fuck you!' Simon's voice rose considerably, anger and frustration bursting out in a torrent. 'Fuck you...in fact, I'm glad you are doing nothing because nobody likes you, and you'll be gone soon.' Spinning on his heels, he threw the rubber artefact over his shoulder and marched out of the kitchen.

'What was all that about?' Colin emerged from the living room covered in glitter and paint.

'I have had it with that shithead.'

'Which particular shithead?'

Gesturing toward the kitchen door, Simon crossed his arms defiantly. 'Jost. He wasn't interested in doing the willy thing; only wanted to blow me off when he saw my cock. He is so predictable. And after all the trouble I took over his...I've just had enough.'

Affably, Colin put an arm around Simon's shoulders and led him into the living room, ignoring the mess that he and Jackson had created. 'Don't worry about it. Look, it's obvious that living in this artificial environment will get to us sooner or later. Try to relax. Ignore it...it's not your problem if he doesn't want to join in. Come on now, it's nearly time for the judging. Go and get your willy, and wake up any of the lazy bastards who aren't up yet.' He planted a kiss on Simon's forehead.

'OK. I'm just being silly, I know.' He sighed. 'Still, I think I'm with a good chance with the willy I made. I'm very proud of it, even though I don't like the model very much.'

'Good boy. Off you go, then.'

The various moulded rubber cocks were placed in the large cardboard box and left down by the main gate for collection by the production team, and the guys went back to enjoying the rest of their Saturday. Jost and Simon didn't speak for hours, until Colin persuaded them to shake hands and make up. This they did grudgingly, but there was still a palpable tension between them. As the guys settled down in the living room, waiting for their supper to be announced by Peter who had created an 'Italian special' for them – lasagne, garlic bread and a mozarella cheese salad – the hidden speaker crackled into life again.

'Good evening, Boycam house. Matt speaking. Thank you all for your efforts over the first challenge. The results have been noted and marks awarded accordingly. For the moment the totals will be kept secret, as we do not want them to affect the way you react and exist with each other. But good efforts from you all. Obviously some put more effort in than others, but moving on...' He paused for effect. The seven guys in the living room and Peter in the kitchen listened intently. 'As you are aware, tomorrow is the first eviction vote. In the morning you will find a small metal box outside the door. At six o'clock precisely you will place your confidential, hand-written votes in the box, fasten the padlock and leave it at the gate. The result of the vote will be announced to you all at eight o'clock exactly. The first person to be evicted will then have one hour to pack his belongings and make his way to the gate. Is that clear?'

A sea of nodding heads answered him.

'Good. And so that you enjoy the magnificent repast that Peter is preparing for you tonight, you will find half a dozen bottles of wine outside the front door. Have fun!' A cry of delight went up among the housemates. William leapt to his feet and ran to the door, returning wreathed in smiles and carrying a case of wine.

'Very nice...three red and three white. Should make the evening go with a swing, eh chaps?'

And indeed it did. All the tension that had built up over the last six days vanished as the alcohol worked its magic. The guys relaxed, started opening up and for the first time bonded as friends.

'What's the time?' Jackson asked the room, looking over the pile of recumbent bodies populating the sofas, chairs and in one case slumped against the wall.

'Half past two.' Skye, sitting next to Jackson, lifted his hand and showed Jackson his wrist watch, dropping his arm and letting it land on his neighbour's thigh, giving it a squeeze. 'I don't know why it has taken so long for us to get to know each other.' He twisted his head so that he was looking up at the handsome features of the black guy, un-aware that he was slurring his words a little.

'Neither do I. Although...' Jackson stuttered to a halt, and bit his lip. 'Go on...'

'Well...it's just that you do come across as arrogant sometimes.'

'I don't mean to.' Skye scanned the room until he found Rhys, fast asleep, curled up in a foetal ball in one of the armchairs. 'Rhys!' His voice pierced the quiet, making Peter and Simon, who were dozing in each other's arms, wake with a start. 'Rhys!'

'Wha's the matter?' The Welsh lad mumbled, rubbing his eyes and looking blearily at Skye.

'I'm a nice guy, aren't I?'

'Course you are.'

He smiled triumphantly up at Jackson. 'There you are. I'm nice. Rhys says so, and everyone trusts Rhys...bless him, little innocent Rhys.'

Shifting a little in his chair, Rhys turned to stare at Skye, drinking in his stunning good looks, and shaking the image of his naked body from the forefront of his mind. 'What are you saying about me?'

'Nothing, flower. Just that I'm nice, and you're nice and that you are sweet and innocent...and that's nice.'

Something clicked in Rhys' brain and he sat up, rubbing his fingers against his temples, trying to bring some clarity to his thoughts. 'Why do you keep on saying that? OK, I'm not as experienced as you, but what's wrong with that? And at least I'm not a slag. I haven't lost count of the number of guys I've slept with, and that's no bad thing.'

Through the alcohol-induced state, Skye realised he had gone too far. 'I'm sorry, baby. I didn't mean it.'

'Good. Now talk about something else.' Rhys stopped, an idea formulating rapidly in his head. 'How about we play a game?'

'Sure.'

'A truth game.'

'A what?' Jackson sat up, suddenly alert.

Rhys was now warming to the idea. 'A truth game. We ask each other questions, and we have to answer truthfully. If we reckon someone's lying, then they have to pay a forfeit.'

William, who had been listening to the conversation without speaking, nudged Jost in the ribs, waking him. 'Sounds fun,' he said, aware of the possibilities such a game could throw up.

Simon and Peter, also now wide awake, disentangled themselves from each other and sat up too, Peter throwing a cushion at Colin, who had earlier slumped against the wall in a drunken state. 'Come on sleepy-head, time for some fun.'

Soon all eight guys were awake, in varying stages of intoxication, and waiting for the game to begin. Rhys looked around the room, seeing the seven expectant faces, knowing that they were all waiting for him to start the game. As if a thunderbolt had struck him, he saw that he had a role to play in the Boycam house. He wasn't just a naïve hanger-on, a passenger along for the ride, but he was equal to the others, as important as them, and with as much to give to the life of the project as they had. He took a deep, soothing breath and spoke.

'Right then...we ask a question each of one other person in the room, and they have to answer with the truth...and I mean that, the whole truth...'

'So help me God!' Colin tittered and raised his hand mockingly.

'Ssshh.' A chorus of hushing sang out like a pit of snakes and, chastened, Colin sat back in his chair.

Continuing unabashed, Rhys said, 'If we think you aren't telling the truth, then you have to pay a forfeit decided by the one who asked the question. OK?'

All heads nodded their understanding. 'Who wants to go first?' Rhys scanned the others housemates, his eye lighting on one of his fellow participants. 'You, Simon?'

'Sure, why not?' He leaned forward in his chair. 'Jackson...' He gazed at Jackson, who lay back on the sofa, his arm still around Skye's shoulders. 'Is it true what they say about black cock?'

Without saying a word, Jackson stood up and unzipped his trousers, dropping them in a swift motion.

'In this case, it is,' he said, raising an enquiring eyebrow.

With a shriek, Simon stared at the purple-headed giant being waved at him, and collapsed in a heap of laughter.

'My turn, my turn!' William waved a finger in the air and pointed it at Simon. 'Tell me about that piercing of yours. Why did you have it done, and did it hurt?'

'I don't know, really. It wasn't something I thought about for ages. I just woke one morning and decided to have it done. I had plenty of anaesthetic, and the actual piercing didn't hurt a bit. The only time I regretted it was the first few times I needed a piss, and fucking hell it hurt! Like trying to piss several large razor blades. But it eased quickly and now I love it. I wouldn't be without it. It enhances my love-making and sometimes comes as real surprise to a partner, because they aren't expecting it and I say nothing in advance.'

William hesitated for a moment, then asked the obvious question. 'So how about a quick look?'

Sighing and realising he had no other option but to agree, Simon stood and pulled it out, letting everyone who wanted have a good look. Pleased by the reaction and rather flattered by the impressed comments, Simon sat down, a huge grin creasing his face.

'Me next.' Peter raised his hand. 'This question is for Jost. When did you know you were gay?'

'I can't remember a time when I wasn't. I suppose whilst at school – I was about twelve – I recall having strange feelings about one of the older boys. I was fascinated by him, and used to hang around just to get a glimpse of him, and would usually get this churning in my stomach whenever I saw him. I never did anything about it, though, until I was much older. My turn now. Er...Colin, who do you think will eventually win this show?'

There was a joint drawing in of breath around the room. Although it wasn't in the rules that they shouldn't discuss the show and its possible outcome, they had not deliberated it between themselves. This question had taken them by surprise. 'Don't say you haven't thought about it...because if you say you haven't, I know you'll be lying.'

Colin sat still, marshalling his thoughts. 'Well, since you ask I will answer, as I have no choice. I won't name names, but I will say this. I think the person who wins will do so through his personality. Those of us who try to make a big impression or who cause trouble will find themselves voted out. I think it will be the strong silent type who'll eventually win through. That's all I have to say. Now then...William, what was your most bizarre sexual experience?'

'That's easy. I've never really had one.'

The room exploded in jeers and disbelieving cat-calls.

'It's true. In all my years on this planet I've never really experienced anything that I would classify as bizarre – cross my heart and hope to die.'

Colin inched forward and fixed William with a steely gaze. 'I'm afraid I don't believe you!'

The others yelled triumphantly, ready for the game's first sacrifice. 'OK, your forfeit...I want you go into the kitchen, bring back a cucumber and give it a blow job...'

'You are joking!'

'No...go on. I'm waiting...' Colin sat back and crossed his arms.

The group watched and yelled as William performed his forfeit. Jackson and Simon were reduced to quivering heaps, rolling on the floor laughing hysterically.

'You bastards!' Throwing the cucumber into the corner of the room, William sank into his chair, his face reddened with the acuteness of his embarrassment.

Rhys took his turn, saying 'Peter...what's the biggest cock you've ever had?'

Grinning, Peter looked at the carpet. 'Well, there was the one in Amsterdam when I was in this sling in a darkroom. One of the guys who fucked me was huge, although there is someone closer to home...' He tailed off and glanced at Colin, waiting for a reaction, before he burst out laughing and fell back into Simon's arms.

'Right, who hasn't had a go?' Rhys looked round the room.

Slowly Jackson raised his hand and smiled down at Skye who sat nestled against his side. 'So tell me Skye...firstly, is it really true that you have done live sex shows, and if it is, tell us all about them.'

All eyes turned in the blond's direction, eager to hear the answer.

'Yes, it is absolutely true. I had done some modelling for gay magazines, you know the kind of stuff, general bum and soft-cock shots, and met this guy called Fabio who owned a club in Barcelona. He was looking for guys to go out and dance in the bar. I thought it would be a good laugh and so said yes, plus the money was really good. When

I got there I was surprised at the seediness of the place, quite dingy, but full of the horniest guys. So me and this guy from Manchester, called Dan, started dancing on the bar top, letting the guys fondle us and stick money in our G-strings. After a while Fabio wanted to diversify and asked Dan and me if we'd consider doing some live sex stuff. Well, Dan was cute, and so I said yes immediately; Dan soon agreed. Fabio set up this stage at one end of the bar, draped it in black velvet and directed a few lights on it. We hadn't really got anything planned; we just winged it. We went up on stage dressed in our normal clothes and slowly undressed each other to the music – Jean-Michel Jarré I seem to recall, all a bit eighties, I know. Anyway, we were down to our undies and both quite hard – that's the exhibitionist in me, I suppose – and soon we were naked and sixty-nineing on this raised plinth, and the audience was going wild. We became a regular Saturday night feature.'

Rhys raised his eyes and shot him a glance from under hooded brows. 'It's Saturday today... how about a demonstration?'

He couldn't believe what he had just said. He hadn't expected those words to come from his mouth. Perhaps it was the alcohol talking, perhaps something deeper. The seven other guys stared, surprised at the young lad, amazed that he was speaking in such a straightforward manner. But all were eager for an answer from Skye, all curious to see this blond bombshell in action.

It took a few moments for Skye to respond, but his eventual answer was direct and plain. 'OK, I'll show you, if you'll answer my next question truthfully.'

Rhys gulped, his throat suddenly dry, now only aware of himself and Skye, and the tension that had built up between them. 'Sure...' His voice cracked as he spoke.

'Then tell me the truth. Would you like to be performing with me?'

'No.'

'The truth now...'

'No.'

'I don't believe you... and I am sure none of the others believes you. So it's time for a forfeit, I think...let me see...something worthy of the situation...I know...has anyone got a scarf or towel or something we can use as a blindfold?'

Rhys shivered as a gust of cold air scuttled across him. 'What are you going to do?' Now he was nervous. Unsure of himself. The situation had been his to command, but now things were out of his control. Anything could happen.

'You'll see. Ah, thanks Colin.' Skye took the scarf that had been brought from the hallway and gestured for Rhys to come closer.

'Down on your knees before me...come on...you made up the rules of this game and so you have to do it.'

Slowly and with an unsure gait, Rhys stood and crossed the room, sinking to his knees in front of Skye, who stared down at him, his eyes exuding a shining light, twinkling with an exultant intensity. 'Turn round.'

The lad obeyed and found the scarf being wound tightly around his eyes, the woollen fabric soft against his skin, cutting off all vision. Again he shivered, his nerves in shreds, his heart beating a loud tattoo in his chest, his mouth dry.

'Now...' Skye said, 'this is your forfeit. You are going to suck my cock, here and now...but you have to find it. Stand up.' Shakily, Rhys did as he was told, and without warning someone grabbed his shoulders and spun him round and round. He was roughly pushed down to his knees again, and he put out his hands. His fingers made contact with someone's leg, but they were immediately brushed away. Something banged against his cheek, warm and solid...he knew what it was and he knew what he had to do. Opening his lips slightly, he awaited the object which he knew would soon be approaching his mouth, and instantly it arrived. He widened his mouth, his mind a riot of conflicting thoughts. Should I be doing this? Think about the cameras...they'll be watching your every move. Everyone will think you are a tart, do you want that? But Skye's cock is so beautiful. Don't you want to suck it again? Would you be doing this if you hadn't got drunk?

He had no chance to change his mind. The cock-head pushed at his lips and slid inside. For a moment Rhys sucked and then the revelation hit. Skye's cock was circumcised; the one in his mouth still had a foreskin. The man he was sucking was not Skye. He pulled away, wiping his mouth with the back of his hand, but someone gently pushed him toward the cock again. What the hell. He went for it and began to suck the cock, a tiny thrill coursing through him; a thrill caused by the notion that he was sucking a cock, and he didn't know who it belonged to. Perhaps he never would know.

Another dick slapped against his cheek and Rhys turned to it, opening his mouth wide to let it in, feeling it slide inside, along with the first one, until he felt his mouth being stretched to its limit, both cocks vying for attention. He twisted his head and back and forth, going down on one and then the other, determined to give as good as he was able. He could hear groans, and still he wasn't sure who they came from.

He heard a scuffling sound and the two cocks pulled away, to be replaced by two more. One he recognised as Skye's, the perfect symmetry of that wondrous phallus still fresh in his mind, the other of a reasonable size, not huge, but a nice mouthful, but with the addition of a cold metal ring through the end. At last, he knew two of his tormentors – Skye and Simon. With the mental pictures of these two uppermost, he opened his mouth even wider, and sucked for all he was worth. Skye's cock slid in and out smoothly, whereas Simon's, which was slightly bumpier, with the veins and arteries creating a rugged landscape, and the steel ring at the tip, gave Rhys a completely new sensation. The cold heaviness of the piercing dangled across his tongue, rhythmically pushing against the back of his throat, giving

Rhys the urge to gag. He knew he was doing well. He could hear the grunts of pleasure and he could feel the pounding of the cocks increasing. Suddenly Simon pulled himself out of Rhys' mouth and he heard a small yelp and felt a warm splatter across his cheek. His lips were forced wide open as Skye pushed his way back inside for some last few sucks before he too shot his load, the cum falling in gentle pats on Rhys' face and hair, around his mouth and neck.

For a couple of moments he just sat, dazed, stunned by what had just happened, completely amazed that he of all people had done such an outrageous and daring thing. And in front of the Boycam cameras too. He imagined Matt rubbing his hands – or even his cock – with glee, seeing the possible ratings figures rocketing.

'Guys...?' Rhys waited patiently for an answer, but none came. 'Guys...? Pulling off the scarf he saw that he was alone, kneeling in the middle of the carpet, his face and hair covered with newly shot spunk.

Sunday

Rhys tried hard to act as though nothing had happened, but all day he found the other guys watching him out of the corner of their eyes and then quickly looking away embarrassed. Skye was friendly of course, and would occasionally give Rhys a big, amiable hug, tittering to himself under his breath. The day had passed quite quickly for the eight housemates; an impromptu game of rounders had provided much amusement after lunch, and the pitchers of home-made lemonade that William brought out into the garden went down a treat. Everyone seemed relaxed about the impending vote and had apparently put it from their minds. Dinner had been a great success too, with Peter providing a casserole that had everybody applauding its flavour. Jost sat disconsolately with a plate of tuna salad, and watched the guys wolfing down their supper with gusto.

Rhys looked at his watch. Five minutes to eight. The voting had happened quickly and efficiently. All of the eight had written the name of the person they wanted evicted on their voting slip and placed them in the metal ballot box, which was then safely delivered to the main gate. After the fun of the day, the last two hours had been hell, with most of the guys going to their rooms, or doing solitary activities, eschewing company and conversation.

'Hello, Boycam house.' Matt's voice rang out. The eight assembled guys looked around the room, nerves jangling, stomachs and mouths dry with anticipation. Who would it be?

'I have the result of the first vote here in front of me, and there is a clear winner...or I should say loser. One of you will have an hour to pack and be ready to leave. A car will be waiting for you outside the gate to take you home. Now if you are all ready...the first person to leave the Boycam house is...Jost Van Dijk.'

Interview with Jost Van Dijk

'I have to say that I was very disappointed to be the first person to go. I actually thought I would last longer than that. The other guys seemed OK. I liked Colin and Peter, and hadn't really got to know the others that well before I was forced to leave.

'I probably think that the reason they voted me out was that they couldn't cope with my alternative views and my attempts to live my way of life in the house. In that respect they were all very cloistered, if that's the word. I had only been in the house for one week, but I have to say that it felt like a year. Living with seven other guys, all with attitude problems of one sort or another was difficult, and I was glad to get back to normal life.

'I suppose in a way I was glad of the experience. It taught me that I am a man who likes to live on his own, who needs his own space. If I do eventually settle down with a guy, then it will be on my terms. It will be someone who is prepared to live my way.

'Who do I think will win the show eventually? That's tough at this stage. I think it has to be a guy with strength of character, someone who is prepared to fight to be there at the end. Possibly Simon or Jackson. I'm not sure. Anyway, the whole thing has been good for me. After the eviction I was offered a job at a gay health centre teaching Tantric sex classes, and I am now quite happy.'

WEEK TWO

Monday

The seven remaining housemates all assembled at breakfast the following morning with an air of badly concealed relief. All were glad that the voting had happened without a hitch and one of their number – one who had done little to endear himself to his fellow inmates – had gone. There had been little ceremony. At the announcement of his name, Jost had looked around the group, noting the heads hung in embarrassment and discomfort and the eyes that studiously avoided his angry gaze. 'Fuck you all,' he had said in a bitter tone, rising and stalking from the living room, stomping upstairs to pack. He had remained in his room until the appointed hour and just swept away in a cloud of resentment without saying goodbye to any of the watching guys. The general consensus was that he would not be missed, and that life – for the next week at least – would be a lot more harmonious. After he had left, the house had retained an uneasy air, with most of the housemates either keeping their own company or going to bed early.

'So what do we fancy doing today?' Jackson surveyed his compatriots.

'I fancy a spot of sunbathing. Take in a few of those delicious rays.' William looked through the kitchen window at the glorious sunshine bathing the verdant lawn. 'Slap on a bit of tan factor fifteen and improve my general desirability. Anyone else coming?'

There were a few enthusiastic murmurs and a plan was made to have a lazy day just enjoying the warmth, with a picnic for the late afternoon.

And so it happened. All the guys could soon be found stretched out on towels or blankets, taking advantage of the wonderful summer sun. It was Skye who had pottered inside to get a glass of water, who returned clutching a sheet of paper which he brandished like Chamberlain after his meeting with Hitler. 'Look what I've got! This week's challenge.'

'Oh, I'd forgotten about that.' Peter shielded his eyes and raised himself on one elbow, looking, so Skye thought, rather dishy in his tight red and white Speedos. 'Read it out, then.'

The other five also sat up and waited expectantly as Skye cleared his throat dramatically and began to read. 'This week's challenge is less exacting than last week's and should prove to be a lot more fun.' He paused and licked his lips.

'Go on, don't stop, you rotten shit.' William picked up a small stone and lobbed it playfully at him.

'Now girls, if you don't behave you won't hear any of this. Are all quiet? Good, then I'll continue.' Enjoying this minor moment in the limelight, Skye looked back at the sheet and continued. 'You will have all week to plan and prepare a dinner party to be held on Saturday evening. All food and drink and accoutrements will be provided to your specifications, with no limit as to what you can have. But...' Skye paused for effect, his eyes scanning the inquisitive looks from the others.

'But what?' Rhys couldn't help but burst out.

'... But you will all assume the personas and characters of famous film stars, alive or dead. You will have to create a costume and be in character from seven o'clock until midnight when the dinner party will end. Extra points will be awarded to those who show imagination and wit in their choice of star and who create the most appropriate costume. Leave any requests for materials or props at the gate for collection every morning and they will be delivered the following day. You can work alone or with others. Have fun.' He folded the paper and handed it to Peter who was nearest to him, then burst out in a peal of infectious laughter.

'What a brilliant challenge. This could be a real laugh.' Colin sat cross-legged, a huge smile on his face. 'But who to choose? That'll be really difficult. Do you pick a star you admire, or one whose voice you can mimic, or just go for one with the silliest costume? Tough call.'

The rest of the day was spent chatting amiably about the party, planning what kind of food they should eat, what the decorations should be and most importantly, who they wanted to come as. All the gloom and despondency of the previous evening had vanished and strong friendships were developing in the hot rays of the summer sunshine.

Wednesday

The box that sat on the tarmac by the front gate was bulging with materials and props, wigs and hats. And when Simon had carried them into the games room and dumped them on the pool table, the others fell upon them with cry of excitement, carrying the various bits to their rooms to start work on creating their costumes.

'Any good with a tape measure?' Simon gazed up at Jackson who towered over him by at least twelve inches.

'Possibly...if you are any good with scissors.'

'Done.' Simon and Jackson grabbed an armful of stuff and raced up the stairs giggling.

'Shut the door. We don't want any spies.' Simon gestured with his head, his normally immaculate black hair slightly dishevelled this morning after a poor night's sleep. Strange dreams had invaded his slumber; images of monstrous snakes everywhere, and his mother marooned in their house unable to get out, calling his name, needing help. He woke bathed in sweat, wrapped in his duvet like a modern-day mummy. After that, he found it difficult to get back to sleep, so he just lay awake watching the sun come up, listening to the tuneful babble of the dawn chorus mixing with the sounds of heavy breathing from Jackson, who always seemed to sleep well.

'Sure. Listen Si, I'll help you, if you could help me. I'm not very good with all this making costume thing, and would appreciate a hand. What do you say?' Jackson sat on his bed, still clutching his bundle. He looked up at Simon who stood, hands on hips, his tongue poking out at the corner of his mouth, waiting for his answer.

'OK. I don't see why not. If we can come up with something extra special it might earn us a few extra points. And I do want to look spectacular. Come on, then. If I hold this material up, can you measure it and cut it to the right length?' He draped a vivid yellow cloth around him and let it hang in generous folds, watching as Jackson fell to his knees and began to measure.

After a few minutes, Jackson looked up, a frown corrugating his brow. 'It's not hanging right. Can you take your sweater off?'

Simon let the cloth fall to the floor, and with a swift yank, pulled his sweater over his head so he stood in his jeans and a South Park T-shirt. Then without being asked, he shucked his jeans and sandals. Naturally, since they shared a room, Jackson had seen Simon in various states of undress, and so there was nothing new or intrinsically arousing in his current appearance, but there was a change in the atmosphere. Simon stared down at Jackson, squatting at his feet, perhaps for the first time noting the chiselled features of this friendly black guy.

Over the last week, Jackson had quietly found himself developing a silent fixation on Simon. More and more he lay in bed at night fantasising about Simon and wondering what he was like as a lover. He certainly had a good body. Broad shoulders, with a muscular if slight frame, his muscles flat and trim, and nicely defined under his pale skin. He had what popular gay culture called a swimmer's body, with strong lean legs, his arse compact. His nipples were round and brown, quite large, larger than would be expected. The pectorals were firm, and the ridge below them led down to the washboard stomach which was rippled and well worked on. Today his hair wasn't so neat. It had that just washed springiness about it, with a small tuft that refused to lie down and look perfect. He had created scenarios in his mind where he would walk into the room and find Simon naked, and they would find themselves locked in a fearsome, fervent embrace. He had imagined being alone with him late at night, when all the other housemates had gone to bed and their passion would erupt. But even so, in all his erotic wondering he had never pictured Simon with a hard-on. He had seen his cock of course, having had a good look when they were playing the truth game and Simon had whopped it out for the boys, but in his mind he had resisted the temptation to picture the erection; somehow it would be cheap, and spoil the delight in seeing it in reality.

'What are you waiting for?' Simon looked down inquisitively, one eyebrow raised.

'Nothing. It's just that...' his voice trailed off as he sat on his haunches, staring up at the perfect body, and the deep, dark eyes. His mind was again assailed. He thought about holding Simon and caressing him, letting his fingers explore every inch of his lean torso. He thought about kissing his lips and then sucking on his cock. He could feel a stirring in his own loins and he knew he should clear his mind and get on with the task in hand.

As if Simon were psychic, he moved closer to Jackson, his light blue briefs now just inches from his housemate's face. 'It's OK. I know.'

'Know what?'

'I know that you have been watching me. I know that there is something between us. I think there could be. Why should Peter and Colin be the only ones getting a shag in here?'

Jackson's mouth was suddenly dry. In all his imagining he had never expected something like this to happen. 'In fact,' Simon continued, 'I think it would be a bloody good idea. I think you are really handsome. I reckon we could have some fun. What do you say?'

Silence hung heavy in the bedroom, as Jackson weighed up his answer, although somewhere in the back of his mind there was a nagging thought...something wasn't right. Then it came to him in a flash. The cameras.

'But what about them?' He gestured with his eyes to the ceiling, indicating their faceless observers.

'What about them?'

'They'll be watching.'

'So?'

'So do we want to do this?'

For a second he could see a spasm of indecision cross Simon's face as he considered the situation carefully. Then, as if a monumental judgement had been reached, he put out a hand and stroked Jackson's cheek.

'I actually don't care. Let them watch. Let them see two young studs in action...it'll send the ratings soaring. Besides...have you never wanted to be watched having sex? You must have had some kind of latent fantasy or you wouldn't have applied to be on the show.'

Jackson knew he was right. He had nothing else to say. He took in a deep breath and inched his face closer to Simon's crotch. He was so close now he could feel the heat from the Chinese guy's body, and could smell the fragrance of the soap he had used earlier. He inhaled deeply, and pushed his face into the crotch, letting his nose and mouth push against the mound of confined flesh. He opened his mouth and felt with his teeth and lips for the cock slumbering in the pale blue cotton. His teeth rested on something hard. The piercing. Then with small nipping bites he pulled on the ring through the cotton, hearing gentle whimpers of pleasure escaping from Simon's mouth. Then, slowly, he sucked on the head of Simon's cock, feeling his saliva moistening the cotton briefs, and with his teeth he felt along the length of the shaft until his nose was nestled at the top, his forehead rubbing the elastic waistband. Sitting up a little, he gripped the band and gently tugged it down, revealing the first wisps of dark bushy hair, and the beginning of the shaft. Inch by inch he tugged, letting the cock emerge from its confinement, until it bobbed free, and Simon was able to step out of the briefs and stand before Jackson, naked and ready.

The cock was beautiful. Very nice, quite large. It hung, half hard now, between his legs, not that thick but quite long, culminating in a symmetrical head, adorned with the monster Prince Albert piercing, the weight of which seemed to pull the head down. It would need to be a monster hard-on to raise that fucker, Jackson thought to himself with a wry smile.

'What's the matter? Don't you like it?' A frown of concern twisted Simon's normally placid features.

'No, it's very nice.'

'Well, go on then. Have fun.' Jackson smiled again as Simon echoed Matt's usual parting words to the housemates. Have fun. He certainly would. This was a golden opportunity and he was determined to enjoy himself, cameras or no cameras.

Jackson put out his tongue and flicked it across the heavy, silver piercing. It felt cold but smooth. This would be a first for him. His first pierced dick. Letting it slip inside his lips, he allowed the head to pop inside, immediately feeling it swelling with blood, feeling the tell-tale rush that signalled excitement. The ring felt odd, but somehow strangely erotic, lying on his tongue. As the cock grew and hardened, it pushed along and slipped further down Jackson's throat, until it had reached its maximum solidity, and filled his mouth nicely. The ring dangled over the base of his tongue, banging against the back of his throat, and happily not causing him to gag. This was wonderful. Wanting to show Simon his oral prowess, he began to suck his cock.

Simon closed his eyes and started to moan as Jackson went to work, his thick, smooth lips closing over the tip of his cock, enclosing it and then sliding down the length of the hardened shaft. He put out his hands to grip Jackson's shoulders, twisting the material of his shirt between his trembling fingers. He had hoped for a blow job from this attractive guy, but never one so good. He felt the heft of his piercing nudging the back of Jackson's throat, then slipping across the surface of his lapping tongue. He certainly knew his stuff. The suction seemed to increase with each in-thrust. He squirmed as Jackson left the cock for a moment and moved his tongue to the compact balls hanging beneath, licking and sucking them into his mouth, pulling them away from the body, almost stretching the skin to breaking point. Simon was compelled to cry out a little as the discomfort finally became too much and, as if he knew he had gone too far, Jackson let them plop out, immediately resuming his attentions on the dripping cock. Simon burned with desire and lust as he concentrated his mind on the wet, slippery feel of Jackson's lips and tongue all over him, focusing his thoughts on the blow job, trying to think of nothing else, to be nothing else but his cock and Jackson's mouth. He felt Jackson's hands sliding up and down his thighs, caressing them lovingly, then reaching up to gently knead his nipples, tweaking them into two erect points, before slowly drawing his fingers down the smooth, muscled stomach.

Jackson was now really enjoying this. He usually described himself as versatile sexually, and was willing to try anything, but his ultimate favourite activity was sucking cock. And this cock was a gem. Stunningly hard, beautifully shaped and perfectly adorned. It felt so good and so natural to suck it and he knew that Simon was enjoying it too, from the moans he was making and the tight pressure of his hands on his shoulders. Suddenly he knew that it was time to move on. To accelerate this coupling into the next gear. He wanted to be fucked. He wanted Simon's cock to push inside his arse. And he wanted it now. Fuck the cameras, and fuck the programme. And fuck me. He had a mental image of the producers sitting in their viewing gallery, eyes glued to the monitors, all willing them to go the whole way, all with secret stiffies, all longing to bash away at their pent-up juices. Well, now he'd give them something to watch.

He pulled away and sat back on his heels.

'Why've you stopped?' Simon looked puzzled and a little hurt.

'I want you to fuck me.' Blunt and to the point. Jackson had nothing else to say.

A smile creased Simon's face, his eyes narrowing, his mouth widening in understanding. 'I see. You'd better strip then.' He gazed delightedly as Jackson rapidly undressed, throwing his clothes in a heap by the bedroom door.

He was also quickly standing there, naked and erect, watching Simon's eyes travelling over every inch of his body. He was proud of his physique, and knew that his exertions at the gym had paid off handsomely. He looked down with pride at his swollen organ, raising his eyes to meet Simon's impressed gaze. He knew it wasn't the biggest cock in the world, but it was sizeable. Some of the porn videos Jackson had seen featured actors with some of the hugest cocks. Cocks that somehow never really got hard. Cocks that had to be squeezed tightly round the base to even give a semblance of a hard-on. All the grunting and groaning and faked fucking looked so unerotic. But he never had that problem. His cock was big enough and hard enough to always give pleasure. But this afternoon that would be a purely arbitrary statement. This afternoon he wanted a cock up inside of him, to stretch and fill him utterly. And it looked like it was going to happen.

Simon crossed to his bed and took a toilet bag from inside the bedside cabinet, reaching in and pulling out a tube of lubrication and a condom, Jackson seeing from where he stood that it was an extra-strength protective.

'Do you wanna give me a hand?' Simon held out the condom and the lube and waited. Nervously, Jackson took them and knelt before Simon, giving the cock-head a tiny lick before tearing open the foil pack and beginning to roll it down the length of Simon's enraged shaft until it came to rest at the base, snugly encasing it.

'Ready?' The words sent a shiver down Jackson's spine as he knew what was expected of him. Nodding he climbed onto his bed, kneeling and spreading his legs wide, feeling a cooling gust of air from the slightly open window play across his hanging bollocks, making him shiver again. He turned his head to watch Simon spreading some lube on his cock, until it glistened in the natural light of the room, before kneeling up behind and positioning himself. Jackson gasped as he felt a finger at his hole, greasy and cold, which began to probe and smear the lube all around him, pushing inside and greasing the inner ring of his arse. The ring tightly clenched around the finger, and he heard a low chuckle from the guy kneeling behind him.

'Hmmm. Someone's tight. Someone needs a good stretching. I wonder who that could be!'

Bowing his head so it met the embroidered duvet, Jackson prepared himself, pushing his arse up into the air, waiting.

Carefully, Simon placed the tip of his firm cock against the pulsing ring of muscle, the metal piercing held down by the encasing sheath. He slowly began to push.

For a brief second, Jackson had second thoughts, the image of this solid rod plundering him, ripping him apart. Sensing his anxiety, Simon placed a hand on his smooth back and cooed gently. 'Just relax. You know you want this. And in a few moments you'll be loving it.'

And Simon was right. His cock-head breached the entrance, feeling the muscles grip and relax alternately as they became more accustomed to the invasion. The lube was certainly doing its job, helping the stiff pole to slide ever upwards, further and further inside. Jackson felt the urge to scream out. It had been a long time since he was last fucked and he was still unsure whether he could take the waves of pain that rippled around his arse. But momentarily the pain developed and became pleasure, the exquisite feeling of a man inside him, filling him and making him whole. He didn't want to cry or make much noise, in case Simon thought him any less of a man. His own cock was now totally rigid, standing up from his groin, slapping against his stomach.

Simon kept pushing, taking it gently, waiting until Jackson was used to the sensations before carrying on, until finally he was up to the very hilt, and he could fell his pubes brushing the velvety skin of Jackson's buttocks. He reached round and grabbed hold of Jackson's cock, which he started to wank up and down, loving the solid warmth of the tool in his grasp. The soft heat of Jackson's hole was now encasing him utterly and he knew he was in for a great time. Pulling out, and watching the muscles contracting as he did so, he let himself push inwards again, making Jackson cry out and bury his head in the duvet. He now knew he was doing well. He had hit the target. His actions started to increase, growing rapidly, like a steam piston, fucking the aching hole with all his strength and energy. Soon he was panting and beads of sweat fell from his brow and landed with silent splashes on the already-glistening skin of Jackson's back. In and out, Simon worked his cock inside the smooth arsehole, pounding with a strength he didn't know he possessed. This couldn't last forever.

Sounds of several of the guys playing with a frisbee in the garden filtered through the window, obscuring the gentle whimpers that were now coming from deep within Jackson. He couldn't hold back any longer. Simon was soon going to explode.

Jackson was oblivious to everything. All he was aware of was the acute splitting sensation in his arse; he heard and felt nothing else. He also knew that he couldn't take it for much longer. Soon he would be forced to grab his own rod and jerk it into life. He tried to do this, but couldn't, as Simon was still holding him tight. He pushed the hand away and began to wank himself off, hearing Simon's breathing growing harsher, signalling that he too was on the brink of climax. As if one creature, their cocks sprung into action, shooting out semen in a vast gushing flow, Jackson pumping out over the duvet cover, Simon still deep within his prey; the fierce orgasm inside Jackson's arse sending ripples of delight through Simon's dick. Falling forward and gasping for breath, Simon felt his chest slapping against Jackson's sweat-drenched back muscles. For an eternity they lay like that, their breathing now rhythmically rising and falling.

'Wow.' Jackson had nothing else to say, wincing as Simon pulled back, letting his still-hard prick gently ease out of the tender hole.

'I know.'

'I needed that.' Jackson turned over, and lay on his back looking up at the man who had just given him such pleasure.

'So did I. It's been ages since I had a good fuck.'

'Me too.'

'Perhaps you'll return the favour sometime?'

Jackson gave a deep, resonant chuckle from somewhere in his chest. 'I think that would possible to arrange. Any plans for the next six weeks?'

'Hmm. Let me check my diary and get back to you.' Simon smiled and threw himself down on the bed, taking Jackson in his arms and planting a big, wet kiss on his lips. 'Whatever happens with this show, I'd love to keep in touch with you when it's all over.'

'Sure. I'd like that a lot. I really would.' Returning the kiss, Jackson snuggled down into Simon's arms. 'So are we going to lie here all day or are we going to make some costumes?'

Friday

The house was a hubbub of excitement and activity as the dinner party drew near. The decision had been made to have a full English roast, with beef, potatoes, vegetables, Yorkshire pudding, accompanied by many bottles of rich red Australian Ironstone wine. A sherry trifle was to follow. The dining room was to be decked out like a sheikh's tent, with chiffon hangings and candles, in homage to Rudolph Valentino. The atmosphere amongst the housemates had seemed to be cordial and convivial, with scarcely a cross word spoken between any of them. They were unaware of the undercurrents which had begun to seethe and bubble. Which is why the argument, when it happened, came as great shock.

'Can you not clean the bath out after you've used it?' William's voice was tremulous but direct. He stood at the breakfast bar staring defiantly at one of his housemates.

'I beg your pardon?' This had come out of the blue and Skye was surprised.

'I am fed up with wanting a bath and finding your filthy scum around it every morning.'

'Fuck you. How do you know it's me?' Skye wasn't going to stand for such an unfair accusation. William was a pleasant enough guy, occasionally a little extreme but always even tempered. But there were times when he could be a prissy queen and Skye wasn't prepared to be spoken to like this.

'Because I check these things. This morning we passed each other on the landing, you came out of the bathroom and I went in. The bath was in a disgusting state, the floor was sopping wet and you hadn't flushed the toilet.'

'Well pardon me, Miss Perfect, but that's the way I am. Live with it or embalm me. Or better yet...use the downstairs bathroom.'

This was like a red rag to an extremely angry bull. 'How dare you! I am just as entitled to use the upstairs bathroom, as well you know. And if you cannot show any respect for the other people in this house, then we have a problem.'

'Fuck you.' Skye repeated himself and stalked from the kitchen.

William stood for a moment breathing deeply, resentment and fury bubbling inside of him, full of hatred for Skye's casual attitude towards living with others. There had been other things that had annoyed him too. Rhys, although a sweet lad, was very lazy about the house, and tended to ignore the washing up. Several times he had to be ordered into the kitchen when it was his turn to perform this routine chore. With his desire of neatness, he was finding the lack of hygiene disturbing.

But he wasn't the only one in the house to have a secret grudge. Peter was of the opinion that William should lighten up and stop clearing up after everyone, constantly straightening cushions, or cleaning out cupboards. He would have to talk to him about it. Even Colin had been getting on Peter's nerves at times. He had taken to waylaying him at odd moments and trying to steal kisses, or he would hang around Peter and constantly paw and pluck at him like some old favourite teddy bear. There was one thing that was guaranteed to drive Peter mad and that was being pawed at. Many times he had had to tell Colin to back off and he had turned away hurt. Still, it had to be done. Peter was being forced to admit that the fun and excitement of his fling with Colin was beginning to lose its charm. He was also slightly peeved that he had chosen to work with Colin on creating matching costumes for the dinner party. Still, that would have to be done. He didn't want to be the one who brought the party down.

A meeting was called for early on Friday evening to air any problems and annoyances. The whole house gathered in the living room and sat waiting for someone to get the ball rolling.

'Shall I start?' William took the floor. Six pairs of eyes watched him intently. 'Right. There are people in this house who have seemed to forget that they are living in a communal situation. They don't help around the place; they refuse to tidy up after themselves and delight in leaving the house in a complete mess. I do not want to name names yet –' he paused '– but I will if necessary.'

Peter piped up from the corner of the room. 'I think you should.'

Urged on, William took a deep breath and continued. 'As you wish. Skye...you are a disgrace. You seem to think that everyone else is here to clean up after you. I have no idea if you live with anyone outside of this programme, but I am sure if you do, they are stupid if they let you treat them in such a way. Rhys...darling...I know you come from a closeted Welsh family, but you must learn to do your share of the chores. And while I am having a moan...could you two keep the sounds of your nightly fuck sessions quiet? Some of us want to sleep at night, you know.' With a frown of displeasure at Simon and Jackson, he threw himself down into his armchair.

'Well, that's opened up the conversation.' Colin's sardonic comment went ignored as a tumult of angry responses burst out.

'How dare you comment on my life? You hardly know me,' Skye blazed at William, who sat arms crossed saying nothing.

'He is right though,' said Simon. 'You are a messy bastard. I wish you would clean up after yourself. I hate going in the bathroom after you've been in there...it's like a bomb has gone off.'

'Must you be so fucking perfect all the time?' said Skye, his eyes now full of self-righteous anger. 'Why do you need to spend so much time in the bathroom anyway? Who are you preening yourself for? Or is it that you want to look your best for Mr Black Stud here?'

Jackson stood and crossed the room, standing before Skye, his eyes blazing with fire. 'Stand up, you sick bastard, and say that to my face.'

'With pleasure.' Skye hoisted himself to his feet and squared off to his angry housemate.

'Please...calm down.' The reasonable voice of William filled the furious silence, cutting through the tension. 'A butch display of fisticuffs will achieve absolutely nothing. If we have grievances, then I suggest we all sit down and calmly discuss them. No good will come from shouting at each other.'

'You started the whole fucking thing,' said Colin bitterly, biting a fingernail with casual abandon.

'I know...so let's finish it properly. I have stated my grudges. Has anyone else got anything they'd like to let off steam about?'

'I have.' Peter raised his hand, and all eyes turned to him. 'Does anybody else think it would be a good idea to swap bedrooms every now and again? I just think it might be fun getting to know others in the house, rather than just sticking with the person we chose to share with on day one.' He lowered his eyes, purposefully not looking at Colin, knowing that he would be feeling hurt by this announcement.

No one else spoke. After a few moments rumination, Rhys cleared his throat. 'I don't see the point in doing that, actually. Sorry.'

Crossing his arms and saying nothing more for the rest of the meeting, Peter looked down at the carpet with a sigh.

'Look, can I make a suggestion?' Simon said quietly.

'What?' Skye's belligerent tone made Simon narrow his eyes and give him a long hard stare.

'That we all try to think about others in the future. We clean up after ourselves, and we do our best not to leave a mess. We ask others if we are going to do something that might affect the house, and if something gets on our nerves, we say so to the person involved. I hate all this bad feeling, and I think you all do. So let's clear the air and get on with it. We've got a party to look forward to tomorrow and it would be a shame to have a miserable evening.'

'He's right,' said Colin. 'Let's just kiss and make up.'

The guys stood and shook hands and hugged. Some with more reticence than others, but the wounds had begun to be healed. It was an important event in the Boycam house. The first big clouds of argument had billowed about them and the storm had been weathered successfully.

Saturday

The preparations for the dinner party had gone well. The dining room was looking wonderful, and the food – cooked by Peter and William – gave off delicious odours from the kitchen. At five minutes to seven the housemates started to gather in the living room, whoops of amazement and delight filling the air as the next guy made his entrance, resplendent in his chosen costume. The screams of recognition were almost as loud as each star was identified.

William and Rhys arrived first, William in hired thirties-style suit and trilby hat, carrying a violin case, while Rhys looked very attractive in tight black leather jeans and biker's jacket, complete with a peaked cap and sunglasses. They grinned and introduced themselves.

'Cagney...James Cagney...you dirty rat!'

'Marlon Brando.'

'In *The Wild One*...am I right?'

'Yes. Does it suit me?'

'I'll say. I like to see a man in leather...very sexy. Yes, very sexy. In fact I'd go so far as to say rather horny.' He smiled as Rhys' cheeks glowed a deep scarlet, and he crossed to stand beside the fireplace, sunglasses in hand.

'Ay-ay-ay-ay-ay...I like you very much...ay-ay-ay-ay-ay...I think you're grand.' A high, mock-Spanish voice floated in from the hall-

113

way, and into the living room flounced Simon, in a long frilly costume, and a head-dress bedecked with plastic fruit.

'Carmen Miranda!' William screeched appreciatively, admiring the wonderful get-up.

'Happy birthday to me...' In the doorway stood Jackson, a blond wig on his head, his lips daubed perfectly in red lipstick, his muscular body encased in a sheer white frock. 'May I come in?'

'Certainly, Miss Monroe. Allow me.' Putting out his arm in the most gallant manner, William escorted Jackson to the sofa, where he sat demurely, knees together, a most outrageous pout on his square-jawed features.

'We seem to be the only men here so far,' said William to Rhys in his unbelievably bad American accent, hunching his shoulders then crossing and standing beside the lad, who had put on his dark glasses and had assumed a 'far-away' air of smug superiority.

'Yup.' Rhys nodded at the two ladies who sat side by side on the sofa, giggling like girls.

The door slammed open and in strode Skye, his legs in black tights, his head in a blond ringletted wig and his torso looking astonishing in a silver sleeveless bodice with two large conical breasts.

'Strike a pose.' He stood in the doorway fanning himself, the perfect Madonna clone.

The others screamed in shock and surprise, gathering round for a feel of his pointed boobs. 'What the fuck are we missing?' His voice had adopted a nasal Detroit twang to accompany his persona, taking a long swig from a water bottle clutched in his hand. 'It's vodka...I have to replenish my fluids.'

'Somewhere over the rainbow, way up high...' A voice trilled outside the door, punctuated by small growls and barks. Skye pulled the door open and stared open mouthed at Peter in a blue gingham dress and plaits, carrying a basket, glittery red shoes on his size 10 feet, and Colin who sat at his feet, swathed in brown fake fur, his face painted like a dog, with false ears flopping down the side of his head.

'Come on Toto, let's see where we are.' Peter skipped into the room and put his hand to his mouth. 'I think we're not in Kansas any more. Do any of you know Dorothy?'

The other five automatically raised their hands before bursting out laughing. This could turn out to be a good evening.

And indeed it was. The wine had flowed, as had the conversation, all the seven guys trying very hard to stay in character, and mostly succeeding. The food was enjoyed by all, and the sherry trifle was guzzled down with gusto. At the end of the meal, there was still an hour to go until the end of the party, and so Skye suggested they all adjourn to the games room for a game of snooker. The two 'men' – Cagney and Brando – willingly agreed, whilst the ladies took just a little persuading.

Grasping a bottle of brandy that had been provided to finish off the meal and gesturing to the tray of glasses on the serving table, Skye stood and sashayed his way through to the games room. Rhys picked up the tray and followed, and the rest trotted after them, still chattering, laughing and swerving slightly as the alcohol swirled through their systems. Colin and Peter, after their initial entrance, had sat at opposite ends of the dinner table, and had hardly spoken to each other, just joining in with others around the table. Rhys again had let his hair down and thoroughly enjoying the admiring glances he was getting, had become suddenly sure of himself, aware that his costume had enhanced his appearance tremendously, even made him feel attractive. William was in his element, assuming the role of host, bumping up the conversation whenever it was in any danger of flagging, his constant use of the phrase 'You dirty rat' evincing groans from the others every time he uttered it. Jackson and Simon were totally in character, both giving convincing portrayals of the women they were dressed as, Jackson being kooky and utterly feminine whilst Simon was loud and jolly, his Spanish accent wavering a little though, once the wine took hold. All agreed that moving to the games room would be a good idea, having already ignored Skye's suggestion that they play the truth game again.

'Aww, shame on you guys,' he whined, 'I could have shown you all how I do a blow job.' Images of the scene in the movie *In Bed With Madonna* filled the guys' minds and they all fell about laughing again.

'So who is playing who?' Rhys was buoyed up, anxious to start, not wanting the fun of the evening to end.

'I'd rather just watch all you strong men playing. I don't have the strength to lift those big, heavy sticks.' Jackson pouted and put his finger to his lips. 'Who wants to keep me company?'

'I will...you dirty rat. I've remembered that I can't play. I'll sit and keep the lady amused.' William took Jackson's arm and led him to a high bar stool along one wall where they perched, watching the others decide on partners. Colin appeared from the hallway, having just been to the bathroom, saw what was going on and gave a small bark, kneeling at Jackson's feet, panting, his tongue lolling from his mouth.

'There's a good doggy-woggy. You like being tickled don't you?' Colin gave a small yelp of pleasure as Jackson began to ruffle the fur around his neck. Colin rolled over and spread his legs, giving Jackson easy access to his more intimate areas. With a small, feminine gasp of appreciation, Jackson grabbed a handful of fur and gave Colin's cock and balls beneath a good squeeze.

They all watched as a coin was tossed and it was agreed that Rhys would play Simon and Skye would play Peter. The first two chalked their cues and positioned the balls on the table, Rhys making the break. The young Welsh lad hardly noticed the appreciative moans from the spectators as he bent low over the table, his leather trousers tightly encasing his pert arse cheeks. When he did realise that he was being ogled, he began to play to his audience, pushing out his arse, hearing the murmurs and delighting in them. For the first time in his life he knew that he was looking good and that his appearance was totally appreciated. He knew that his housemates were seeing him in a new light, and they liked what they saw. Perhaps this was the start of a new Rhys, someone who could get whatever he wanted from life, and from the six others in the house. It would be worth a try. Surely they wouldn't vote out someone so young and cute as he, especially if he made it worth their while not to do so. He took his shot, and watched disconsolately as the white cue ball missed its target.

'Hah! You no good, meester.' Simon took a shot, his frilly dress rustling as he moved, the plastic fruit teetering precariously on his head-dress. As he bent over his cue, an apple detached itself from the foliage and fell onto the table, bounced and rolled into the corner pocket. Everyone roared with laughter and William declared the match null and void, freeing up the table for Skye and Peter.

Each shot Peter took was accompanied by a muffled curse from him, as his aim was hampered by the puffy sleeves and swirling skirt of his costume. Ignoring the calls of glee from the others, he hoisted up his skirt and tucked it into his belt, revealing that he was wearing no underwear beneath the gingham folds. Jackson gave a very unlady-like wolf-whistle and Skye let the end of his cue poke between his thighs, all of which didn't help with Peter's aim. Having missed a shot, he threw his cue down and stalked to the corner of the room. 'You are all bastards, and I hate every single one of you.' His face belied his words and he grinned like a Cheshire Cat, lifting his skirt again to the encouragement of Skye, who wanted a good look at his equipment. As drunk as Peter was, he saw no reason not to oblige.

'What 'bout you?' His voice was slurred, as he pointed to Jackson, seated demurely on his bar-stool, glass of brandy in hand. 'Are you wearing any?'

With a sly lick of his lips, Jackson grinned back. 'That is something you'll never know.'

Rhys had a sudden thought and raced from the room, returning moments later with a large electric fan from the kitchen. He uncoiled the flex and plugged it into the wall socket, placing the fan, facing up-wards, on the floor at Jackson's feet.

'Your air vent, Miss Monroe.'

Aware that all eyes were now expectantly on him, Jackson took the challenge, passing his glass to William, who swigged down the brandy in one gargantuan gulp. He stepped down from his stool, placing his feet either side of the fan, and waited. The updraft of air, when it came, could not have been more perfectly aimed. In a stunning simu-lation of the infamous Monroe pose, it lifted the white skirt – which billowed about Jackson's waist to reveal the lack of any other item of clothing. Everybody gasped and applauded the slumbering black cock hanging free for all to see.

'My turn now...get 'em off.' Jackson pointed a finger at Skye, who was absently fingering the conical points of his bra.

'Whatever you say, Miss Monroe.' Skye unzipped his bodice and stepped out of it, watching carefully as the other six gazed, entranced. Here was a chance to show them what he was made of. They knew he had had an intriguing life, including acting in porn movies. They knew he had done live sex shows. So why not give them a quick demo? He sat down on the edge of the snooker table and began un-rolling his stockings, first one and then the other, grasping the toe sec-tion and pulling them off his legs in a crude copy of some tarty pub stripper. He stood before them in just a jockstrap and wig, still quite groggy from the amount he'd drunk earlier. He started to gyrate his hips to the beat of an imaginary tune which he could hear pounding in his head, thumping through him, pounding like his heartbeat. His head was swimming, and the room seemed to whirl before his glazed eyes, but through all this he knew that he was the star of the show, that everyone was scrutinising him. He stared around for Rhys, who was leaning drunkenly against the fireplace, looking a real stunner in his tight black leather biker's outfit, his cap at a jaunty angle, his mouth open, his eyes wide and absorbed in the show being played out before him. Jackson was showing signs of arousal, a small mound visible beneath the cotton of his dress, one hand lightly placed there, gently stroking it with his fingertips, completely unaware of anyone else. Simon had placed his arms around Peter's shoulder, and was almost imperceptibly brushing his cheek, whilst Colin sat lounging against the wall in boxer shorts and T-shirt, his Toto costume now discarded. He also watched, engrossed, although still throwing the odd adoring glance up at Peter, who seemed not to notice.

William started a slow hand-clap, encouraging Skye to a more erotic finish. A couple of the others joined in. Reaching high, Skye clasped his hands together behind his head, puffing out his chest, displaying his musculature for all to admire. Then, with a sensuous, circular sway of his hips, he began to spin around slowly, spreading his legs and bending forward, so that his arse was on view to the housemates. Reaching round with his hands, he grabbed his buttocks and spread them too, giving the guys a clearer look at his rose-pink hole. Bending over more, he grabbed his ankles and soon was doubled up, the relaxed muscles of his thighs feeling no strain. Behind the taut elastic of the jockstrap, the guys could see the base of his snugly nestled bollocks. Some of them were really turned on by this, and Skye knew it. He was so aware of his prowess, and so proud of how easily he could get men going. As he uncurled himself upright and turned back to face the front, his own cock vaguely swelling, he could see with satisfaction that his performance had done its job. Beneath Jackson's dress was a sizeable erection forming a tent, his hand grasping it tightly at its base. And the same was obvious beneath Peter's. Rhys had unzipped his leather jacket so that his smooth chest was showing, and he was fingering his nipples with ill-disguised lust. Colin had moved his position so that he was squatting at Peter's feet, one arm clutching at his left leg. William had placed a hand at his crotch level, and was taking surreptitious squeezes at his growing cock when he thought no one was noticing. This could turn into an interesting evening, thought Skye, now sober and now seeing that his housemates were all aroused and ready. Anything could happen. He looked down at his wrist watch. Five minutes after midnight. The party had officially ended. They could throw off their characters and be themselves again. He twisted his wrist to show the others the time. Simon threw off his fruit head-dress and swiftly stepped out of his frock, so he too was standing naked.

As if all of the same mind, the others followed suit in a welter of wine-sozzled activity until they were all naked, some semi-aroused, some not, and some proudly sporting hard-ons. Was this the crunch time? Was this the moment when all guards would be let down and they would feast on each other?

It was Peter who made the first move, realising that things had perhaps gone a bit too far, and he padded from the room, throwing a casual 'good night' over his shoulder. Colin waited for as long as he could and then sprinted after him, bounding up the stairs and slamming the bedroom door shut after him.

'This has been the most delightful evenin'. I hope we can do it again sometime.' William assumed as much dignity as his nakedness would allow and left the other four to make his way gingerly upstairs. 'I'll pick up my clothes tomorrow.'

Jackson, Rhys, Simon and Skye said nothing, but looked at each other. The erections that Jackson and Simon sported were extremely alluring, and Rhys had to fight the desire to fall down on his knees and suck them.

'I...I think we should go to bed...' Rhys managed to stammer out, dropping his eyes and covering his nudity with his hand. He had seen with his own eyes the hard-ons of the other three and was slightly embarrassed at the size of his own. He had thought himself well endowed, and perhaps he was, but he didn't quite measure up to these three.

'Is that an invitation?' Simon gave Rhys a sly grin, noting that he had had a hard time looking away at his solid manhood.

'No...I meant...sorry.' He ran from the room, now hideously ashamed and cursing the effect of alcohol, and wondering why he hadn't learnt his lesson after last week.

'Oh well. Fancy a fuck?' Simon turned to Jackson, who put out a hand and grabbed the pierced dick fondly.

'That'd be nice. Care to join us?' Jackson cocked his head on one side, and waited for Skye to respond.

After a few pondered moments, Skye ran a hand through his crumpled hair and smiled. 'I don't think so. Maybe another time. Enjoy.' He picked up his costume and left the other two behind, heading for the stairs and a night of dream-free sleep.

Sunday

Most of the housemates slept in late, and it was past one o'clock in the afternoon when they were all downstairs, wishing desperately that their headaches and hangovers would go. The cleaning up operation was well in hand, William being Commander-in-Chief, and soon the house was looking spotless and all the costumes had been collected and placed down at the main gate. Again there was an air of nervous tension about the seven guys – the knowledge that one of their number would be voted out that evening. It was an unpleasant task, but it had to be done. Once everything was cleared away, the housemates dispersed to various corners of the house and garden, and so consequently a whispered conversation went unheard by anyone else.

'Well...?'

'I don't know.'

'It's a simple enough proposition.'

'I don't like it.'

'What's not to like? Just make sure we all vote the same way and we could be the surviving two. Then we split the money. And we both win. Think about it...'

As the clock approached the dreaded hour of six, the housemates were gathered in the living room. All conversation had ceased, and there they sat, waiting for Matt's voice to reverberate around them.

'Hello, Boycam house. This is Matt speaking. It is almost time for this week's vote. Like last time, you will write the name of the person you want evicted on the voting slip provided and place them in the ballot box. That box will then be placed at the gate. The results will be announced this evening at eight o'clock. The evictee will then have one hour to pack and be ready to leave the house. It is now six o'clock. Please cast your votes.'

The next two hours seemed to crawl by, and nothing any of the housemates said or did could make it pass any quicker. Any attempt at conversation was snubbed and no one appeared relaxed or calm at all. To a man, they watched the hands of the clock tick by, anxious to know the news, to know whether they would be remaining and still in with the chance of winning serious money or if they would be out of the show and back to their routine existence.

Rhys pleasured himself with thoughts of the other's reaction to his appearance at the party, revelling in the knowledge of his attraction. He had noticed that the guys seemed more attentive to him, and his confidence had grown because of this.

The coolness that had existed between Colin and Peter had been exacerbated by Peter's refusal to have sex with Colin after the party. He had thrown himself into bed and gone straight to sleep. Even in the morning, when they usually had some of their most energetic shags, he had still had a cold exterior.

William had never felt better. He had done some thinking in his bedroom last night, and had put several things about his attitude to the programme into perspective, whilst Skye was his normal self, the memory of his success at arousing the others having plastered a silly grin on his face all day.

Simon and Jackson had obviously had a good night, for the sounds of their love-making had kept Rhys and Skye awake for quite a while.

So it was that these seven men assembled in the living room for the announcement that would shape the next week of their lives.

'Hello, Boycam house. This is Matt. I have the result of the second vote here in front of me, and unlike last week it was more of a close-run thing. But there is one name that emerged as the eventual loser. One of you will have an hour to pack and be ready to leave. A car will be waiting for you outside the gate to take you home. Now, if you are all ready...the second person to leave the Boycam house is...Colin Crisswell.'

Interview with Colin Crisswell

'I was sorry to go, as I had really been enjoying myself. Things had settled down after Jost had gone and we all seemed to be getting on well. I was getting on very well with Peter, in fact had grown quite attached to him. Still, I suppose it wasn't meant to be.

'I have no regrets whatsoever about doing the show. I am just glad that I was one of the lucky ones chosen to do it. Few people get the chance to take part in such an extraordinary event. Of course I wanted to stay until the end, but that wasn't to be. I'm not bitter, just a little regretful perhaps that the others wanted me out. I thought I was quite easy to get along with, and was surprised at my eviction. I think that there was some tactical voting going on, to keep certain people in the house.

'The first week was relatively easy, as it was like a big holiday, away from home with lots of other fun people, but then in week two the boredom began to kick in. There wasn't actually much to do. The tasks were quite fun and I liked doing stuff like the willy moulding, but the days did start to drag quite a lot. We hadn't reached a stage where we were all completely comfortable with each other, and so we were never able to fully relax in each other's company. Everyone kept sloping off for solo naps, to get away from the others and have a bit of time alone to think and balance oneself for the rest of the day.

'I think I'd be happy to meet the guys again, only because we all have a common bond, been through something that no one else has, and it'd be fun to go over old memories.

'As to the winner, I think it might be someone innocuous – like William – who sneaks through.'

WEEK THREE

Tuesday

Peter had breathed a sigh of relief when the name of the next evictee was announced. He had gotten on well with Colin, but had quickly tired of his constant attentions. Sorry though he was to see him go, he was glad that he wouldn't have to put up with his peckings and stolen kisses and frequent pinches of his arse again. Monday had passed quickly and easily. Once more the six remaining housemates exuded a relaxed air, as they knew they had at least another week of life in the Boycam house. Snooker was played, as was Trivial Pursuit, one of the board games in the games room. The inane and trivial questions the game posed had the six housemates laughing and cheering well into the early hours of Tuesday morning.

They were all aware of the new challenge. Matt had come through just after lunch that day, his voice as efficient and crisp as always. 'Hello, Boycam housemates. So now you are down to six. I hope you are now all adjusted to the rigours of living in the house together. The dinner party on Saturday was a great triumph and, as with the moulding competition, marks have been awarded for wit and originality in costumes, and for those who we think managed to "be" their characters most successfully. These accumulated marks will be taken into account when there are only two of you left. The person with the most marks will then be declared the winner. But now to this week's task. It is slightly more creative than last week's. You will be provided with Polaroid instant cameras, and a large supply of instant film. You will pair off and create life-size photographic replicas of each other. You can use as many shots as you like to make this photo montage, but it must be an exact replica of the other person, in size and height and so on. Marks will be awarded for artistic integrity and for dress sense, or undress sense. Large boards will be provided for you to fix the finished portraits to, which you will leave at the gate on Saturday afternoon at six o'clock. I hope that is all clear. Have fun!'

The six guys looked at each other for a brief moment, then burst out laughing. So far the tasks they had been set had been fun, just as Matt had said they would be. Life in the Boycam house wasn't as bad as it could have been. Almost.

'Who has taken my hairbrush?' Simon stood, hands on hips in the doorway to the living room. William and Rhys stared back, a large sheet of paper on the floor between them, the plans for their body montages well in hand.

'I haven't touched it, my darling.' There was a slight sneer in William's voice as he answered. 'I have my own, besides I think it terribly bad form to use another person's hairbrush. Don't you?' He lowered his eyes to the recumbent form of Rhys, flat out on his stomach, in just a T-shirt and briefs – white briefs, which encased his buttocks snugly.

'Er...right.' Rhys had nothing else to say. Since his and William's name had been drawn out of the hat to work together, he had been full of enthusiasm for the task, and his mind tuned out any distractions.

Simon was unconvinced. 'Well, some bastard has. Where are the others?'

'I believe Peter and Jackson are in the garden, and Skye is still in bed.'

'Thanks. Sorry to have bothered you.' Pausing before he marched outside, Simon turned back into the room. 'You can get back to grips with each other now.' The mischievous twinkle in his eye returned momentarily.

Rhys looked up and tutted. This was no time for silly jokes.

'I think we should do each other at the same time.'

'Hmmm, sounds interesting.' William raised and eyebrow and wet his lips suggestively.

'I'm being serious.'

'So am I, gorgeous.'

Rhys stared up at William with a sigh. Would this coupling work? He doubted it. Although William was a nice enough guy, he wondered how he had ever risen in the heady and serious world of stockbroking – he always seemed to have a joke ready about everything the house-mates talked about, and he always had some suggestive comment, lowering the tone, making base and lewd inanities. Most of the time they were really tiresome. Because of this, Rhys had never paid much attention to William, just categorising him as the middle-class twit of the house, someone to just tolerate rather than interact with, but this new task had changed that. He would have to make an effort to get on with him, as he would be spending a lot of the next week in his company.

'I mean if we both start at the head and move down, photographing the same body part at the same time.'

'Fine by me. And what body part would you like me to start on first?' Again his voice held that vulgar tone.

'Don't you ever tire of making crude comments all the time?

'What do you mean?'

Rhys took his time answering. This could be tricky. 'I mean...why do you always have to make rude jokes about everything? Life in this house would be a lot easier for everyone if we didn't have to watch what we say all the time...in case there is a smutty comment from you about it.' He stopped, wondering if he'd gone too far.

'I see...' William's voice petered out, his eyes boring deep into

Rhys, daring him to continue. This was the first time any of the house-mates had spoken to him like this. The first time anyone had begun to make a deeper contact above the facile niceties they always uttered. It would be interesting to see what this spunky young Welsh dish had to say. Perhaps it would be worthwhile letting down his guard, to show a little of what he had inside. After a few seconds he continued. 'Carry on...'

'Well, that's it, really. Why do you do it? We'd all like you a lot more if you were more like one of us.'

'Perhaps the problem is I'm not like one of you. The producers of this show seem to have seen fit to place only one chap like me in here, a sensible bloke, from a privileged background, one who obviously speaks in a more up-market way – and then expected me to just min-gle. It's difficult, you know. All my life I have mixed with my kind of people, from the same kind of background, with similar antecedents. At work I mix with the same kind of people too, all well brought up, all from moneyed families. The great majority of them are straight, as straight as hell. Homosexuality appals them and so to make my work-ing life easier I adopt this façade, a joke-telling, all-round good chap. I thought that it would work just as well in here as out there. I had no reason to think that it wouldn't.' He looked down at his beautifully manicured nails and lapsed into silence.

'Oh. I'm sorry. I didn't mean...' Rhys also went quiet, unsure of what else to say.

It was William who broke the tension, giving Rhys a pat on the back, and a huge grin. 'How about if you could help me? I'll try to mix a lot more, and I'll try and drop the jokes. It'll be hard, because that's how I've been for so many years, but if I could rely on you to be there, to hold my hand as I dip my toe in the water, so to speak, well...what do you say?'

The helpless look on his face immediately gave Rhys his answer. He stared up, for the first time seeing that there was probably more to

William than he knew. There were great depths to him, and he wasn't bad looking either. He was kind of lean, and it looked as if his body had been worked on. From what little he'd seen of William, he appeared to have taken care of himself, and that was a good thing. He always came down to breakfast well groomed, although there was a small tuft of hair that was frequently sticking up at some annoying angle, defying the best attentions of his comb. That was sort of endearing. It showed he wasn't perfect. But then who was?

'Sure. It will give us a chance to get to know each other better. And I think I'd quite like that.'

Lying flat out, sunbathing, Jackson and Peter were side by side, both completely naked. Their towels had been spread on the grass by the tree at the bottom of the garden, a gentle breeze just managing to sway the old rope swing attached to its branches back and forth. They were deep in conversation and didn't even notice Simon approach.

'Could I have a word?' His voice made them look up, both shielding their eyes against the dazzling rays of the sun.

'What is it, mate?' Jackson gave him a crooked smile, and rearranged his genitals so that they lolled against one dark-skinned thigh.

'Have either of you seen my hairbrush? I left it where I usually do and now it's gone.'

Both Jackson and Peter looked blankly back.

'Sorry, no,' said Peter cheerfully. 'Wait a minute, though...I did see Skye going into your room when I went up to get my towel. About twenty minutes ago.'

His lips pressed together in a firm line, Simon nodded his thanks and stalked away.

'He doesn't look happy.' Peter flicked at a fly which was buzzing round his head.

Jackson lay back down with his hands behind his head, stretching his legs and pointing his toes, feeling the warming sunshine covering his body. 'The smallest thing can get you pissed off in here; I'd have thought you'd have realised that by now.'

'I guess so.'

'I mean, didn't Colin get on your nerves a lot? That's how it looked to me.'

Taking a moment's thought, Peter said 'Yes...I suppose the unnatural closeness in here made him want to be even closer. And between you and me, he became too close. There were times when I wanted to scream because he was always at my elbow, always asking me what I was doing, always wanting to know where I'd been. I can't live like that, always being interrogated like some suspicious criminal.' A small smile appeared on his lips. 'Still, it was nice at times. He was very good at...' He stopped, his cheeks reddening.

'Don't stop there. What was he good at? And I want the whole truth.'

'Well...he was great at...' He lowered his voice as if aware that he might be overheard, forgetting the microphone carefully positioned in the branches above them. 'He gave great head. I can honestly say that Colin gave one of the best blows I've ever had.'

That familiar deep chuckle bubbled from within Jackson's throat. 'Really...and I bet you've had some good head in your time, eh?'

'Yes, I have and what business is it of yours?' said Peter, giving his housemate a playful nudge in the ribs. 'I thought you and Simon were an item?'

Picking up a daisy from the grass, and sitting upright to pull the petals off one by one, Jackson smiled down. 'Sort of. We made a connection and have been having some great sex recently.'

'I know...we all know...we can hear you through the walls, you know. They aren't that thick.'

That chuckle again. 'Sorry. We just get carried away. He has such a lovely body and such a nice cock, especially with that piercing...I've never had a pierced guy before...and he seems to like me, so why not?'

'No reason. We have to get as much happiness and satisfaction as we can in here, otherwise I think we'd all go mad. That's why Colin and I hooked up, I suppose. Just think of it...seven weeks without sex...a nightmare!'

'Well, if you ever fancy a bit, you know where to find me.' Jackson's tone had assumed a sudden seriousness. The change in his voice caused Peter to sit up and give his housemate a quizzical look.

'Are you serious?'

'Always.' Jackson threw down the limp remains of the daisy and leaned in towards Peter his lips slightly parted, his eyes narrowing. Before he could respond, Peter let himself be kissed. It was surprisingly gentle for such a big powerful man. Pulling away and looking around to see if any of his fellow participants were watching, he then leaned in and returned the kiss, his tongue exploring every inch of Jackson's mouth. As if a light had been switched on, he suddenly saw what a horny man Jackson was. And as he had made the first move, had Jackson been secretly desiring him? He had to find out.

'Whoa...stop for a moment.' He sat back, wiping his mouth with the back of his hand, noticing from the corner of his eye that Jackson was slightly aroused; the lolling organ had raised its purple head. The atmosphere in this quiet corner of the garden had unexpectedly changed. There was a sizzling tension, a tautness that was almost a sentient, living being. And Peter didn't know what to do. The opportunity to make it with this handsome guy was being offered to him, but from deep in him he knew that it didn't feel right.

'I think that we should take a rain check.' His voice was cracked, his throat dry.

'Why? I thought you were up for it?'

'I was...I am...but I really would like to make sure that it is OK with Simon first. I don't want to mess things up.'

'Don't worry about that. Leave Simon to me. Now come here.'

Unable to resist for a second longer, Peter felt himself being embraced by strong, masculine arms, being held tightly, and being loved.

Simon rapped at Skye's door.

'Come in if you're pretty.' The voice floated through the woodwork. 'Oh, you are. What can I do for you?' Skye was lounging on his bed, in just a tight pair of cotton trunks, reading. He looked up as Simon entered, and put down his book.

Simon didn't have to answer, as he saw what he was looking for and pounced on it, picking up his hairbrush from Skye's bedside table and brandishing it in front of his nose.

'This. And if you dare take any of my stuff again without asking, there will be hell to pay.'

Skye closed his book and threw it down on the table, his casual air beginning to really annoy Simon intensely. 'Look, I'm sorry. You weren't around to ask, and I just forgot to put it back. Friends?' He put out his little finger in a mock handshake.

'Oh all right.' Simon sighed and flopped down on the bed beside Skye.

'All right, out with it. What's the matter?' As though he knew that something weighty was on Simon's mind, Skye became immediately serious. This particular housemate wasn't the kind to get upset over a hairbrush and it was obvious that frivolity and jokes would be unwelcome right now. 'You can tell me, you know. I'm quite a nice guy really.'

Simon grinned. 'I know you are. I just need to talk to somebody. If you will promise to keep it to yourself...' he trailed off listlessly, all his energy and spirit gone. He really did need to talk to someone, and he supposed that Skye was as good a candidate for his woes as anyone in the house. Through all his bravado and show, Skye had a sensible character. He didn't let it out too often, but Simon had caught brief glimpses of it on several occasions. Perhaps he would be the best person to talk to.

'It's very simple. I think I'm falling for Jackson.'

Skye raised an inquisitive eyebrow. 'Is that all?'

'All? I think it's a problem.'

'Why for God's sake? He's a single man and so are you. He obviously likes you and you like him…what's the problem?'

'It's this fucking place. I hate it.'

'But I thought you were happy here? You've always seemed calm and content.'

'Yes, well…I am a good actor. I've never really been the type to moan about things. I've always tried to look on the bright side. To be positive. But somehow I just can't any more. I have got some deep feelings for Jackson and in this rarefied situation I think it would be unwise to show them.'

'Why?'

'Oh, because people might think I'm just doing it for votes, or that I am not serious, just caught up in the whole Boycam thing.'

Skye put a hand out and rested it on Simon's shoulder, drawing him close until they were nestled in each other's arms. 'I wouldn't think that. And I'd be surprised if any of the others would, too. They are all decent blokes in their own ways, and I don't think any one of them would vote you out for falling for one of your housemates.'

Simon felt warm and safe, snuggled in Skye's arms, safer than he had in a long time. It felt nice. 'Really?'

'Really. If you have feelings for someone, you should tell them.'

Simon spoke so quietly that Skye had to strain to hear him.

'But what if I make a fool of myself? What if he doesn't feel the same way?'

'Then that's an end of the problem and we go on as before and you forget all about it, and we try to finish this bloody stupid show in one piece. OK?'

'OK.'

*

The hallway was empty. Jackson peeked out through the kitchen door and made sure that there was no one about. 'Come on.' He raced ahead, certain that Peter was right behind him. Peter gazed upwards as they sprinted upstairs, seeing the muscular thighs with just a tantalising glimpse of hairy bollocks.

'In here.' Jackson leapt through the door to Peter's room and shut the door firmly, then crossed to the window and pulled down the blind, silently cursing for a moment that he had left his towel on the grass beside Peter's. As he turned back, he cannoned into his new friend, who had come quietly up to stand at Jackson's side.

'There you are.' They stood facing each other, now both fully erect, their cocks hard and rampant, standing out from their bodies, and butting against each other. Peter looked down with sheer delight. Their two solid dicks were about the same size and dimension, both proudly possessing a cock that was almost certain to give pleasure. He let his hand drop and touch his housemate in that most private area, and he shivered as he realised that special tingle, the excitement of holding another man's cock. The skin felt warm and velvety as he grasped it tightly about the shaft, his thumb massaging the head around the slit, rubbing the small drop of oozing semen into the glans. Peter moaned. Not only was he experiencing the joy of another man in his grasp, but that man was doing the same to him, giving those same wonderful sensations in return. He couldn't wait any longer. Falling to his knees, Peter opened his mouth, and with his tongue tentatively tasted the sticky juice all around the spongy head. He heard a soft whimper from Jackson, and so he pressed on, taking the head inside, enclosing it in his warm, moist mouth.

Jackson was filled with lust and desire and found it very hard to resist and, with a thrust, pushed his cock down Peter's throat. The young guy didn't stop or gag; he took it all, swallowing each inch as it descended, his tongue massaging the skin as it went. It didn't take long. Soon Peter had taken all of Jackson's cock in his mouth, and he could feel the wiry pubic hairs brushing against the underside of his nose.

'Oh wow, that's fantastic!' Jackson gasped, grabbing Peter's shoulders and holding him in position, encouraging him to continue. He felt he was going mad with excitement, the sensations that Peter was providing were just right. This boy certainly knew how to suck cock. His hands moved from the shoulders to the back of the head and he held fast, letting his fingers entwine themselves in the hair, pushing himself forward, grinding his cock as far down Peter's throat as possible without making him choke.

With his lips and tongue Peter worked back and forth, as Jackson's groin thrust inside. Peter started a sensational new action, as he sucked in the slathered prick, using a rippling massage with the insides of his saliva-filled cheeks, whilst pressing down hard with his tongue, and forcing the cock to the roof of his mouth. This sent Jackson wild. He threw his head back and a strangulated cry bubbled from his throat. He could feel an orgasm starting to accrue itself deep in his loins, and he tried to pull away, wanting to shoot his load across Peter's smooth-skinned face. Peter could tell what was going on and slipped his hands behind Jackson's arse, holding him firm. He wanted to suck this guy to within an inch of his life. To bring him to the edge and hold him, hold him looking over into the blackness of a withheld climax. Drawing his mouth around the cock-head, Peter swirled saliva about it, making Jackson's body quiver and goose-bumps break out over his skin. Peter went lower again, taking the cock down, using more of the same massage technique, until he heard a small whimpering from above and he knew Jackson had reached that moment when nothing else mattered. He stopped and pulled away, gripping Jackson's wrists tightly, stopping the black guy from beating at his twitching, sloppy meat.

'Aaah! I want to come...'

'Well, you can't. I haven't finished with you yet. Deep breaths…let it all subside…'

Jackson obeyed, letting the primal urge to shoot go away, his dick still ramrod straight and stiff.

'Fucking hell…you know how to make a guy feel good.' Jackson's eyes were moist as his breathing grew slower.

'Thank you, kind sir.'

'You can let go of my wrists now. And I can definitely see what Colin saw in you…you are a right little raver.'

'Thanks again. But I didn't want us to finish so soon. If we are going to give them a show, I think we should go the whole hog.' His eyes motioned to the small cameras positioned around the ceiling. 'Is there any fantasy that you've never had fulfilled? Anything that you'd like to try? Because I am willing to have a go at anything…'

Jackson thought for a moment. 'Not really. I do have this thing about uniforms, but we can't do anything about that here. What about you? Any little kink that you'd like ironed out?'

A light twinkled in Peter's eye as he responded slowly. 'Yes…there is something I'd love to do with you…if you'll trust me…?'

'It's not too messy, is it? That sort of thing doesn't turn me on.'

'Oh no. Lie down on the bed.' Peter went to his chest of drawers and after rummaging round for a few moments came back with two ties and a two belts. 'OK baby…spread 'em.'

Jackson looked on amused as he let Peter do his thing. Deftly and with nimble fingers he took each of Jackson's hands and tied them to the bedposts with the belts, then did the same with Jackson's ankles, using the variously coloured ties.

Throughout, Peter noted with delight that Jackson's cock was rigid and ready, a sight that sent shivers of expectation coursing through him.

'Comfy?' He waited for Jackson to answer before making his next move.

'As well as can be expected, thank you.'

'Good.' He returned to his bedside cabinet and fumbled around in his sponge bag, triumphantly pulling out a condom and a sachet of lube. 'We'll be needing these shortly.'

He jumped up on the bed and settled himself down between Jackson's spread thighs, letting his head fall until his lips were inches from the trembling cock-head. Again he started to swallow the beautiful glans. He wanted his captive to be once more brought to the edge, eased into the situation where he would beg for mercy. He had had many dreams about such a scenario, where he had someone powerless in his grasp, ever since he had been in such a situation in that Amsterdam sex club, and he had been fucked by those silent bikers. He had thought about that evening often and had wondered what it would be like to turn the tables and experience it from the other side. And so far he was loving it. His eyes never strayed from watching Jackson, whose head thrashed from side to side on the pillow, breathing in short gasps. This guy had wanted sex and now he was getting it, and Peter was in control.

When he sensed that Jackson was not far from exploding, Peter sat up and reached for the condom, ripping open the packet and slowly rolling it down the stiff pole with some difficulty; it would be a tight fit. As he reached the base of Jackson's cock, he ripped open the sachet of lube and slowly oozed it over the waiting tool, slipping and sliding it around until it covered the whole of the sheath. Taking a deep breath, he sat up and squatted over the cock, holding himself in readiness for the great moment. He looked down and saw Jackson squirming, his eyes bulging in his head, anxiously preparing himself mentally for what was to come. Peter paused. He had wanted this cock up inside of him for a long while, but now that the time had arrived he had a pang of nerves. Could he take it? Of course he could. With one hand he held the rod tightly about the shaft and positioned it at his puckered hole, feeling it push against the resistant ring of muscle.

'Well, go on then...what are you waiting for?' Jackson's voice cut through the silent tension, as nervous as Peter, if he but knew it. There was always those few seconds of doubt as he prepared to fuck someone; would he be able to do it? Would his cock let him down and go limp? Would he be able to perform as well as he was expected to? These questions frequently floated across his mind in such situations, but here Jackson had no alternative. Although he would be the one to do the fucking, he was in a suppliant position and was helpless to do anything about it. He just bit his lip and hoped. The leather belts were beginning to chafe at the skin on his wrists and an ache had begun in his neck muscles. But instantly these uncomfortable hindrances were forgotten.

Peter lowered himself, feeling that exquisite pain as the cock-head breached the entrance, forcing the hole wide. He stifled a cry as it ate into him, a searing spasm of mind-blowing joy ripping him apart. The lube was certainly doing its job as the cock inched its way upwards, farther and farther inside Peter's arse. His own cock had begun to harden and fill, and soon it stood upright. He kept on sliding himself down, feeling his hole being stretched until it was up inside, to the hilt. He was finally sitting on Jackson's midriff, and he was thoroughly stuffed.

Jackson so wanted to reach up and take hold of Peter's cock, but he couldn't. He had never had such feelings, never known such an intense wave of pleasure flow through him. His cock was being tightly gripped and massaged by his housemate's arsehole, which was now bouncing up and down, taking the whole length inside, then sliding up, until just the head remained inside, then sinking back down until it lay buried deep once more. Jackson had fucked guys before, many times, but this was so different. Being unable to control his powerful cock as he normally would, and unable to move to stop the pounding, or to manipulate the session as he wanted, was bizarre. He felt like a small child, someone not in control of his own life, and strangely he found it mind-blowing. He loved the submission, and he was so completely in Peter's thrall.

'Oh... my... God!' Peter cried out, as he bounced up and down, alternately feeling the cock filling him and then receding before plunging upwards again. Peter's ring screamed for peace, Peter's cock throbbed for release, as his fist gripped it and began pummelling. The movements quickened, as piston-like, he felt Jackson's cock fucking him utterly. He loved all the sensations – the burrowing stretching of the cock inside him, the rapid wanking of his fist about his cock and, most of all, the fact that he was in command, he was the one in control, and he would be the one to end it – which was something that would happen very soon.

With a simultaneous gasp, both lads stiffened, as an orgasm rolled through them, making them both cry out in ecstatic yells. The come shot out of Peter's cock, landing in creamy globs across Jackson's chest, while he pumped his seed deep inside Peter. After an ear-splitting scream of elation, Peter fell forward, collapsing onto Jackson's chest, the cock still firmly embedded in him.

It felt wonderful to Jackson, the searing hotness of that dick inside him, the smoothness of the chest, and the stickiness of his own come squelching between them.

They lay there for a few seconds, breathing deeply, enjoying the afterglow of that climactic moment when the door was suddenly banged open.

'I heard a cry. Is anything the –' Simon looked down at the two of them, and without a word spun on his heels and ran down the hall. The sound of his steps descending the stairs rang clearly through the house.

'Fuck.' Jackson was the first to speak. 'I think you'd better get me out of here, and then I've got some serious arse to kiss.'

'Sure.' Peter clambered to his feet. 'And if that fails, then you are welcome to come and kiss mine anytime.'

He didn't see the scowl that momentarily flicked across Jackson's normally placid features.

That evening the atmosphere in the house was odd, to say the least. Rhys was puzzled to see Simon being extremely off-hand with Jackson, while Peter was slinking around like a cat who had just devoured a whole carton of cream. Rhys had had a good day though, and his collaboration with William was going well. They had done quite a bit of photography of each other, both having agreed to be shot in just their underwear. He had been very surprised, when William stripped off, to see that there was a rather well-kept body under his clothes, with a hint of muscle about the stomach. He had been wearing loose boxer shorts, so Rhys had not been given any chance to tell what the equipment was like underneath. Rhys grinned to himself as he caught himself wondering that perhaps he liked William more than he thought. You don't want to know the cock size of someone you don't like, do you? Skye had been absent most of the day, either reading in his room, or in the garden. Rhys sat on a bar stool alongside the snooker table, with a large sheet of board covering its green baize surface, arranging some of the instamatic photos of William, trying to make it look as realistic as possible. He looked up at the clock, which said it was nearly midnight. Time for bed.

'Goodnight.' He looked up as he reached the landing, and saw William coming out of the bathroom.

'Goodnight. Sleep well.'

'I shall try.' William paused for a moment, grasping the towel that was round his neck. 'It's very odd you know.'

'What is?'

'I sort of miss Jost.'

Rhys wasn't quite sure what to say to that. He stammered a reply. 'Oh...really?'

'Yeah.'

Rhys felt that William was desperate for company, and was dragging this chat out unnecessarily. 'Why?'

'Well, I sort of got used to sleeping in the same room with him. It was quite nice having someone to talk over the events of the day with, you know, lying in bed, nattering before you turn off the light.'

'Right.'

'And since he left I've been a bit lonely.'

Rhys saw what he was driving at. 'How on earth can you be lonely in here? There's never a moment's peace. There is never anywhere else to go. Wherever you do find a quiet corner, someone comes in and ruins it. And we are always being watched.' He stuck his middle finger in the air and waved it at the camera that clung to the landing wall, knowing that it would bring a smile to Matt's face when he reviewed the tape in the morning.

'Well, I am lonely. You may not have noticed it, but I'm not that much of a party animal.'

'Neither am I. But I make the best of it.'

William looked down at the carpet and spoke with an assumed casual air. 'Are you tired? Because I fancy a drink, and wonder if you'd like to join me?' The request was so sweet that Rhys hadn't the heart to refuse.

'Sure, why not?' He draped his towel over the banister rail and followed William down the stairs and into the kitchen, where they sat up on high stools, side by side at the breakfast bar, a glass of brandy in hand.

'Cheers.' William raised his glass, watching the strip lights that illuminated the room sparkle in the cut-glass splendour of his brandy balloon.

'Cheers.' Rhys didn't normally like brandy and so he took a tentative sip, bursting out coughing as the fiery liquid reached the back of his throat.

With a wry smile, William rushed across to the sink and poured out a beaker of water, passing it quickly across, then began patting Rhys' back. 'Take it easy. You could have had a cup of coffee, you know. You didn't have to have brandy if it disagrees with you.'

'I know.' As his coughing fit subsided, Rhys' face assumed its normal colour, but he was still aware that previously he had gone a shade of deepest vermilion. 'Thanks for this.' He nodded at the water, grateful for it.

For a few moments the two of them sat in silence, Rhys dreadfully conscious that he didn't have much to say to William. Thankfully he didn't have much longer to wait.

'So are you glad you did this show?' A hint of hesitation was clear in William's voice, as he sipped his drink and watched Rhys intently, his eyes bright.

'I think so.'

'Why?'

That was a tough one, and Rhys didn't know if he was up to a deep discussion about his motives right now. He sighed and tried to answer as best he could, given the lateness of the hour and the tiredness that had suddenly started creeping over him.

'Well...I hadn't done anything exciting at all, and this seemed like an interesting thing to do.'

William swirled this piece of information round like the remnants of his brandy. 'But are you glad you did it?'

'Yes.' His voice was guarded, as though there were still doubts.

'You don't sound sure.'

'Well, we aren't even halfway through it yet. I'll have more of an idea if it was worthwhile when we are out of here.'

'But so far you have no regrets.'

'I don't think so. Although...'

William pounced. 'Although what?'

'Although it has taken me a lot longer to get to know people than I thought it would. I've discovered that even in extreme circumstances such as these, people are closed. They don't let others see their true selves. I think I'm easy to read, you get what you see with me, and that's not true with everyone else here.'

'Including me?' Fixing his eye on Rhys, William waited.

'You are the worst.' A slight smile started twitching at the corner of Rhys' mouth.

William raised his hand in mock horror and placed it across his chest. 'Well, I'll be damned,' he said in a Southern American drawl.

'That's exactly what I mean. You still make a joke out of everything; you take nothing seriously, and let nobody in.'

Suddenly hushed, William downed the last of his brandy, before putting the glass on the counter and staring at it. 'That's probably because I've never met anyone that I want to let in.'

Rhys said nothing. He had hit a nerve. He waited for William to continue.

'I make jokes and put up a front because I'm afraid that if I let anyone in, let anyone get to know the real me, then eventually I'll get hurt. And I couldn't bear that.'

This was an important moment. Rhys was certain that William was the kind of guy never to admit to such emotional stuff, and now here he had shared a deep, personal secret. He just kept changing before Rhys' eyes. When he first met him, he didn't like William. He thought him crude and obvious and full of self-satisfied smugness. But over the past few days he had come to see that there were hidden depths, and underneath the bluff exterior was a nice man. A man with foibles and neuroses and a man beset with angst, just like everyone else he knew. It wouldn't hurt to really get to know him, to see if he could get those emotional barriers to come tumbling down. But now wasn't the time. It was something to try in the clear light of day.

'Look...it's late. I think we should get a good night's sleep and perhaps we'll talk more tomorrow, OK?' Rhys slid himself off his stool and stood close to William, who sat still as a rock, his eyes now firmly fixed on Rhys again. A small muscle twitched at the side of his temple, and his lips were grimly pressed together.

'I'll see you in the morning, all right?' Without a sound, Rhys placed a gentle kiss on William's forehead, and padded from the room.

Friday

'Can I have a word?'

'Sure. What's up?'

'I just wondered if you'd given any thoughts to who you'll be voting out this weekend.'

'Not really. Why?'

'Well…it occurred to me that if we pool our resources we could end up making something from this.'

'What do you mean?'

'How can I put this? If we make sure that we vote for the same person, then we'll be in with a good chance of staying 'til the end. And we could make a pact…share the money. What do you think?'

'I think that's a totally dishonest, underhand thing to suggest. Have you spoken to anyone else about this?'

'I'd rather we kept it to ourselves, if you don't mind.'

'Hmm. I'll think about it.'

The photo collages were almost complete. Peter sat back and surveyed his handiwork with pride. The montage of Jackson had turned out superbly.

'Let me see.' Jackson stood in the living room doorway, his arms crossed and his eyes closed tightly as bidden.

'And *voilà!*' Peter held the board upright so that Jackson could see his likeness.

A huge burst of delighted laughter erupted from him. 'Brilliant! I look like the Hunchback of Notre Dame!' Tears rolled down his face, as his laughter showed no sign of dissipating.

'What's so funny?' Frowning, Peter put the board down and stared at Jackson. 'I think it's bloody good.'

'No, it is. It just looks kind of odd, that's all.'

'Have you finished me off yet?'

Jackson raised one eyebrow at this unintentional double entendre. 'Not yet.'

'Well, you'd better get moving. We haven't got long.'

'What's all the laughter about?' A voice from the doorway made them look round. Simon stood there watching proceedings.

'Nothing, really. We were just discussing this week's task.' Peter gave Simon a big grin, hoping that this was the first sign of melting the icy reception he'd been giving them lately.

'Huh.' Simon grunted and turned away, shooting a look of disdain at them as he went.

'He's really upset.' Peter's statement of the obvious made Jackson sigh.

'I know.'

'Well, can't you make it up with him? We've all got to live together in this damn place. If one of us isn't speaking, then it'll get very unpleasant.'

'I know.'

'I think you should go after him and try and talk.'

'I know.'

'Stop saying "I know" and get on with it, then.'

Shrugging his shoulders, Jackson could think of nothing else to do but acquiesce.

*

He found Simon in the games room, sticking the photos of a totally naked Skye onto the board, Skye at his elbow marvelling at his artistic touches.

'That looks so good. Have you ever thought about doing this kind of thing for a living?' Skye was impressed.

'Not really. I did art at school and was always getting top marks. I guess it's all about having a good eye. Knowing what makes something worth looking at.'

'I still like that bit best.' Skye pointed at the exaggerated shots of his cock and balls, which he had insisted Simon take in close-up, so as to accentuate their size and make them appear even larger than they were.

'I still think there was no need for that. Surely they're big enough already?'

Skye put an arm around Simon's waist and drew him close to him. 'You can never have too big a cock.' He had assumed a dark, Bette Davis voice, and crossed his eyes comically.

'Fool,' said Simon laughing.

'Er...can I interrupt?' Jackson cleared his throat.

'What do you want?' Glowering, Simon stood and turned to face him.

'I'd like to talk to you, if you have a moment.' He angled his head to one side, giving Skye a look that said 'Do you mind?'

'You two carry on...I've got to spend a penny.' With a cheery wave of his hand, Skye departed.

'Well?' Simon was immediately on his guard. He had nothing to say to this bastard. This bastard that he had begun to have feelings for. He knew that the situation they were in was a false one, made up for a television programme, and that whatever happened within its confines should be looked on as vaguely unreal, but he couldn't help the way he felt, and was angry at himself. Why did he feel this way? Jackson was just another nice guy, who he had only known for a short period of time. Sure the sex was great, but was that any reason to suppose that Jackson was in any way smitten with Simon in return?

'Well...I don't quite know why you are so angry with me. We didn't have any kind of exclusive thing, did we?'

'No, but...'

'And we never said that for the rest of our time in the house we wouldn't be tempted to go with any of the others, did we?

'No, we didn't...'

'So why the attitude?'

'Because I was – I mean, I am – falling for you.'

This statement hit Jackson like a bullet from a gun. 'Wow. I don't know what to say to that. I thought we were just mates, having some fantastic sex, enjoying each other while we could. I didn't realise you felt like that.'

'It's not your fault.' Simon was beginning to thaw. He could see that it was ridiculous to hold a grudge in such a weird atmosphere, and that life would be a lot more bearable if things were back on an even keel. 'I stupidly let my defences down and began to become emotionally involved. Daft, but there it is.'

'It's not daft. It's kind of nice in a way. I've never had anyone say they've fallen for me like that before. I'm touched.'

Smiling, Simon moved closer. 'Would you like to be?' He raised his eyebrow and gave a suggestive wink.

'It's not beyond the realms of possibility. Come here.' Jackson opened his arms and enfolded Simon in his embrace, then tilted his head so he could plant a wet kiss on his housemate's lips.

'That's nice.' Simon could feel himself becoming immediately aroused. His cock started to fill and press against Jackson's warm thighs. He groaned deliriously as Jackson dropped a hand and gave his swelling a squeeze, manipulating and massaging his hardness with a gentle, pulsing strokes. Simon's legs began to tremble. Why did this man affect him so? It wasn't just the sex, surely? But whatever the reason, he found himself falling again, plunging headlong into those dark, vibrant eyes, desperately wanting to be taken and made love to by this powerful man.

'I see...you really are fickle, aren't you, Jackson?' A voice made them stop what they were doing and look up. Peter stood in the doorway, hands on hips, defiantly watching the action.

Simon spoke first. 'Piss off and leave us alone.'

This immediately annoyed Peter, who strode forward and pulled Jackson away from Simon's clutches. 'I don't think so.' His fingers grabbed at Simon's arm.

'Let me go.'

Peter's hand withdrew from Simon's shirtsleeve. 'I don't know what's been going on here, but Jackson and I have something going. You were just a casual fling, so get lost and leave us alone.'

This was the wrong thing to say. Simon, who up until now had been a fairly placid member of the Boycam house, exploded with pent-up ire.

'How dare you! Jackson and I have become close recently...until you came along and sunk your grubby claws in him. I can see what you are up to...just after sex. Well, let me tell you that it won't work. He is mine and you can't have him.'

Anger boiled over in Peter now. No one spoke to him like that. He was going to have his say.

'Listen...Jackson and I have something special...I give him more than you can. At least he knows what a real man is like...in fact, he probably was grateful for it after having your anaemic body all over him.'

Simon was too stunned to answer, and so all he could was react in the most natural way he knew how. He slapped Peter's face with such ferocity that the sound made Jackson flinch.

'Look, can I say something here?' He tried to come between the two antagonists. This was a ridiculous situation that had escalated out of control. He wasn't the kind of guy to enjoy this kind of thing; he firmly eschewed violence of any sort and he felt very embarrassed by the whole situation.

'This can be easily settled.' He spoke calmly and clearly, his eyes fixing on the intrigued faces of Skye, Rhys and William who had gathered in the doorway, the sounds of the argument bringing them running.

'I don't see how.' Simon was now like a small, belligerent child. He was not prepared to back down. Jackson was his and was going to stay his. 'The only way to settle this is for you to choose. Me or...' He gestured with a dismissive hand. '...Or that.'

This was what Jackson had been hoping wouldn't happen. He liked both Simon and Peter and enjoyed both their company. He had had great sex with them and the thought of choosing between them would prove to be extremely difficult.

'Well...?' Both Simon and Peter now looked at him, both beseeching and both demanding. Jackson knew that there was only one thing he could say to keep the equilibrium in the house and to keep everyone happy, or relatively so.

'You are making this very hard for me.' He started to talk to the two aggressors, a hand on each one's shoulder. 'But how can I choose? This isn't fair. We are in this bizarre situation, with every move we make watched by thousands of faceless strangers. Our behaviour in here isn't how we would normally react. You have to remember that. I don't know why you two are so worked up over me. It's very flattering of course, but very silly.' He paused and took a deep breath before continuing. 'There is no way I can choose between you. I would rather have both of you as friends than one as a lover and one as an enemy, so I choose neither. We've got a long time to go yet, and the atmosphere in here will be intolerable if we are all at each other's throats.'

Simon and Peter looked at each other, the wisdom of Jackson's words starting to slowly sink in. They had to spend time with each other in the house and such arguments made it hard for everyone.

'So how about a group hug, and we forget all about this?' He raised his eyes and smiled at the other three clustered by the door, watching the proceedings with ill-disguised interest. They moved in and stood behind the warring couple.

Peter put out a hand. Someone had to make the first move. 'Truce?'

'Why not? Aardvarks.'

'What?' Peter looked puzzled.

Simon grinned childishly. 'Oh, it's something we used to say at school. Aardvarks...it means truce.'

'Then aardvarks it is.' Holding his arms open wide, Peter waited for the five others to join him in a hug.

Sunday

The photo collages were a great success. All of the housemates admired the results of each other's handiwork and said very flattering things about them. The general mood had improved immensely since the argument two days before, and all the six guys had resumed an air of contented comradeship.

'I am going to ask if I can have my collage when this is over,' said Rhys jovially. This was the first time he had had such an article made of himself and he was pleased with how handsome he looked. Nods of assent took place all round. One by on they carried the life-size boards down to the main gate for collection and marking, and once this had been done they returned to the house. The rest of the day had passed by uneventfully, with the majority of the guys chatting, or playing canasta in the living room.

Sunday, as always, was more tense than the rest of the week put together. The imminent eviction of one of their group put a huge strain on the usually mundane Boycam life. By now it was getting harder and harder to choose which of their number was to be voted out, as they had become a tightly knit group and, arguments aside, were getting on well.

Eight o'clock was but a few minutes away as William sauntered into the room, the last one to arrive, and he plumped himself down in a comfy armchair. Rhys was sitting at one end of the sofa, hugging his knees tightly, and gently rocking back and forth. He just wanted this to be over. He had voted this week as his head had told him to do, not his heart, and was wondering now if he had made the right decision. Jackson stood by the large window looking out over the garden, his mind full of thoughts of the argument that had taken place over him, and wondered if that was enough to see him voted out. Surely the others wouldn't be so petty as to do this spiteful thing? Simon sat cross-legged on the floor in front of the marbled fireplace, quietly awaiting the announcement, not communicating with any of the others, whilst Peter sat next to Rhys, biting a fingernail nervously.

'Well, it's nearly time.' Skye broke the silence, scrunching up the empty crisp packet from which he'd been assiduously munching, and tossing it into a corner. 'Are we all ready?'

'As ready as I'll ever be,' said Peter quietly.

'Listen guys...when this is over...' William started to say, his voice trembling slightly with emotion. 'I mean, when we are all out of here...I hope we'll all stay in touch. There are people here I'd like to get to know in more normal circumstances. What do you say?'

There was a barrage of nodding heads, which ceased as Matt's voice came booming out through the hidden speakers.

'Hello, Boycam house. This is Matt speaking. I have the result of the third vote here in front of me, and unlike last week it was more of a close-run thing. This week the voting was very interesting, with votes being cast widespread, but there did emerge one person with more votes than the others. That person will have an hour to pack and be ready to leave. A car will be waiting for you outside the gate to take you home. Now if you are all ready...the third person to leave the Boycam house is...Jackson Leroux.'

Interview with Jackson Leroux

'I suppose I am not that surprised that I was voted out when I was. The whole thing with Simon and Peter did get a bit much. I like an easy life and things were getting out of hand. I did like Simon a lot, but then I also grew fond of Peter. I mean, what's a boy to do when he has got two men available and interested? He makes the most of it, doesn't he?

'Anyway...despite all the drama, I did enjoy my time in the house. It was odd being in such a closeted atmosphere, where you felt that your every move was under surveillance. There were odd little spots where you realised that the camera couldn't quite pick you up, or where you were just out of earshot of the microphones, and that meant that there were places to go if you needed a bit of privacy, or wanted to talk to someone without the world knowing. There was nothing I missed when inside, perhaps a television set...I am one of those guys who puts the telly on as soon as he wakes up. I like having it on all the time because it's like a friendly voice about the place. I can't stand silence. And I will enjoy catching up on the soaps, which one of my mates has been videoing for me.

'Looking back, I wouldn't have changed a thing, except perhaps I might have been a bit more cautious when seeing both the guys, having them fighting over me really didn't help the balance of the place, and I think it made some of the other guys dislike me for my attitude. That's probably the reason I was voted out, for my behaviour over Peter and Simon. I hope that the other guys liked me in the main, though. I would have also liked to have got to grips with Skye. He was such a stud! And a cock to die for. I would have really loved a session or three with that.

'What do I remember most? Probably the sexual energy about the place. It was like living in a gay bar, full of handsome guys, all exuding charisma, all seemingly available for sex. There were times when you just wanted to grab the nearest guy, rip his clothes off and go down on him, but of course you didn't. Having the cameras there was inhibiting at first, but after the first couple of weeks you just forget about them, and that's when the real fun and games started. I mean I wouldn't have dared do that being-tied-to-the-bed thing knowing that I was being filmed, but it just happened and I didn't care. The most important thing was having the sex.

'I'm not sure who will win; I think the whole thing is still wide open. I would like Simon to win, if only to make the whole thing worthwhile for him after the upset I caused. I would like to see him again after, and I hope we can be friends. And I won't be sorry if I don't see Jost again. He was a really stuck-up, narrow-minded arse-hole. The meals he used to make for us all were terrible, full of healthy stuff, tofu and beans and organic soya milk...give me a steak any day!

'I've been inundated with letters and invitations since I left, loads from guys wanting to date me, and I might take up a few of the in-vites...and I've been offered a job presenting a daytime TV show about learning to swim, can you believe it?! I was totally gob-smacked when I got that call. I have had to get an agent, and it looks like my life is going to be totally changed. So I have Boycam to thank for that.

WEEK FOUR

Monday

There was not a great deal of surprise among the housemates at the result of the vote. Somehow it seemed appropriate that Jackson would be the next person to leave. He was a nice guy, but had caused upset amongst them, albeit unwittingly, and the five remaining guys thought that it was the best outcome for the stability of the house.

His departure had been emotional. He had packed his stuff quickly and efficiently, hauling his case down to the front door with plenty of time to spare before the car arrived to take him home. Peter and Simon had wisely stayed out of his way, and it was William that offered to lend a hand, staying cheery and helping Jackson to keep his spirits up. At the main gate, as he was about to leave, the guys all stood around offering words of comfort and hugs, secretly glad that they were still in with a chance, but a little saddened to see this open and friendly man going. Peter held out a hand and then pulled Jackson to him, giving a big, sloppy kiss, and a farewell grope of his packet, quickly followed by Simon who whispered something in his ear, something Skye thought he overheard, as 'I'll ring you when I can.'

The rest of that evening was spent with several bottles of wine and a curry, kindly provided by the production team, and the guys went to bed, drunk and emotionally drained.

Up bright and early the next morning, Skye decided the day was pleasant enough for him to do his exercises in the garden. The sun was shining with a vivid intensity already and a plethora of birds had set up residence in the tree, giving him a tuneful serenade as he sauntered down to the bottom of the lawn. This was his quiet time, usually when the others were still in bed and, as all was peaceful, he could do his sit-ups and press-ups and not be disturbed. As he worked up a sweat, he cogitated on the current state of the house. Now that Jackson had gone, Peter and Simon should relax a lot more as the source of their recent animosity had been removed. Rhys was also becoming a nicer guy, having seemed to have done a lot of growing up in the last couple of weeks. His sexual experiences at the party when he was blindfolded had been a rude awakening to his sexuality and he although he had appeared shocked at the time, he struck Skye as being more able to cope with such a scene now. Perhaps it would be worth experimenting.

Skye's thoughts stayed with Rhys, as he curled himself up from the ground, hugging his knees tight and then lying back down repeatedly. Rhys was an attractive lad, and one who needed to see what life could offer him. realised that he had been thinking about Rhys a lot lately. Did he have feelings for him? Perhaps he did. There was definitely something there to think about. He kept finding the image of Rhys in his Marlon Brando outfit in the forefront of his mind, and the possibility of what lay beneath intrigued him. Was this young stud a goer? Did he thrash his head against the pillow when he was being fucked? Did he cry out, or was he the silent type who just lay there and waited for satisfaction? He doubted that.

And what about the others? Simon was a nice guy, if a bit easily led. The whole Jackson thing had shown that. It would have been obvious to even the most stupid person that he was head over heels about him. And when Jackson started making overtures to Peter, it was clear that there would be fireworks. And Skye had been proved right on that one. Perhaps they would settle down a bit now. Perhaps they'd even get it together themselves. That would be interesting. Even more interesting was Simon's appendage. His cock. Skye had admired it before, and his mouth had watered at the shiny metal addendum. He had a thing about pierced cock; the very mention of it started the machinery of arousal in his loins. And to have one so close at hand and not be able to get his hands on it annoyed him. Simon hadn't shown the slightest sexual interest in him at all, but there were ways of changing that. He made a firm decision. He would have a mouthful of that knob before he left the house.

William was a different matter. Skye had never really liked him. There was something about his middle-class attitude to things that pissed Skye off. He had a superior air, assuming he was better than everyone else simply because he went to a posh school, and because he spoke like Prince William. And those jokes! He seemed incapable of opening his mouth without some form of naff comment, some crude remark about cock or sex or spunk...it really bored Skye. But he had to admit that William had toned a lot of that down lately and had appeared more relaxed and like one of the lads. Skye appreciated that he'd made the effort. And, after all, he was the first one to offer to help Jackson out with his packing when all the others seemed a little reticent. Maybe there was more to William than met the eye, and maybe it would be worth finding out what. He certainly seemed to have a reasonably nice body, and there was something quite endearing about the way his hair always looked like he'd just got out of bed. That was sweet. And he had nice eyes. Yes, perhaps Skye would make an extra effort with him too this week.

But Peter puzzled him. He was young and good-looking in a kind of Mediterranean, swarthy way, and knew how to look after himself. He must also have been good at sex, owing to the ecstatic noises that came from his and Colin's room during the height of their passion. He struck Skye as the type of guy who needed others around. He needed other people to justify his existence. He desired company all the time, someone to talk with, or to sleep with. He was a nobody when on his own. He was the sort of guy who'd happily set up home with a man, and spend his day cooking and cleaning and then be waiting at the door to say 'Did you have a nice day at the office, dear?' and have a gin and tonic waiting for hubby as he massaged his tired feet. He wanted to be wanted. That's probably why he latched onto Colin and then Jackson so soon after his departure. He probably put up a show of resistance at first but secretly adored the chase. He was a bit of a tease. And probably the one person in the house not to be trusted.

Life here was bearable at the moment. Skye had surprised himself by being quite entertained by the last challenge, and had taken real pleasure in creating a marvellous portrait of Simon. He had had fun, and that was a revelation. Up until now it had all been a bit pathetic, and he had gone along with the challenges and everything because it was expected, and he realised that he would need to put on a show and expend some effort if he was to be in with a chance of winning, and that was something he was determined to do. After all he had done and was going to do, it would be too humiliating to have to walk away empty handed.

At the end of his fiftieth sit-up, Skye fell back on the ground, looking up, watching the clouds floating relentlessly by. He would definitely have a holiday when he won the money. A month on a beach somewhere hot. A place full of palm trees and handsome bronzed men who'd enjoy the privilege of being fucked by the attractive blond stranger. He'd sit on a balcony overlooking the sea and drink exotic cocktails, then dress up in a tight white T-shirt and expensive trousers and go out strolling the town, revelling in the admiring glances of men and women alike.

His nose was assailed by an odorous whiff and he knew that a shower was now in order. Jumping to his feet, he strode inside and up the staircase, noting still that nobody else seemed to be up yet. He pushed open the bathroom door and halted in his tracks.

'Oh, sorry. I didn't know anyone was in here.'

Through the clouds of steam issuing from the shower cubicle came a voice. 'It's all right, sweetheart. I won't be a minute.' William wiped his hand against the glass cubicle wall and peered through the condensation.

'Hand me a towel, would you?' The glass door slid open a couple of inches and a hand poked through the gap, dripping water into small pools on the cork tiling.

'Sure.' Skye picked a small, fluffy white towel from the rail and placed it in the waiting hand. The door slid open fully and William stepped out, holding the towel modestly in front of him. His hair was slicked back and a tiny glob of shampoo sat by his left ear. His body glistened with water, and he began to vigorously dry himself, keeping a portion of the towel delicately hanging in front of his most private area.

For the first time Skye was able to get a good look at this guy. How old did he say he was? About thirty, was it? He was in good shape. It was clear that he didn't do a lot of exercise, but it appeared as if he didn't need to. His stomach was quite tight, and although there was no evidence of anything remotely resembling a six-pack, he looked fine. His chest was also quite nicely developed, with fairly muscular pecs, and large nipples, which were completely hairless. His neck was strong and bullish; in fact, he looked as though he might have just finished a tough game of rugby and stepped out of the showers. That was another of Skye's fantasies – to be allowed full reign in a football team's changing rooms, watching the invariably cute guys stripping and showering, or maybe diving into the large soapy bath together and being serviced by all of them in turn. Shaking his head slightly to dispel this image, he gave William a crooked smile.

'Better now?'

'Much, thank you. It's all yours.'

'And what about the shower?'

William cocked an eyebrow, surprised at the suggestive comment from Skye, of all people. Here was the one person in the house that he'd had most trouble getting on with. Shame, really, because he was such a hot guy. He had a great body and a delicious cock, and William was absolutely convinced they could make sweet music together. All of a sudden Skye was standing in front of him, a glint in his eye and being suggestive. What did it mean? Perhaps it was time to find out. Throwing the towel around his shoulders, William nodded toward the cubicle.

'The shower.' He watched Skye's eyes momentarily flicker down to his now-exposed genitals, and saw that flicker of interest. The gorgeous blond seemed surprised and delighted. He knew Skye had imagined he didn't have much to speak of down there, but he was wrong, and now he had seen the evidence for himself.

'Catch you later,' he said, sauntering casually from the bathroom, feeling Skye's gaze burning into his retreating back, knowing that he was admiring his buttocks. And why shouldn't he? They were quite pert and well worth a good gawp at. As he reached his bedroom door and closed it behind him, his mind was full of odd conjectures. Why had Skye shown an interest so suddenly? So far he had been polite and friendly, but always distant. This was a fascinating turn up for the books. In his opinion, Skye was probably the most sexually practised guy in the house and because of that the most interesting. William knew that to have sex with Skye would be a wonderful experience. He wasn't ashamed to admit that at times he had haboured secret fantasises about such a thing occurring. The images that filled his mind of Skye, naked and hard, wanting to do almost anything William wanted gave rise to some of William's more energetic early morning wank sessions.

He closed his bedroom door behind him and then stopped, his hand still resting on the handle. Quietly, he pulled it open just an inch, and looked out. From his room door he could see straight down the landing to the bathroom at the other end. Skye had left the door open, and so William was surprised to have a good view of the young blond in the shower. The condensation was starting to build up around the cubicle, but William saw with delight that he was able to clearly make out the stunning body inside. Throwing the towel onto the bed and turning back to the door, William could feel his cock growing. An image of Skye, wet from the shower and erect, flitted across his brain. He watched entranced as the muscular figure soaped and washed himself attentively, giving time to each part of his body, lingering over the genitals. Suddenly William noticed that Skye had turned to face in his direction.

Skye knew from the first second he saw William in the shower that he had been pleasantly surprised. There actually was a nice body under those baggy, shapeless clothes he relentlessly wore. He thought he had seen a glimmer of interest in his eyes too, as he casually dried himself down, and the unexpected, but almost defiant act of throwing his towel around his neck, giving Skye a good look at what he had down below, was certainly an act of enticement. If he wanted to get involved in any way with him, perhaps here was the chance to make an effort. Through the steam in the shower cubicle wall, he could see that William had opened his door slightly, and there appeared to be a slight movement there. Was he watching him? It seemed very likely. So maybe it was time to give him a show. And what a show he would give him.

Skye knew all the tricks, how to bring a man to the edge, to have him drooling with pent-up lust and enthusiasm, and he knew where to let go, to ease off so that his prey didn't reach exploding point too soon. As though he was finding the steam from the hissing shower stream too much, Skye slid open the cubicle door, so that he could be plainly seen by William. He reached again for the cake of soap and began lathering himself all over, starting at the neck and slowly but sensuously working down to his chest, just momentarily lingering about his nipples. Then, as if drawn by some invisible force, he bent forward, soaping his legs and thighs before lastly smoothing the slithery bar around his cock and balls. Taking his time, he took his bits carefully in one hand and rubbed the cleansing froth all over them, feeling that exciting tingle of arousal from knowing he was being watched. After a moment he bent forward again, this time with his back to William, his hands moving sinuously around his firm buttocks. Then with small, circular, probing movements he began to finger his own arsehole. With his slippery hands he pulled at the cheeks, spreading them wide, letting anyone who cared to look see his exposed pink ring. Standing again, he stretched his arms high over his head, feeling the hot water cascading down him, washing away the last remnants of the lather, until he stood beneath its stinging needles, clean and erect. His cock was now hard, and it stood up magnificently. He was very proud of what he had been blessed with, which was one of the many reasons for his entering the world of porn. 'If you've got it, flaunt it to as many people as you can' was one of his mottoes. He had no doubt that his exhibitionistic show had got William very hot and bothered. Half of him wanted to pad his way down the hall and knock at the door to see the results of his performance. The other half urged caution. Wait and see. There were bound to be more opportunities to play around with this guy. Don't rush in and spoil the fun of the hunt. If William was horny, then let him enjoy the fruits of that on his own.

And William certainly was. From his vantage point behind the crack in the door, he had an astounding view of the proceedings. He could not believe his eyes when Skye opened the door to let steam out of the shower cubicle. He can't be aware that he is being watched, thought William to himself – surely he'd be too self-conscious. He was only too conscious of his own state, his cock stiff and begging for some action. It butted against the door, a small droplet of pre-come adhering to the white paint of the door and leaving a sticky string hanging. He watched in mesmerised awe as Skye washed himself, his body undulating as he soaped himself down. His eyes were glued to the sight of the guy fondling his cock and balls, their size and shape quite obvious even from a distance. His hand dropped to his own solid rod, wrapping his fingers tightly about it and gently stroking it from base to tip. His throat was incredibly dry, and his heart was pounding fit to burst. He so wanted to walk the length of the hall and take that man in his arms. But propriety screamed at him not to. Unable to tear himself away, he watched entranced as Skye bent over, fingering his arse. Surely he knew he was being watched? Surely? A thought suddenly struck William with immense force. Skye did know he was being watched and this show was for his benefit. A shiver worked itself all the way down William's spine, and he felt suddenly cold and hot all at the same time. What should he do about it? He wasn't sure. All he felt he could reasonably do was to watch from a distance and see what happened. If Skye wanted to do anything more or to make a move, then William would react accordingly.

Skye felt the blood throbbing in his cock. It was the feeling he loved to experience. To know that he was stark bollock naked and was being scrutinised by a pair of lust-filled eyes turned him on totally. Another thought entered his head, telling him that William's eyes weren't the only ones watching him right now. Several pin-head cameras and a production crew were no doubt surveying every move he made, silently cheering, knowing that as he gyrated and became more worked up, so would their viewers. He would probably be a real wank fantasy for hundreds, if not thousands, of gay men, something that he adored being. To know that guys were beating off, with images of him in their minds and on their videos, pleased him immensely. Indeed, as this thought entered his mind he uttered a groan and grabbed his cock. He had to beat off now himself; this would show William who was boss. A slight fluttering movement from the crack in William's bedroom door showed that they were both of the same mind.

Simultaneously they worked at their cocks, loving the tight grips of their hands about their aching rigidities; for only a few moments they jerked them with a fierce intensity they'd not known for some time. Breathing through his mouth, small gasps escaped William as his vision clouded and his eyes closed momentarily as he shot his load in one long stream, splattering against the door. As he came, the weight of his body fell against the door and banged it shut.

Skye knew he had done his best and in a second he was also at boiling point and he let forth an arc of spunk which landed in globs in the shower stall, immediately washed away by the force of the gushing shower.

Reaching across and turning off the water, Skye stepped out and onto the bathroom floor, grabbing up a towel which he wound round his midriff. And not a moment too soon, as Peter's door swung open and he came blearily and full of sleep down the hall towards him.

'Morning.' Skye heard how bright and ringing his own voice was, the kind of voice that was utterly irritating when you had just woken.

'Humph.' Peter grunted a reply of sorts and went straight into the bathroom, slamming the door behind him.

An interesting start to the day, thought Skye. What else could it bring? He pondered this as he padded into his room, closed the door and started to dress.

After the amazing events of the morning, William decided the only way to behave was to be extra cheery and act as though it hadn't happened. If Skye wanted to raise the subject, then he would wait for him to do so. It was completely clear that Skye wasn't interested in him sexually, and had put on that show for some vain reason of his own. Until he owned up, William would say nothing.

'Morning, chaps.' William strolled into the kitchen and surveyed his housemates. Rhys and Simon were seated at the breakfast bar eating bowls of cereal, while Peter and Skye stood by the toaster waiting for some freshly browned bread to pop up.

Rhys looked up and gave him a wide smile. 'Morning, William. Sleep well?'

'Remarkably so, thank you.' His tone held a hint of something secret, which he and Rhys shared, after their late night chat. 'Any orange juice left?' He hauled a large plastic container out of the fridge, then poured himself a healthy-sized glassful. This was going to be an interesting day.

Chewing on his flakes, Rhys watched William intently. In the early hours of Friday morning they had shared a moment, when a confidence was told and their relationship had taken another step forward. Ever since, Rhys had looked at William differently. Not always the brash, lewd snob, but a man with a soft centre, who was often lonely, and had a tendency to get hurt. Someone who had tried to live up to the expectations of his background and occasionally found it difficult.

Skye caught the happy smile that Rhys gave to William and wondered what that was about. Had they talked already? Had William spilt the beans about their early morning shower liaison? If he had, then he was the owner of a very big mouth. And something would have to be done about that. He was all for a bit of sexy fun, but if the recipient started bragging about his conquests, then he'd have to be taught a lesson. He turned and looked at William, who had finished his juice and sauntered from the kitchen, whistling an annoying tune through his teeth. Skye's eye wandered over to Rhys, who was staring at him, but then quickly flicked his gaze away and went back to his breakfast.

As he waited for his toast, Peter looked at the loaf of bread that sat on the counter before him. He was fairly relieved that Jackson had been voted out. Although he was a terrific guy and lots of fun, he was also a liability. Someone like Jackson was capable of upsetting the entire house with his bed-hopping antics, and making the housemates lives uncomfortable because of them. The sooner everything settled down again, the better he would feel. He had a strategy for remaining in the house, one which he'd settled on in the last couple of days. As he had made it to the last five contestants, he was prepared to do anything to stay inside. He would be friendly and helpful; he would make himself an invaluable member and be the best chum of his other housemates. Surely they couldn't be so cruel as to evict Mr Niceguy?

Simon was also deep in thought. For him, it had been a strange few weeks in the Boycam house. For all his cheerfulness and his normally placid exterior, inside he was a mess. For the first time in ages he had met a guy that he had started to develop strong feelings for. Up until he had met Jackson, the men in his life hadn't stayed long. He had had his fair share of relationships, many good ones, but none of them had lasted. In Jackson he had found a guy who he knew was very attractive, friendly, charming, sensual and open. Simon had closed his mind to any faults that he may have possessed, including a desire to fool around. Peter was a tart who had a devious nature and had done his best to entice Jackson into his lair. It was just a pity that Jackson didn't have the ability to say no to this back-stabbing slut. He had agreed to a truce to keep Jackson happy, and had voted for Peter to be expelled, and so was extremely upset when the last eviction announcement was broadcast. He had confidently expected Peter to be the next guy to leave, and was truly shocked by the news. As a result, he had slept badly, tossing and turning all night long, full of bitterness and regret, and had come to a momentous conclusion in the early hours, as he listened to the smug twitterings of the dawn chorus outside his window. He missed his own bed, and he desperately missed his own friends. Yes. He had made his decision. He wanted to leave the house.

Standing and taking his bowl to the sink, rinsing it and placing it on the draining board to dry, Simon faced the others and cleared his throat purposefully.

'Excuse me, guys. I want to talk to you all.' He took a deep breath.

'Look what I've got, girls.' William ran back into the kitchen, a sheet of paper clasped in his fist. 'It's our next task.'

The room burst out with an excited babble of voices. All eyes turned to William expectantly. All except one. Simon sank back down on his stool with a sigh.

'Sorry, Simon...what were you going to say?' Skye put an encouraging hand on the young Chinese guy's shoulder.

'Oh...it doesn't matter. It can wait.' Crossing his arms, Simon waited to hear what William had discovered.

His eyes quickly scanned the sheet, and his broad shoulders drooped somewhat with disappointment. 'Oh dear.'

'What is it?' A chorus of voices beseeched William to stop dithering and read the task to them.

He took a deep breath and began. 'Boycam housemates. Now that you are well into the project, we feel that you have no doubt become a little lethargic, with perhaps too much time spent lazing in the sun. To this end, this week's challenge is the Boycam Olympics. Tomorrow we will be delivering an electric running machine, some weights, and other sundry athletic equipment. Your task will be to compete against each other to find out who is the fittest member of the house. All are expected to participate, and anyone who does not make the effort will find points deducted for slothfulness. All events must be finished by four o'clock on Saturday afternoon. You will be provided with suitable Olympian attire to compete in and will be rewarded with the prospect of a Roman toga party on Saturday evening. Have fun.'

William put down the paper and stared at his housemates, dismayed. He did do the odd bit of jogging, but to be forced to compete for fitness supremacy worried him enormously.

'Well, I guess we have all got a bit lazy,' said Rhys, not noticing Skye lifting his shirt and patting his firm, flat stomach smugly.

'Speak for yourself.' The tone of Skye's voice made them all turn to him; he seemed completely unconcerned about the challenge. In fact, it looked like he relished the chance to show his stamina. 'If you guys did daily exercises like I do, then you wouldn't be so in awe of this task. Come on...it'll be fun.'

Simon watched the others without saying a word. He wondered if he'd get the chance to speak to them, now that they were full of this new assignment. He had wanted to speak so badly before, but the news of their task had soothed him somewhat. Perhaps a week of mindless exertion would help him to put things in perspective. That was it. He'd stay another week, and decide then. If he got voted out, then great; if not, then he might be in a happier frame of mind. He was not averse to a bit of physical exercise, rather enjoying the occasional trip to the gym or the local pool. It would be a good thing.

'Sorry, Simon...you wanted to say something?' Peter swung the group's attention back from the new task.

Simon dropped his eyes and stood up from the stool, heading for the kitchen door with emphasised casualness. 'Oh, it's nothing,' he tossed over his shoulder. 'Nothing at all.'

With a shrug, the others began to clear up and head off to various parts of the house, for contemplation, reading, resting or to start a few flexing exercises in preparation for the task ahead.

'Hi. I'm not disturbing you, I hope?'

'No.'

'Could I have a word?'

'I guess so. I think I know what you want, though.'

'Do you?'

'Yeah. One of the guys told me what you'd said to him...about voting.'

'And...?'

'I think it's despicable.'

'That's a harsh word.'

'Well, it is. Trying to sway the voting, which should be completely impartial, is wrong.'

'Wouldn't you like to win, though?'

'Of course, but fairly.'

'If you just thought about my suggestion, then it'd be more of a certainty.'

'I don't know...'

'Look, if we make sure we all vote the same way, then we could be down to the last two and then we could share the money. Think about it...that's all I ask.'

'I don't know.'

'Just think about it.'

Skye pushed open the door to the living room and fixed his eye on William, sitting curled up in an armchair, reading a book, oblivious to the rest of the world. No doubt the denouement was about to commence and the detective was on the brink of naming the murderer. William jumped as Skye cleared his throat forcefully, but he put down his book and looked up at his housemate.

'You gave me a start.'

'Sorry about that, but I'd like word with you in private.'

'Fire away.'

Skye wet his lips before he cleared his throat again, this time more nervously. 'It's about this morning's...er...bit of fun.'

'Oh yes.' William had wondered if Skye was actually going to say anything about it. Up until now, William had decided that it was just that – a bit of fun. There was nothing more to it. Skye was an attractive man, although William knew that he himself wasn't bad looking, but it was clear that there was absolutely no sexual tension between them. He would say nothing about it to anyone and just enjoy the memory. A small section of William's mind was a little surprised that Skye was bringing the subject up. 'What about this morning?'

'You enjoyed the show, I take it?'

William was unsure what to say to that. Skye knew that he had been watching him, so it was much better to admit it and pass it off as a bit of a laugh. 'Yes.'

Skye stood still for a moment. He had expected William to be more demonstrative and not so cautious in his replies.

'I assumed that it would be our secret.'

'It is.'

'I don't believe you, actually. You have talked to Rhys about it, haven't you?'

This was an unexpected development. 'No. Why should I have?' A bemused William sat up and crossed his arms in a vaguely defiant manner.

'Those looks the two of you were giving me over breakfast said it all. And in future I'd appreciate you not telling all and sundry what goes on in private between us.' Skye's face had darkened and the tone of his voice had dropped alarmingly. 'You do not want to see me when I'm angry.' With that, he turned and stomped away, leaving a stunned William to sit totally mystified by what had just happened.

Tuesday

A large brown box sat ominously down by the gate when Skye emerged from the house for his early morning exercise. Carrying it into the house, he dumped it on the snooker table and decided to leave it for when he'd finished. He wasn't an impatient man. He was fairly sure that the box contained the athletic outfits for their new challenge. The lure of his impending sit-ups had more of a pull than what ridiculous colour their shorts might be.

Later, heading downstairs after his shower, his ears were assaulted by a barrage of shrieks and screams. Sometimes, he thought, the others could be real queens. He sauntered into the games room and watched the proceedings dumbly.

'Look at these.' William held up a pair of pink satin shorts and a clinging vest, cut low to emphasise the chest muscles. He threw a pair of the outrageous coloured items over to Skye who examined them with a feigned air of disinterest. 'Let's try them on!'

Without a moment's hesitation, William stripped off and jumped into the outfit. 'Christ, these are tight.' And they obviously were. The shorts were cut high on the thigh, showing a lot of leg, and gave added prominence to the groin, making the cock and balls nestled inside look rather impressive. 'Hmm. I look quite good. I wonder if they'd let me keep them afterwards?'

The others chattered away gaily, ignoring Skye, who stood some distance away. After a moment's hesitation he spoke.

'Er...guys...if you'd care to follow me outside, you'll see what else we have been given.' He spun on his heels and disappeared into the garden.

Sitting proudly on the lawn was a motorised running machine, some weights, and a set of parallel bars. They looked brand new, glinting fearsomely in the bright morning light. Attached to the running machine was a sheet of paper. Skye grabbed it and read the contents. 'Well...it seems that we are expected to run a marathon, lift beyond our body weight and give a demonstration of complete physical prowess. Excellent. This could be a lot of fun!'

'Fun!' William spluttered, his eyes wide with amazement and dismay. He knew that there was no way he could lift such things and as for the parallel bars, he dreaded the thought of using them, his upper arm strength not being great. 'I can't think of anything worse. OK, I do go jogging occasionally, but to run the equivalent of a marathon, just for a few lousy points...in the unlikely event that we get through to the end of this show...well, I just think it's ridiculous. Anyone else agree?' He surveyed the group, all deep in their own thoughts, all except Skye, who was staring at the running machine control panel, trying to work out how it operated.

As no answer came, he snorted derisively and stormed inside the house. Trust Skye to be enjoying all this. Still, it suited his nature. He'd be in his element, looking stunning in his tight shorts, beating everyone at every athletic event. Since the contretemps yesterday, he had avoided talking to the beautiful blond, still puzzled by his over-the-top reaction. And today was not going to be any different.

'Arsehole.' Everyone looked up at Skye, who was now triumphantly taking his place on the ever-quickening running machine, his face a beaming smile, jogging along in time with the speed of the rubberised track.

'Yes, well...we are not all as athletic as you, Skye.' Peter shook his head. He also had grave misgivings about the task, and wondered silently if he should go after William and cheer him up. There was something on William's mind lately, his personality seemed changeable. One moment he could be happily trying on his Olympic outfit, the next he could be angrily stomping away. Only yesterday he had come down to breakfast in a jolly frame of mind and then later in the day he had been seen dashing upstairs to his room, deep in thought and deaf to any calls. Perhaps the whole Boycam experience was finally getting to him. Peter knew how he felt. Since the Jackson debacle, he had been wary of the others, Simon especially. But William was the one guy he hadn't really got to know yet. Possibly it was time.

The rest of the afternoon was slightly strained. Skye had gone to work immediately on the task, climbing enthusiastically into his shorts and vest, setting the running machine on a fast speed, and jogging away without the slightest loss of breath, or at least that's how it appeared to the rest of the house. Peter had also changed and was toying with the weights, trying to lift the lightest possible amount, and succeeding easily, this giving him the confidence to add more weight to them. Simon had retired to his room with a semi-hard wank magazine, uninterested in the task, but vowing to have a go later when he felt more ready.

Rhys, who knew from the others' reactions that he looked amazingly cute in his figure-hugging shorts, drifted toward the parallel bars for a practice. In his youth, he had been quite good at such activities at school, even competing a couple of times in the inter-school championships, and had won a bronze medal for parallel bar work. He was also quite good at rope work, amazing his then sports teacher Mr Evans with the speed at which he climbed up to the sports hall ceiling. He knew he had strong arms; all they needed was a little practice, and they'd soon be back in shape. He had offered to help William and Simon with the bars, but as yet they'd shown no interest in this particular task. All in good time. He was certain they'd be glad of his help.

As he hoisted himself up between the bars, he watched Skye on the running machine, mindlessly listening to music on his personal stereo as he jogged relentlessly on, his mind in some other place, his eyes glazed over. He did look good in his outfit, though. Rhys' eyes were drawn to Skye's groin. As he jogged, the cock and balls bounced alluringly, encased as they were in the tight pink satin. The effect was mouth-watering and Rhys was very impressed. He knew from personal experience that Skye was definitely well endowed, probably the biggest cock in the house, and it was a joy to watch it in action, and bring the memory of it in a more excited state to the forefront of his mind. If Skye had performed in porn movies, then perhaps it might be fun to try and find some of them out once the show was over. As he swung between the bars, his muscles beginning to ache slightly, he closed his eyes and thought about that first blow job he had given Skye during the willy moulding. It had been fabulous to have that cock in his mouth, but then to be given the chance again during the late-night drunken truth or dare session was more than he could have hoped for. He wanted it again.

Ever since he had arrived at the house, with his own insecurities and foibles, plus the inability to be as expressive as he wanted, he had found himself drawing closer to the people in the house. He hadn't much liked Jost, and hadn't really had much of a chance to get to know Colin or Jackson. But he liked Simon and was also finding that William was worth spending some time with. Peter was still a bit reserved but was basically a nice guy. But Skye. He rolled the name silently around his mouth. Skye. He was something else. A man with self-assurance, who didn't let the world tell him what to do, who did exactly what he wanted and enjoyed every second. He was attractive, he was confident, and he had something wonderful between his legs. The man had everything. And Rhys wanted to be just like him. It hadn't always been like this, though. In the early days he had seen him as arrogant and insensitive, someone with a tacky lifestyle and who made a living through immoral means. But now he had begun to change his mind. Earning money through sex had a twinge of excitement about it. To be paid large sums to simply have some guy suck your cock, or for you to fuck some other hot stud seemed incredible. The images of Skye in such situations blasted themselves in front of Rhys' eyes and he gulped, dropping down to the ground from the bars and massaging his arm muscles. He could feel a slight swelling in his groin. His overactive imagination had begun to arouse him. Christ, he needed a wank. Feeling Skye's gaze boring into his back as he headed toward the house, he decided to stroll upstairs and relieve some tension.

'Doesn't his smug attitude get on your nerves?' William sat at the breakfast bar, slowly and repeatedly stirring a cup of coffee. His eyes were intently scrutinising Rhys, who had wandered in for a glass of water. Rhys had worked up quite a thirst this afternoon, first with his parallel bar work and then a rather energetic bout of masturbation, his eye not wavering now from behind the curtains, glued to the sight of Skye's bouncing packet.

'Whose attitude?' Rhys didn't really have to ask.

A snort accompanied William's answer. 'You know who. Skye, of course. Miss Fucking Schwarzenegger out there. The one with the washboard stomach and nothing between her ears. Don't you get a tiny bit pissed off by her superiority sometimes? Strutting about the place showing off those muscles, preening and posing, knowing that if anyone finishes the task, it'll be her.'

'I guess so.' Rhys sank down beside William and took a long deep draft of the cool water.

'Well, it's really getting on my nerves. He's nothing but a show-off. I think it's time he was taught a lesson.'

'What do you mean?'

'I think he should be sent to Coventry.'

Rhys paused in mid-swallow and put his glass down decisively. 'Not talk to him, you mean?'

'Yes. Show the smug bastard that we are all pissed off by his attitude.'

'But are we all?'

'Sorry?' A puzzled expression passed across William's face. He had expected nothing but complicit agreement from this young man.

'Are we all pissed off? I don't think Peter or Simon are. I think they are more pissed off by each other at the moment.'

'Really? I hadn't noticed.'

Rhys decided on a few home truths. 'No, well, you are still a bit selfish, aren't you?'

Shock registered on William's face and he gave Rhys a stare, his brow furrowing. 'What are you saying?'

'I'm saying that at times you are so bound up with what you want that you don't think about the others here. I thought after our recent talk that you'd try to be more relaxed and normal. You don't seem to have got very far.'

William didn't know what to say. When he'd started this conversation he had hoped for a bit of sympathetic nodding and some agreement from a fellow Skye hater. But it hadn't happened. Rhys was being more outspoken than he had ever been before. And William didn't like it.

'Up yours.' Standing, William strode manfully out of the kitchen and upstairs.

'Oh, sorry.' Simon spoke involuntarily as he bumped into Peter coming out of the front door. He silently cursed himself; he had not wanted to talk to this pig.

'Watch where you're going.' Peter's tone was quite sharp, and without another word he pushed past and out into the garden.

Anger flared in Simon; he did not allow others to speak to him with such a casual disregard, and he wasn't going to let Peter do it, of all people. He was going to get this off his chest, and he didn't care who heard it.

'Come back here! You can't talk to me like that.' The anger turned to outright fury as the other guy stopped and, after a deep breath, turned to stare balefully at him.

'What did you say?' Simon was really getting on his nerves, and the edge in his voice only served to arouse a deep resentment in Peter.

'You heard. I want an apology.'

'Well, you won't get one from me, so why don't you just piss off?'

Scarlet flashes of indignation and rage filled Simon's head. This had got to stop. He moved forward until he stood a few inches from Peter, his eyes bulging, a small vein throbbing at the side of his neck. He had never been so angry.

'You arrogant bastard.' Like a dormant volcano at the moment of eruption, Simon lashed out. He pulled back his fist and let fly, landing a punch on Peter's nose, the sound of the crunch louder than he'd expected. He watched aghast as blood gushed out, soaking the front of his shirt.

Peter was so shaken by what had happened that he stood still, water springing to his eyes, a dull throbbing resonating around his head.

'Here, take this.' Skye rushed up, holding out a handkerchief. He'd seen the whole thing and decided it was time to help. 'Let's go inside.'

He put his arm around Peter's shoulder and guided him up to his room.

'What was all that about?' Rhys emerged from the front door looking shaken. The sight of blood had always made him go cold, and seeing Peter being helped upstairs, covered in the stuff, had shocked him greatly.

'Nothing,' said Simon.

But the look on Rhys' innocent face broke down Simon's barrier and he sighed. 'I hit him.'

'Why?'

'Because he deserved it. I've had enough of his attitude, all smug and superior.'

Rhys had heard all this before, but from William's lips. And not about Peter. Perhaps he had had his head in the clouds lately, but he hadn't realised there was such bad feeling in the house. All this anger had come as a bolt from the blue.

'But what has he done to you?' Rhys asked.

Simon didn't know how to reply, but stood staring at Rhys' ingenuous face, his eyes wide and questioning.

'Oh, all sorts of things. Especially taking Jackson from me.'

So that was it. Rhys knew that Simon had got close to Jackson, but hadn't an inkling how close. He decided to chance his arm.

'But he wasn't yours to have, was he?'

'What do you mean?'

Rhys continued. 'He was a member of this house, and a man in his own right. He wasn't owned by anyone. I'm sure he was enjoying a flirtation with you, but in such circumstances you can't expect people to be faithful. It's like asking a nymphomaniac at an orgy to only have sex with one man. It can't happen. It's not possible.'

Of all people to speak his mind so directly, it wasn't supposed to be Rhys. Simon stared at him, wide-eyed and open-mouthed. A part of what he said did ring true. Had he been blinded by lust? Was he acting like a stupid love-sick teenager? Of course Jackson wasn't his to have. But all the same, it hurt that he'd gone and spent time with Peter. But was that Peter's fault? Or Jackson's? Or nobody's? The only thing he was now certain of was his confusion.

'I need a hug,' was all Simon could say, his voice soft and slightly tremulous.

Opening his arms, and smiling broadly, Rhys obliged. He may have been the youngest member of the house, but he was learning fast, and his reconciliation skills seemed to be working brilliantly. In spite of his earlier bout of self-abuse, he was still feeling horny, and the warm strength that exuded from Simon's body began to affect him. Again he could feel the uncalled-for swelling down below, and in this most awkward of positions, too. He prayed that Simon wouldn't notice. But he did.

'I see.' Simon grinned, as something semi-hard butted at the top of his thigh. 'Someone's excited!'

'Sorry,' Rhys mumbled and pulled away, his face now the colour of a beetroot. He damned his reproductive system for letting him down badly at such a time.

'Nothing to apologise for. I was always getting a hard-on in the most embarrassing situations, especially at school.' Simon chuckled.

'Really?' Grateful of a change of subject, Rhys tried hard to make his erection subside, mentally picturing his mother in an attempt to help it along.

'Yeah, really. I even got a stiffy during a science lesson. Luckily the work benches were very tall and there was no one on my bench, and so I pulled it out and whacked off into a hanky. No one knew. Except perhaps the teacher. He looked at me strangely, and seemed to have a twisted smile on his face. I'm sure he was gay too! So you see, there's nothing to be ashamed of.'

Simon pulled Rhys close again, and with one finger idly flicked a nipple that was made visible by the thin shoulder strap of his athletic vest.

This was not supposed to happen. Half of Rhys wanted to pull away, but the other half dared him to stand his ground, to see what would take place next. The finger became two, pinching the nipple, holding it firm between thumb and forefinger, pulling at it slightly, easing the fleshy lump, rolling it around and toying with it. It had to happen. He couldn't help himself. The blood began to flow, and in a second he was getting hard again.

Rhys wanted to speak, to say that he didn't think what they were doing was wise, but his throat stayed dry. The words that rose in him would have to stay unspoken. He had objections, but his lust won the day. His libido screamed out that it wanted satisfying, right here, right now, and wouldn't be content with just the rather rapid jerking off and climax of earlier. Shutting his eyes and praying that Simon would stop and go away, Rhys fell back against the side wall of the house, his trainers scrabbling against the gravel that filled the gap between lawn and brick wall. The brickwork felt rough and harsh against the smooth skin of his back, and scratched the synthetic material of his vest. He kept his eyes closed, even when he felt a hand start to work its way down his chest, heading south with a purpose. In an inkling the hand had reached the object it desired, and began to rub Rhys' cock through the satin shorts. There was nothing else to do but surrender to the passion, and so he did. He opened his eyes and stared at Simon, whose deep brown eyes gazed back, narrowing as his hand continued to rub the bulge in Rhys' shorts.

The Welsh lad looked down and watched what his housemate was doing, fascinated by the slow undulating rhythm of his hand, and the constant squeezing and relaxing. It felt so incredibly good that he did not want it to stop.

Simon knew he had succeeded the moment that Rhys closed his eyes. He now knew that this young man wanted sex. So did Simon. He was a highly sexed individual and wasn't one to turn his back on such a golden opportunity. He had the lad in the palm of his hand. The pinching of the nipple seemed to have worked its magic and so he felt his way down to the crotch and struck treasure. The cock snuggled in the slippery satin had reacted to the touch and begun to swell, and quite nicely too. This boy was a real find. He wondered if he was a virgin, if anyone had parted his gorgeous arse cheeks and plundered his tight hole. He wanted to do just that, but not here. Later. Simon's hands manipulated the growing cock until he could feel its swollen length, bursting for some action and desperate for release. He reached a finger up the leg of the shorts and hooked it round the cock and balls, pulling Rhys' cock out so that it stood straight up, proud and hard from under the elastic. Simon stared at it with desire, and knew he had achieved his goal. He inclined his head and leaned in towards Rhys' chest, his tongue making wet contact with a nipple, tickling the tip, and then licking around the darker outer ring. He put his mouth to the lump and sucked it into his mouth, teeth nipping at it, listening with pleasure at the gasps of pure amazement that burst out from Rhys' lips. He spent equal time on one nipple and then the other, sucking and licking, teasing and nuzzling, while a hand kept the other one busy.

Then, without a moment's pause, and ignoring the movement of the camera placed on the wall above their heads, he knelt and in one swift, determined motion took the cock in his mouth in one gulp. He heard a cry of pleasure escape the lad's lips, as he sucked deep and long, then drew back and made circles all around the trembling head, wetting the velvet skin; making the lad's legs go weak.

Rhys grabbed Simon's head and began to pump his mouth. For him, this was astonishing. This was the very first time he had been given such an expert blow job and he could not believe what the guy was doing to him. It was as if an electric tingling was surging up and down the length of his dick, and coming to a stop at the head, the tender part, where the sensations were at their most extreme. Part of him wanted the blowing to stop, as the feeling was too much to bear, but then again it also felt wonderful. And he needed it to continue.

As he sucked, Simon ran his hands up and down Rhys' thighs, caressing them, then reaching up to stroke and pinch the nipples once more, this provoking another yell of ecstatic pain from the lad. This was what Rhys wanted. He wanted to be sucked hard and deep, to be used and loved like this. Simon knew that he was giving the best blow he had ever given to a guy in his life. Something about the young, firm flesh and the saintly virgin-like quality of the lad made it doubly exciting. Pulling away from Rhys' cock, he dropped down to the balls, which hung heavy and waiting, drawing them into his mouth, thinking for a second that they seemed oddly disproportionate to the size of the cock. Still, some guys did have nice but average cocks and big bollocks and Rhys was one of those. Simon opened his mouth wide to take them in, which he was pleased he could do, rolling them around, wetting and sucking on them, then setting up a small hum which resonated through the orbs, causing Rhys to gasp uncontrollably. With his lips clamped tightly about the two balls, Simon pulled them away from Rhys' body, stretching the skin sac, until it would go no further and then, with a twinkle in his eye he let them plop free, first one and then the other, hearing the wince of pained pleasure as each one was freed. He slid his tongue over and over Rhys' cock, from the swollen and tender glans to the rigid base, surrounded by tufts of wispy brown pubes. With a free hand, he grabbed that shaft and slowly began to wank it, keeping the majority still inside his mouth.

Unable to believe the exquisite phenomenon happening to his cock and balls, Rhys pushed forward, thrusting his hips out, pumping himself into Simon's mouth. Christ. This guy knew how to give a blow job. Rhys knew for the first time in his life what he had been missing. If this is what gay life could offer, then he wanted more. Right now he wanted to come. The vacuum of Simon's mouth seemed to be coaxing the seed out of him and he knew that soon he couldn't hold back any longer. He felt Simon's lips tighten around the head and Simon's fist start wanking with speed, and soon the eruption came, suddenly and without a sound.

Rhys poured out hot semen, which Simon swallowed thirstily, as Rhys' cock strained against the roof of his mouth, bolt after bolt hitting the back of his throat. After a few more thrusts, Rhys felt that there was nothing left inside his balls, and so he pulled away, staring down wide-eyed at the guy who had just given such extreme delight.

'Wow!' His cock was still hard, and a small drop of the pearly white juice ran down from the slit, dribbling down between the saliva-soaked lobes. Simon leaned forward and let the tip of his tongue flick at the drop, then a broad smile brightened his face.

'That was great.' He knelt back on his haunches and looked up at the lad, the cock still hard and standing straight up to attention. 'I really enjoyed that.'

Feeling the intrusive eye of the camera on him, Rhys stuffed his cock back inside his shorts and straightened up. 'So did I. Thank you.'

'No need to thank me. I thought you probably needed a little light relaxation. I'd love to have another go sometime...if that's all right with you?'

Rhys pondered for a minute. Simon was certainly an attractive man and the blow he had just received from him was amazing, but did he want to get into anything deep with him? Simon had seemed to work his way through the guys in the house quite rapidly, but did Rhys want to be just another notch on his bedstead? Something about Simon had the air of a friend rather than a lover.

'Perhaps,' said Rhys. Memories of the set-to caused by the longing for Jackson filled his mind and he shook his head to clear them away.

'No problem. I like you a lot and think we could have some fun together. You know...something to relieve the boredom in here.'

Rhys gave Simon a gentle peck on the cheek and scampered into the house and headed upstairs to the shower.

Saturday

The following few days had also been tense. Peter had ignored Simon with a vengeance and William had walked around Skye as if he didn't exist. Rhys watched all this with a mixture of amusement and concern. He hoped that, once this week's challenge had been completed and the next voting session had happened, that things might settle down and people might start to talk to each other again. In his mind he turned over the various permutations of who it would be best to lose to on Sunday, but he came to no definite conclusions. Assuming that he would be able to remain, he knew that one of the warring couples would still be in the house together.

The task had been all but finished by Skye, who had grasped the opportunity to indulge in some real athletic exertion, and had run endless miles on the machine and lifted a huge amount on the weights. Skye had even surprised Rhys with his ability on the parallel bars. William had decided against taking part. He knew he wasn't a sporty type and so shrugged the challenge off, spending most of his time in his room, or curled up in the living room with a book. Rhys, on the other hand, had enjoyed the challenge, and had done well, finding the parallel bars a doddle and the running machine quite good therapeutic exercise. He had spent quite a lot of time on that electric treadmill, thinking and pondering his life and the direction he would be going in after the show's finish. He hadn't dared think about what he could do with the prize money, not being one to jump to conclusions. Simon had also made a good effort, and done well, although Peter had lost a little enthusiasm for the task after lifting some weights awkwardly and straining his back muscles. Consequently he spent a few days either lying in bed or stretched out on the pool table reading.

In the late afternoon, when the task had been finished by all to the best of their ability or as much as they were willing to do, Matt's voice boomed out through the hidden speaker system. 'Hello, Boycam house. This is Matt speaking. We have been watching your efforts at this week's challenge with much interest. There are only two housemates that we consider to have spent the required amount of effort at the task. The others fell short of expectations. Consequently points will be awarded or deducted accordingly. Because we are disappointed in the group's achievement this week, we have decided to cancel the toga party, and to stop any delivery of alcohol, cigarettes and any other luxury items as have been asked for. This next week will, of necessity, be a frugal one. Your next task will be announced on Monday, when obviously you will be down to the last four contestants. Goodbye.' Curtly, Matt signed off and the speaker went silent once more.

The five housemates sat rather stunned at the announcement they'd just heard. So far life in the Boycam house had been quite cushy and not in any way harsh. They had been given every kind of food or drink they wanted, and as much alcohol and cigarettes as they desired. But to have all that taken away, and for a whole week, seemed really unfair.

Skye was the first to break the silence, pointing an accusatory finger at William. 'Well, thanks a lot, you fuckwit. Because of you we've got a rotten week ahead.' The anger in his voice was apparent to all.

Indignant, William stared back, his nostrils flaring. 'Up yours. There were three people blamed for this, and I didn't hear Matt name any names, did you? Just because you think you are bloody perfect, there's no reason to take it out on me.'

'Yes, there is,' said Skye, his face darkening. 'If you had made some effort, then we'd not be in this mess.'

'Guys, guys,' said Peter in a more conciliatory tone. 'There's no good arguing over this. Besides, I was just as bad, and so blame me as well. The best thing to do is accept what's happened and get on with it.'

Skye was in no mood to be calm. 'Get on with it?' His voice had turned shrill and threatening. 'How are we supposed to do that? Ration everything?'

'Exactly. Those who smoke had better count how many ciggies they have left and we should take stock of the booze, as well.' Peter sat cool and unfazed by Skye's outburst.

'This whole place is a joke and so are all of you. If you can't take part in a simple exercise programme for a week, then God help you all.' He rose and stalked unceremoniously from the room.

'Someone's not happy.' Simon waited for a moment before chipping in.

'I'm not surprised, though. He put in a lot of effort,' said Rhys quietly. He could see Skye's point of view. 'I wonder who the failures were?' He looked around at the other three inquisitively.

'Me, obviously,' chimed in Peter, whose back was feeling a lot better.

'And me.' Simon shrugged with an air of one who didn't really care. 'I was hopeless. I thought I was quite fit, but this task proved me wrong. I could hardly lift those weights...what a pansy.'

William spoke again, his voice slightly softer than usual. 'Yes, well at least you all tried. Me, I just gave up the moment I saw it was something physical.'

Rhys was curious. 'So why did you give up?' He watched William, who sat quite calmly but subdued, twiddling his thumbs rhythmically.

'Oh God...well, if you must know the truth...I was always a sickly child, not very strong, and showed no aptitude for anything sporty. I was always more interested in numbers and words than playing football or tennis or cross-country runs. When I left university, I did make a bit of an effort and forced myself to go to a gym and start to build myself up. I think I did a good job...even if I do say so myself. I got some quite good definition and increased my strength a bit.' He watched the others' heads nodding appreciatively, encouraging him to continue with his tale.

'Even so, deep down inside me there is this demon which says that I am still that small, sickly child...and the thought of having to do something so athletic chilled me. I have this fear of being shown as a failure, especially in such extreme circumstances, and especially under scrutiny as we are.' He motioned with his eyes to the corner of the room, indicating the ever-watchful presence of the cameras.

Nobody else spoke. Rhys broke the silence and sank down on the sofa next to William, slipping an arm around his shoulders. 'Well, that's just stupid really, isn't it? No one here would think you a failure because you couldn't do it.'

'Really?' William's eyes had filled and were brimming over with salty tears. This was one of the first times he had ever spoken of his private fears and wasn't sure what the reaction was going to be.

Peter and Simon, momentarily forgetting their differences, came and squatted by the sofa, each taking hold of one of William's hands.

'You are a fool sometimes. Haven't you realised by now that no-body would care a jot?' Peter's tone of voice was warm and soothing.

'I don't know,' William mumbled.

'Well, it's true. So how about a group hug?'

Looking around the room, William gave a motion with his head. 'But we're not all here.'

'Doesn't matter.' Peter stood and waited for the others to join him. They hugged, all arguments forgotten for the moment.

Sunday

'It's that day again.'

'I know.'

'So who are you voting for?'

'I can't tell you that.'

'Have you thought about what I said before?'

'Yes.'

'And...'

'I don't know. It all seems so dishonest, somehow.'

'Listen to me. This is a gameshow. We are all here to win, not to just take part and become better human beings...that's bullshit. Wouldn't the money come in useful?'

'Yes, but –'

'Then do as I suggest, and vote for who I tell you.'

'I don't know...'

'If we get rid of him, then we are both in with a chance of winning. And as I said before, we could share the prize money. Just think of it...'

'I am...that's the trouble.'

Skye had come down to breakfast wide awake, bouncy and in a completely positive frame of mind. He smiled at the others as he bounded into the kitchen, even giving William a hug and apologising for his behaviour.

'Sorry about that. It was my time of the month. I get ratty every now and then. Forgive me?'

William had little option but to do so. 'Sure, life is too short to bear grudges. Especially with someone as beautiful as you.'

Skye grinned boyishly. 'Thank you. For that you get a kiss, and the promise of more later.'

'I hope you keep your promises.' William pointed to his puckered lips and waited for Skye to do as he'd said.

'The exercise equipment has gone.' Everyone turned to Simon. 'It must have been taken in the night.'

'Oh, well. That's life.' William gave a sardonic grin. 'I'm sure we can live without it.'

'Lazy bastard.' Chuckling, Skye ruffled William's hair in a manner that was almost provocative. He crossed to the fridge and helped himself to orange juice.

The voting came and went with an automatic air, carried out by the housemates with seasoned precision. They had all voted for the one person that they thought would upset the equilibrium of the house. And by the time eight o'clock arrived they were all tense and full of nervous apprehension, awaiting the moment when a name would be called out.

'Well, it's been nice knowing you all,' said William, trying hopelessly to lighten the mood that had settled on the housemates as they sat in the living room.

'Yeah. It's been fun while it lasted.' Skye also joined in with the jollity, aware that any one of them could be the next evictee. 'I don't know how you'll all cope without me.'

'Or me,' said Simon.

'Or me,' Rhys joined in, the beginnings of a smile on his lips.

'No, it's bound to be me this time.' Peter sounded matter of fact, his posture giving the lie to his words. He sat bolt upright, chewing a rogue fingernail.

'Let's face it…it could be any one of us. But whatever happens, let's be adult and just accept our fate, eh?' The reasonable tone of Skye's voice seemed to have a strange calming influence. Just as Rhys was about to reply, the speaker crackled into life.

'Hello, Boycam house. This is Matt speaking. I have the result of the fourth vote here in front of me. This week the voting was very interesting, and we have a clear winner for eviction this week. That person will have an hour to pack and be ready to leave. A car will be waiting for you outside the gate to take you home. Now if you are all ready…the fourth person to leave the Boycam house is…Peter Laurence.'

Interview with Peter Laurence

'I was in two minds about being evicted. I was certainly sorry to miss out on the chance of the money, but I was glad to see the back of a particular person. Life had become very uncomfortable in there and it wasn't my fault. I believe that Jackson was the one who caused the trouble. He set out to win Simon, and became involved with him. Then when he'd grown tired of that guy, he went after me. Now, I'm a fairly easy-going sort of guy and when this nice bloke expressed his interest in me I went for it, wouldn't you? It was just unfortunate that Simon had this unpleasant jealous streak, and the whole thing became nasty.

'I shall miss some of the other guys. I liked Rhys a lot; he was a down-to-earth, natural guy, and I hope he wins. I reckon he was the only one without any pretensions of any sort. And I quite liked Jost in a funny kind of way. He was the weirdest of the housemates, and when he'd gone, it all got a little predictable. I think such a situation needs extreme characters.

'I was worried about the cameras everywhere to begin with; my biggest worry was having to go to the toilet with a camera watching me, and so the first few times I took a blanket with me and covered myself up. Then, after a while, it just didn't seem to matter, so I just got on with it. Silly, really.

'I shall miss the house and the guys, even Simon after our little set-to. I have even forgiven him for hitting me. My nose was a bit sore for a few days, but then you can't hold grudges, can you? I hope we all meet up again, because I think that friendships forged in such extreme circumstances will last for a long time.'

Week Five

Monday

'So I see that you voted as I suggested...very wise, if I may say so.'

'I did not.'

'So how come Peter was evicted last night?'

'I voted as my conscience told me. I thought that with Peter gone the house might settle down a bit; it's been too disrupted lately and I just want everything to be calmer and friendlier.'

'Fair enough, although if you'll take my advice...'

'Look, I don't want any more suggestions from you. I'm fed up with the way you're trying to sway the voting...it's wrong.'

'You didn't seem to mind my suggestions before...'

'Yes, well...I've had time to think about it since then and I don't want you to talk to me about this again. OK?'

'Sure. Just remember...if we are the last two remaining people...we split the money.'

'I don't remember agreeing to that.'

'I think you did...'

'Yeah, well...perhaps.'

Three of the remaining housemates – William, Simon and Rhys – sat quietly in the kitchen eating their various breakfasts. Skye was in the garden making the most of the early morning sunshine and doing his daily exercises. No one had really said much after last night's eviction. Peter had taken the news with good grace and duly packed his stuff, and had been whisked away by the waiting car at the appointed hour. There had been hugs all round for everyone, including Simon, who had been so overwhelmed with relief that he wasn't the one going that he gave Peter a big kiss, and said that he hoped they would still be friends. The house had seemed a better place now that Peter had gone, and Simon had put all thoughts of leaving from his mind. Skye stayed very much in the background, happy to be in the last four, but not one for enthusiastic, if false, goodbyes.

The blond porn star wandered into the kitchen with the almost-familiar sheet of paper clutched in his bronzed hand. The weeks spent soaking up the sun had immeasurably improved the colour of his skin, and he looked as if he should be shooting breakers on some Australian beach, not stuck in a house with three other gay men.

'This is getting quite tiresome.' He waved the sheet of paper at the other guys with a bored look on his tanned features. 'All I want to do is get through the next few weeks with as little hassle as possible.'

'So what does it say?' Simon looked up from his corn flakes.

Clearing his throat, Skye began to read. 'This week's challenge should prove less exacting for those of you who aren't of a physical bent.' He raised his eyebrow, aware of the probably unintentional double entendre.

'Yes...carry on.' William seemed somewhat impatient.

The look of amused contempt that flickered across Skye's face vanished. 'This week we want you all to write an erotic story, which can be as long as you like. It should be something that will turn you on, as well as those that you read it to. It can be as explicit as you like, or can just be plain romantic. But whatever you write should be completed by Saturday evening, when the stories will be read out to each other during the toga party which will be re-arranged for then. We will be providing four laptop computers for you to work on, which will of course be returned to us on Sunday morning. The story can be about fictional characters, or real people; it can be set in any time or place; let your imaginations run riot. Have fun.'

Skye threw the sheet of paper dismissively down on the breakfast bar and snorted with derision. 'Well...what a load of bullshit.'

William smirked slightly, suddenly aware that here was a challenge within his grasp, something artistic and creative that he had a chance to excel at. This would show the smug athletes among them. He had always enjoyed the power of words and the joy of writing, even though his first allegiance was to numbers. He had been raised to appreciate Dickens and Hardy, Wordsworth and Keats, as well as more lightweight authors like Agatha Christie and E.F. Benson, Roger McGough and Armistead Maupin. A smile was growing inside him and without hesitation it broke out over his face.

'This sounds like fun...much better than last week's mindless task. Now here is a chance to exercise our "little grey cells", as Hercule Poirot would say, and put our minds to work. Much better for you than running on the spot. This'll weed the men from the boys, and let us see who has a brain and the ability to use it.' He bolted down the last of his coffee and crossed to the sink, rinsing out his mug swiftly. Turning back to the group, he smiled again. 'I think I'll go and have a quick muse about my story, but be careful, my dear chaps! I intend to be the best in the house.' If William had been wearing a cape, he would have swirled it as he exited the kitchen.

The housemates looked at each other, bemused for a moment, before Rhys broke the silence. 'Are you guys any good at writing?'

Skye spat out a bit of fingernail that he had been industriously chewing on. 'No. I'm not what you'd call a literary bloke. I failed most of my exams, including English. You don't get much call for writing skills if you go into the porn industry. All you need is a big cock. No one ever got anywhere with a big throbbing pen, did they?'

'I guess not.' Simon sat unmoving, his chin resting on his cupped hands. 'Still, it could be interesting, I guess.'

The sound of Rhys scraping back his stool made the other two look up. 'Well, I'm not that good at writing either, but I'm going to have a go. I don't want people to say I'm some kind of thicko who can't string a sentence together. I'm going to have a sit in the garden and make some notes.'

As he left, Simon gave Skye a wry glance. 'Well…we'd better get on with it, I suppose.'

Wednesday

The laptop computers duly arrived on Tuesday morning, and William and Rhys got writing almost immediately. Skye and Simon took theirs to their rooms, along with the pads of notepaper and thought for a while before starting work. The task did not fill them with enthusiasm, rather the opposite. Simon, although a clever young man with plenty of academic qualifications, found that the hardest thing for him was finding a subject for his story. He toyed with a story involving cavemen, then drifted towards a tale of smugglers, before finally settling on a memory that sparked some small amount of interest and could conceivably be considered erotic for his audience.

Skye had no idea at all what to write. He sat for what seemed hours in front of the blank computer screen, unable to even come up with the first sentence. He found his lack of imagination rather disturbing, and wondered if he was actually capable of finishing the task. At dinner on Tuesday evening, William and Rhys had been huddled together conspiratorially, giggling and chatting, excluding the other two from their conversation. Simon and Skye retaliated by pairing off and sitting in the cool air of the evening, laughing loudly and hysterically to imaginary jokes, trying vainly to annoy the two supposed authors indoors.

By Wednesday afternoon, though, all four of the housemates were at work at their laptops, some with more enthusiasm than others. Rhys had discovered that he quite enjoyed the process of sitting at a computer and letting the words pour out of his fingers, creating a vivid scenario with his fingers and his imagination. Simon also had found the action of typing quite relaxing. Somehow he could close his mind to every other distraction and noise and just picture the scene in his mind, and then translate that into valid sentences and paragraphs. The images he was seeing in his mind's eye were hot, and the pictures soon found themselves moving from his mind to his crotch. The erotic tale was actually turning him on.

The sound of the loudspeaker system crackling into life made the guys jump, with its unexpected clamour. Matt's voice echoed about the house. 'Hello, Boycam house. This is Matt speaking. I have an announcement to make to you all, so could you assemble in the living room, please.' The voice vanished and with furrowed brows and shrugging shoulders the four remaining contestants made their way downstairs.

'Hello again.' Matt's voice had a slightly annoyed edge to it, discernible through the speaker. 'I am afraid something has come up. There has been a technical hitch with the cabling that links the house cameras with the production gallery. The signals that are being sent to us are breaking up, and so we have to stop the transmission now for a day or so to effect the necessary repairs. This will mean that the cameras won't be working, and you will all be free from scrutiny for an unknown period of time. When everything is up and running again, we will let you know. All I can say is enjoy the time you get off, and I will be in touch when I have more news. Of course, it goes without saying that we shall expect this week's challenge to be completed on time.' The speaker went silent and the four guys stared at each other in amazement.

They were so dumbstruck, so silent with incomprehension of their situation that the muffled sound of the twittering birds outside permeated the closed windows.

'Wow,' said Simon eventually. 'No one is watching us.'

Leaning his head back against the plush sofa, William said, 'I have forgotten what it's like not to be watched all the time. I feel sort of naked.'

'This is so weird,' chimed in Rhys, clutching his knees tightly. 'I feel like we should do something while we are free.'

'Like what?' Everyone looked at Skye who had one eyebrow raised, Roger Moore style, the intention written clear across his face.

'Not that.' It was Rhys who had spoken. He had read Skye's mind at almost the same moment the thought had set up shop there.

'And why not? Just think of the fun we could have, without old nosey watching our every move.' Pausing and lowering his voice a little, Skye leaned towards the others who watched him, intrigued by his actions. 'Have any of you ever had an orgy?'

William burst out laughing. 'So are you suggesting that because we are "off the leash" as it were, we should immediately dive into some group sex session?'

Nodding, Skye sat back grinning, one hand lightly sitting on his crotch, happily watching everyone else's gaze follow his hand to its resting place, knowing that they wouldn't take too much persuading. It had been a while now since he had got any sex. He had taken to having a wank once or twice a day to relieve the sexual tension that was building up within him, but the prospect of a good old-fashioned foursome filled him with delight. He was even prepared to let William have use of his body, seeing as he was so keen to do so. Besides, William had quite a packet himself. He had noticed the nicely filled shorts last week and stored the mental image for further use. And since his rushed dalliance with Rhys in that first week, he had longed for a chance to get to grips with that lithe young body again. Here was his chance.

'Yeah...why not? Now don't tell me that none of you are thinking about it...because I won't believe you,' said Skye. 'I think we all know each other well enough now... and I think that some of us are bursting at the seams for some hot sex... and believe me, there is the possibility of some very hot sex in this house right now. What do you say?'

Again the room fell silent as the other three weighed up the pros and cons of the situation. Rhys knew that he badly wanted to have sex with Skye again. He had even found his dreams being invaded with images of Skye, naked and willing, his cock towering, and his eyes smiling, until Rhys woke dry mouthed and with an erection as stiff as a pole. He had also toyed with the idea of getting to know William in that way too. He had grown to like the man very much, pleased that his initial acerbic personality had softened, and had noted with delight that he possessed a body that he would be proud to get his hands on. Simon also had an aura about him. He had been tempted to ask Peter what sex with Simon was like but had never plucked up the nerve. Now he might have the chance to experience that piercing for himself.

Doubts flooded Simon's mind. He would be the first to admit that the prospect of hot sex excited him greatly. Since his flings with Jackson and Peter, he had found that he needed sex more and more, secretly wondering if he could officially call himself a sex maniac. He had wanted to have sex with Rhys badly at times, seeing the cute lad wandering around in his underwear, or sunbathing in his tight trunks, and noticing that he had something nice snuggled inside them. Even William had assumed the mantle of a possible partner. He had stopped being a wanker and had become a lot more down-to-earth; he had even impressed Simon with his manly appearance in his Olympic outfit. Perhaps he would be an interesting guy to know.

The thought of a four-way sex session with the other three reverberated around William's mind, his libido reacting in the only way it knew how, by sending a surge of excited blood to his cock. He squirmed about in his chair to hide his embarrassment. He was desperate for some real sex. Since that shower incident with Skye, his waking hours had been full of carnal desires. As he hadn't taken part in the athletics task and just lounged around watching the others' efforts, he had a huge reserve of sexual energy that needed working out. Rhys, Simon and Skye were attractive young men, each in their own way. The brash, knowledgeable sexuality of Skye was immensely appealing, as was the self-assured brightness of Simon, not to mention the wonderful adornment he wore down there. While the naïve charm that exuded from every inch of Rhys was also a strong lure – the youngster had the bloom of inexperience and a body to die for. William knew that he would greatly relish the opportunity to teach Rhys a thing or two, or even more. He wanted to say yes to Skye's proposal, but wondered what the others would think.

'I don't know...' Rhys was sounding tentative.

'Me too...' Simon was also expressing doubts. 'Besides, an orgy can't just happen; it needs the right atmosphere. How about we just think about it and see what happens tonight?'

Skye nodded. Simon was right. If they were to have a great time it should evolve naturally, not be something forced and false. This evening after their supper and remaining bottles of wine perhaps something wonderful might happen.

And something did happen. Although the housemates would have balked at using the word wonderful to describe it. As William finished wiping his lips at the end of dinner, he threw his napkin down on the table and surveyed the other three housemates with interest. The last of the wine had flowed quite considerably and all of them had drunk a substantial amount. Although no one vocalised the fact, there were a lot of nerves floating about the room, as if they were on the brink of a new challenge and they didn't know how to make the first step towards starting it. Simon and Rhys were strangely quiet over dinner, their conversation kept to a minimum and only contributing the odd nonchalant comment. Skye was acting as if nothing was wrong, as confident as ever, whilst William somehow seemed over-enthusiastic, his bubbling stream of chatter pouring out without pause. The guys knew that tonight was an important milestone in their relationships. If all went as expected, then they would soon be entangled in each other's arms and would be enjoying the delights of a four-man orgy. But things were never that simple.

'So.' The word that came from Skye's mouth hung in the air. No one knew what to say to it.

'How about we adjourn to the living room?' Again Skye made the first move, tightly gripping his wine glass and standing a little unsteadily, scraping his chair back, and moving into the other room. He didn't look back; he knew that the others would follow...they had no choice. And he was right.

Crossing to the fireplace, he picked up a box of matches and started to light some candles that he had put there earlier, then, as the other three appeared in the doorway and entered, sinking down on the sofa together, he padded across the room and turned the lights off. The room was now filled with the eerie flickering glow of the candles, one of which was scented, giving off a fragrant aroma of freesias.

Skye lifted his glass and toasted the others. 'Cheers.'

Rhys, Simon and William all threw down the last of their wine and looked at each other uncertainly.

'I know what we need.' Skye tottered to the stereo that stood on a table at the far corner of the living room and switched it on, fiddling with the radio control until he found a suitable station, and slushy music emerged. He then took his position in front of the fireplace again and waited. The other three sat, dumbfounded and unsure of how to proceed. Even though they were free from the intrusion of the cameras, and could do absolutely anything they wanted, they were unable to decide what to do next. Skye made the decision for them. As the music came to an end, and the next track started, he began to slowly undulate to it, moving in time to the song, feeling the other's eyes on him. He hadn't performed for anyone in a while and it felt good to do so. The extrovert showman tendency in him reared its head and took over. With a slow, teasing motion he pulled his T-shirt over his head, revealing his superb chest, which was covered in small beads of glistening sweat. He ran his hands down from his neck, lingering around the nipples, and then feeling his way over the ridges of stomach muscle. He knew he had his audience hooked. In the many times he had danced in the seedy sex clubs of his recent past, he had discovered that he could manipulate an audience, and have them on the edge of their seats with their tongues hanging out and their cocks rigid with desire. He smiled inwardly at the memories of grubby hands stuffing bank notes into his G-string. His talents weren't going to fail him now.

Rhys watched, open-mouthed. The nervous tension and the alcohol had mixed badly and his head was swimming. A churning had started in the pit of his stomach and he wondered if he was about to throw up. He found it hard to decide which of the two Skyes dancing in front of his blurred vision was the real one. He was of two minds. Part of him wanted to fall on the gorgeous gyrating blond and ravish him, while the other half desperately wanted to curl up in a ball and fall asleep.

Simon and William sat bolt upright, the importance of the event happening in front of them not lost on either. Here was a handsome and hung stud making himself available, and if they wanted to, they could have him. They could be soon having group sex. But there was a barrier. In their minds they felt that it was wrong. A small voice spoke to each saying that the time wasn't right, and it felt forced. They should wait for the right moment, and it would make itself known in time.

Feeling that he had lost his audience, Skye went into overdrive. Turning his back on the others, he unbuckled his belt and let his jeans fall to the floor, bending over, showing his muscular arse, encased in the tight white cotton of his briefs. This usually got the guys going. Stepping out of his jeans and spinning around, he smiled as the eyes of his housemates had all dropped and were fixed on the growing bulge in his briefs. A hand dropped to it and gave it a squeeze, coaxing it into its maximum hardness. If this didn't do it for them, then nothing would. With a finger each side of the waistband, he swiftly hooked them down, letting his cock spring free, rigid and to attention. All eyes were now wide open and staring at the monster. A drop of spittle had accumulated at the side of Rhys' mouth, and he licked his lips lasciviously. Skye was convinced that the young Welsh lad wanted his cock, and with gentle swaying movements he inched closer to the sofa and closer to Rhys' watery gaze.

Skye's cock was fully erect, and it felt fantastic. The pumping surge made it swell and throb, and it needed a hot wet mouth to engulf it and complete the equation. Cock plus mouth equals ecstasy. He grinned down at the lad, and waved his solid prick invitingly.

Rhys stared at the mammoth member, his eyes closing drowsily, but then snapping open again, the effort of his will power. He let his mouth fall open and his tongue run around the full lips. Then with a muffled cry of 'Sorry,' he leapt from the sofa and charged upstairs, holding his hand to his mouth. As he banged into the bathroom, the other three could hear the initial sounds of him being violently sick before he slammed the bathroom door closed behind him.

This wasn't good. Sickness was one of those things that Skye had difficulty dealing with. He had tended to always be in a healthy and fit state and so he had no patience with those who succumbed to viruses and bugs which left them snivelling, groaning heaps. He believed that most illnesses were symptomatic of some form of hypochondriac attention seeking. The sounds and smells of other people being ill was something hateful and he blocked his eyes and mind to the noises and images of what Rhys was doing.

It was as if a spell had been broken. Casting his eyes from the sight of Skye's rapidly deflating dick, Simon hoisted himself to his feet and made his way unsteadily to the door. 'I'd better see if he's all right.'

Left behind on his own with a naked stud for company, William didn't know what to say or do next. He had also had a lot to drink, and was feeling slightly queasy himself. There were times when he would have gladly taken this chance to leap upon Skye's luscious form and not stop enjoying it until the sun came up, but this wasn't one of them. His voice was slurred as he tried to ease himself up, his arms giving way and falling back into the comfortable grasp of the sofa's cushions. 'I don't think it's going to happen, old boy.' He pointed with a finger at what was now hanging limply between Skye's legs. 'I'd put it away if I were you. Save it for a rainy day.'

Hands on hips, and with a defeated sigh, Skye nodded. 'Pity. I was in the mood as well.'

'So was I...earlier on. Still thanks for the show...very nice...very nice indeed. Now help me up, will you?' Taking a grip under William's arm, Skye heaved his housemate to his feet, and helped him up the stairs and onto his bed, where William fell immediately into a deep, untroubled sleep.

Thursday

All four of the remaining housemates slept late. Even the persistent clanging of Simon's alarm clock failed to make any dent in their slumbers. It was past noon when they were all assembled in the kitchen having a late breakfast and looking the worse for wear.

'Why do I do it?' Everyone turned to look at William, whose outburst had taken them by surprise. 'Why do I drink too much?' He dropped an indigestion tablet into a glass of water and morosely watched it fizzing. The sound of the bubbling, effervescent water reminded William of younger days, when as a student he and his university mates would stay out late, indulging in drinking competitions, seeing who could down the most alcohol whilst playing the most ridiculous games. He recalled one called 'Rabbits', where a lot of pointing and shouting was involved, the actual rules of the game eluding him at present. He would wake each morning with a lecture to attend and a pounding headache, and fall back on the universal breakfast of a large black coffee, several aspirins and a cigarette. He hadn't woken with such an appalling hangover for a good few years, and this time he silently swore to himself that this would be the last time such an event occurred.

He looked up at the other three, who all seemed in a bad way, hunched over their bowls or mugs, all with bloodshot eyes, all still in pyjamas or dressing gowns, all silently swearing that they'd never drink again...until the next time. Skye stood and stretched himself, his towelling robe falling open inadvertently, revealing a broad expanse of tanned chest and stomach. William noted this with an inward smirk, the recent memory of last night's floorshow superseding his older recollections. He let the image of Skye, undressed and with his cock hard and available, fill his aching head. God, why didn't he take advantage of that stunner last night right there and then? He might never have such a chance again. And without being watched by Matt and his cameras.

With a yawn, Rhys stood and made for the door. 'I'm going to have a long soak in the bath, and without anyone watching me.' He disappeared and his footsteps could be heard sloping upstairs.

'Sounds like paradise,' said Simon. 'I think I might do the same after...unless anyone objects?'

'Not at all,' grinned Skye, his robe now fully open, giving the others a glimpse at what they had missed out on the evening before. 'I'm going for a doze in the garden.' He let his robe hang open, giving a full frontal show of what he had to offer, and moved off, his bare feet slapping against the cold linoleum. Picking up a blanket from the hall, he wandered into the garden and spread it out on the grass, then bundled up his robe into a makeshift pillow, and began to sunbathe, safe in the knowledge that his nude form would now only be seen by the other three inhabitants of the house.

William sat at the breakfast bar, musing to himself, the events of last night clear and fresh in his mind. Before he left the house – and he had no doubt that he would be the next to be evicted – he had to get to grips with Skye. It had become an obsession. The constant proximity of that glorious stud was just too much. He wanted him so badly that it hurt, and a dull ache had set up shop somewhere deep in his groin, probably from the frequent erections he achieved every time Skye came near. Maybe this morning might be the time to try. With no prying presence of those bastard cameras, he might feel a little less intimidated by the prospect. Swallowing hard, he opened his bathrobe and stepped out of his boxer shorts, balling them up and stuffing them into a pocket, hastily fastening the robe and jauntily heading for the garden. He knew that Rhys was in the bath and Simon was occupied up in his bedroom, so he had no fear of being watched. As he stepped outside, his heart almost skipped a beat as he saw the object of his quest. Skye was lying flat out on his back, eyes shut, soaking up the warming rays. His thighs were spread wide.

As if he knew he had audience, Skye let a hand fall gently on his genitals and he gave them a reassuring squeeze, lovingly fondling the bollocks and rearranging the cock from its recumbent position on one thigh to the other.

This was too much to take. William had to make his move. He let the robe fall open and sauntered across the lawn with mock casualness.

'Hi.' His voice was slightly wavering.

Skye shielded his eyes and looked up. 'Oh, hi.' He let his eyes surreptitiously wander down from William's face to the cock and balls that were being carelessly displayed. He again noted that they were rather nicely proportioned. But were they on display for his benefit? He sat up on his elbows and smiled. 'Where are the other two musketeers, then?'

As if he was completely unaware of his state of undress, William squatted down at Skye's side, keeping his gaze firmly on the stud's face.

'Well, as far as I know, Rhys is still in the bath, and Simon is next in the queue. Do you mind if I join you?'

'Not at all. Pull up a blanket.' Skye curled himself up and sat crosslegged, showing off everything he had.

Keeping his gaze firmly on Skye's face, William sat down in the same position, his robe spread around him like the train on a wedding dress. Then, as if he had made a momentous decision, William slid out of his robe and threw it to one side, so both men sat opposite, naked and enjoying the warmth of the day. 'There...it's much nicer like this, isn't it?'

'It sure is.' There was a touch of sarcasm in Skye's tone which William chose to ignore.

'I am sorry about last night.'

'No bother. I was in the mood for a bit of hot cock action...but it obviously wasn't meant to be. I had a good wank after, though.' He paused before running his tongue across his lips. 'Actually, I was wanting a chance to talk to you.'

Furrowing his brow questioningly, William leaned forward. 'What about?'

'This story we have to write. I hope you could give me a few tips.'

'Like what?'

'Well, how do you do it? I'm not one for words. How do you write a story?' Skye flicked at an insect which was buzzing annoyingly around his head, his hand then falling to his chest and lingering around one of his nipples in an almost blasé manner.

Swallowing hard and concentrating on the question, William continued, 'It's quite easy actually. Just think of something horny. A scene which turns you on. It can be something that really happened to you, or you can let your imagination do all the work. Picture the scene in your mind and try to write what you see. Describe the picture as you see it, including sounds, smells, anything which will fill out the images you want to write about.'

Skye's hand had dropped and come to rest on his thigh, just inches away from the crotch.

William swallowed again. 'It's easy.'

'For you, maybe. So how would you do this scene?' Skye had one raised eyebrow, and a look of inquisitive innocence on his face. He had decided to make the most of the situation. Here was William who was obviously gagging for sex, and the other two were out of the picture. And there wasn't the ever-intrusive glare of the Boycam cameras. Now was the perfect opportunity.

'What do you mean?' William's voice was tremulous.

'How would you describe this scene...us here, now, if you were writing it for a story?' Skye knew that he had William's complete attention. He could see the cogs of the brain whirring away, and he knew that William wouldn't disappoint. Already the blood was rushing in his ears and something large was beginning to stir.

Taking a deep breath, William looked around and after a moment's pause began to speak. 'The beams of the sun beat down on the Boycam garden, warming its inhabitants. The sky was cloudless and an azure blue, as it had been from the very start of that day. The only sounds were the joyful cries of the birds at home in the tree, watching the only other two creatures in the garden. A blanket was spread upon the verdant lawn; its chequered smoothness felt good upon the thighs. Thighs of two young men who sat on it, both in the full flush of youth, both supreme examples of how a young man should be. They sat, naked, their bodies radiating in the exalted solar outpourings. Both could see what was special about the other. Their manhoods, prime and ready, lay in their laps, waiting for that surge of excitement that would see that flesh growing bigger, and fulfilling its purpose. Hmm...perhaps that's a bit verbose, but you see what I mean.'

He looked down and could see that Skye was living this prose, as his cock had started to expand, and he could feel his own doing the same. He continued to paint his literary picture.

'They knew that the moment of truth had come upon them, and that time would stand still for them, burning this precious moment into their memories forever. The silken skin of the younger man was inviting, like the calm surface of a lake waiting for someone to dive in and sample its tempting depths. He was a stunning example of man, his blond hair framing the handsome face and blue eyes. His strong neck and shoulders showed his prowess at athletic exertions and his chest and stomach were testament to the trainer's art. His legs were powerful, his thighs beautiful to behold. And above all, the wondrous meat that lay between his legs, growing harder and larger by the second, until soon it would stand proud and mighty, ready to be adored by the worshipper before him.'

This was so much more than Skye had expected. As William spoke, his voice soothing but dark, the words had an arousing effect. He had never been described in such a way and he liked it. The egotist in him was loving every uttered syllable. It seemed to act like an aphrodisiac, sending his life-blood gushing towards his groin, filling his cock. He was unable to stop his erection forming, and he wouldn't have done so even if he could have. And as if bidden, his cock stood up, thick and meaty.

William stared down at this vision of beauty, knowing in his mind that he didn't have a large enough vocabulary to describe its wonder. He wished he had. And he wished that he had such a creation. His eyes dropped to his own cock, which had also grown and swollen, rigidly standing out from his body. Not a giant like Skye's, but a good average solid example of manhood. Something he'd had no complaints about before. There seemed only one thing to do, and so he did it.

'William sat forward, his eyes glued to the huge pole that stood before his wide-eyed stare. He saw its sizeable girth and its monumental head, which seemed a deep purple colour in the bright sunlight. A small drop of translucent juice gleamed at the slit, a promise of what lay boiling in the ball sac below.'

He now moved as he spoke, his actions mirroring his words. 'William slid himself forward even more until he was just inches from the cock. With his head bent low, he knelt down and sniffed at the monster. And then with his tongue he flicked at the droplet, taking it into his mouth and enjoying the bittersweet taste. He luxuriated in the smooth, tanned skin, his eyes following the cock from its velvet-soft head, all the way down the solid, veinless shaft. The hair around the base of it was curly and brown, while the bollocks were themselves beauties, the left one slightly larger than the right, hanging pendu-lously in the skin bag, each capable of filling a man's mouth, both probably able to choke. The overpowering scent was of soap, mingled with the sensual aroma of male muskiness. William looked up, his eyes firmly fixed on the other. They stared at each other with inten-sity. William had to know what was going on in the other's mind. He had to know. He had to know if the other wanted him to suck his big cock. He had to know.'

His mouth was now level with the pulsing cock-head, and he des-perately wanted to swallow it whole. But something in him kept him back, as if he needed inviting. As if to take Skye in his mouth without being asked was to commit a social faux pas. He waited, his mouth growing steadily drier, his nerves jangling.

Skye looked down at William's face. It was wide and almost youth-ful, the eyes brimming with both doubt and lust at the same time. Then, as if a light-bulb had been switched on in his brain, he realised what kind of game William was playing. He knew he could play that game as well as this man. And so he smiled and began to speak.

'Skye looked at William, who was kneeling before him. He so wanted to have this man here and now. And he nodded to William to show that everything was all right. William let his tongue run around his lips, wetting them with his saliva, then he let his lips just brush the tip of Skye's cock, and in one slow exhalation of breath he took the cock in his mouth, sliding it down to the back of his throat...'

Skye found it hard to continue to talk, his whole body shivering with delight, as William swallowed the cock. Not many men had been blessed with the ability to take it down totally; they usually gagged as it hit the back, or found their mouths aching from the stretching of its engorged width. But William was a jewel, an accomplished cock-sucker who was giving great head. Skye's legs felt as though they would buckle under the pressure, and he wanted to cry out, shouting the ecstatic feelings to the sky. The story switched to present tense.

'Oh God, it feels great! William is eating my cock, taking it right down. His mouth is working up and down my cock, sort of rippling along it, clamping it in a kind of series of waves, right down until his nose is buried in my pubes, and then he slides back until he has just the head in his mouth. He is now running his tongue around the rim of the head, teasing and licking it, then...ah! Oh God, he is now blowing cool air on the head and I can't stand it! I want him to keep sucking it hard. Oh...now he is sucking me again. His hands are now on my arse, and they are squeezing it, rubbing it round and round, pulling my cheeks apart so that I can feel the gentle breeze blowing across my arsehole. Oh God, I'm shivering...no, don't stop...I am now looking down at William, whose eyes are closed; he is sucking my cock with such intensity. I can see that he has grabbed his own cock and is now stroking it; it looks hard and nice. I think I'd like to suck on it soon. I am now grabbing the back of his head and fucking his mouth, which keeps up the pressure, sucking and licking frantically; his lips and mouth are now full of saliva, and my cock slides in and out easily and smoothly; his lips cling to the outside of my cock, feeling every inch as it goes down. I think it's one of the best blow jobs I've ever had. I can hear the sounds of slurping, as well as the groans of pleasure that he is making...oh God...he has buried his nose in my pubes again and has taken it all down. He's like a vacuum pump, sucking and pulling at the same time. I can see his hand is wanking and I think he wants to come. So do I, but it is too soon...'

Skye stopped speaking and pulled himself away from William, gazing in awe at the mouth, ringed with spit and pre-come. The whole scenario was becoming too hot to handle. Free from the camera's piercing glare, these two men suddenly had no alternative than to go the whole way.

'I don't want to come yet...and I was nearly there.' Skye's voice held a trembling quality, unsure yet determined to make the most of this situation.'Lie down.'

It wasn't an order, but William found it difficult to resist. He obeyed and waited until Skye joined him on the blanket, head to toe in the sixty-nine position, ready to suck each other's dick.

Skye saw the head of William's cock; saw that it was a nice rounded shape. As their bodies met, he open his mouth and closed his lips about the head, the warmth of it suffused from the insistent sunshine. In a second he had let the cock slide down into his throat, hard and manly, and it felt wonderful. William did the same and the two men had no choice but to suck each other as best as they could. Skye's lips rubbed along the length of the shaft, feeling the persistent banging of the head against the back of his throat and, as if a switch had been flicked, he started pumping quickly and with vigour.

The massive rod of flesh that Skye proudly possessed pushed down into William's mouth; it filled him. William knew that he had never been privileged to have such a beautiful man before, and never had the chance of sucking on such a stunning cock. He tried to let his tongue lick beneath the two hanging balls, but he just couldn't reach. He decided to concentrate on the cock and the double sensation he was being subjected to; the delicious attentions of Skye's mouth on his cock, and the utterly incredible feel of the young stud's meat deep inside his mouth and throat. Skye's head and mouth had begun to move around, working him back and forward, so that the skin of William's cock made contact with every part of his mouth, lips, tongue and teeth.

A groan of pleasure started from somewhere in William's stomach, and it grew, coming in rhythmical moans in time with the actions of his and Skye's mouth. He was on the point of coming. He pushed at Skye's muscular chest and rolled him over onto his back, so that William was now lying on top of him. Their heads were now working furiously, sucking and sucking together, each other's cock being the only thing in their minds. Skye opened his eyes and looked up, seeing William's balls rising and falling in front of him, a glorious sight, and relished their weight as they regularly banged against his nose. He too was about to come. But did he want to just yet? It seemed he had no choice. Their mouths were working so fast and furious that it seemed inevitable. William's groans increased dramatically, and the heaviness of his body pressed down onto Skye's torso.

The blond porn star felt the first sudden splash of come hit the back of his throat; at exactly the same moment he too shot his load. He swallowed hard as each jet flew straight down past the working tongue. William ejaculated with urgency, huge wads of come streaming out, hot and sweet. His own juice flowed with a harsh regular beat, also swallowed by William's insistent mouth, not wanting to waste a drop. He could feel the surge along the shaft of the cock with each grunt that emerged from Skye's chest. The hearts of both men had assumed the same rhythm, as they clung hard to each other, not wanting the experience to end. But soon it did. William fell back, almost wincing as his still-solid cock slipped from Skye's mouth, and Skye's organ did the same from his.

They lay still, side by side, both speechless, and both totally amazed by what had just happened. Of all the people in the Boycam house, they would have laid money on their incompatibility. It just didn't make sense. William and Skye. They didn't naturally go together. But after their exhausting exploration of each other, they both wondered why they hadn't done it before.

'That was amazing...' William's voice trailed off, as he couldn't think of anything else to say.

'I know.' Skye was equally lost for words.

Simon and Rhys sat on the Welsh lad's bed, deep in conversation and story writing. Somehow the lack of camera intrusion had made them closer. They no longer had to act up for their audience, and could now be their real selves, free of pretensions. The sex they had enjoyed in the garden the week before had cemented the friendship in Rhys' eyes, and he had begun to really warm to Simon's company. It looked as if Simon felt the same way.

'So, are you glad you did this whole Boycam thing?' The gentle inquisitive tone of Simon's voice made Rhys look up from his laptop.

'That's a tough question.'

'So what's the answer?' Stretching out beside Rhys, Simon reached his hands behind his head and grasped the struts of the bed, his T-shirt riding up on his stomach a little, showing a small area of smooth flesh.

Averting his eyes, Rhys looked back down to the myriad words on his computer screen, which momentarily merged into one block of indecipherable symbols.

'I think so...no...I know so.'

'Explain.'

Sighing and setting the laptop down on the bedside cabinet, Rhys turned his gaze on Simon's dark eyes. 'I never really had much of a life before. OK, my family is lovely and all of them accept that I'm gay, but nothing exciting ever happened to me. I needed something to make me sit up and realise that the world is a wonderful place, with many wonderful experiences in it.'

'And has this place helped you?'

'It really has. Living in such closeness with the other guys has made me realise that the world is made up of many types of person. I was closeted in Wales; you only got to see the local mentality, but here...meeting Jost and Jackson...and you and Skye, has opened my eyes.'

Simon chuckled. 'I hope that's a good thing!'

'It is.'

'In what way?'

Rhys stayed silent for a few moments; a jumble of thoughts bounced around his mind. 'It has given me confidence. When I arrived, I wouldn't say boo to a goose, let alone try to chat to a guy. And being here, having to exist in this strange place, has made me able to speak up for myself.'

It was obvious to Simon that Rhys was telling the truth. For the first couple of weeks of the Boycam experience, Rhys had been a quiet, nondescript nobody. All right, he was cute, but then so were others in the house. Having to fight to be thought of as an equal had given him an edge. No longer was he the timid one, told what to do by the others. He was now a man with real strength of character. And it looked good on him. Simon had never been one to be turned on by fecklessness. He liked charm and warmth and great strength. And all of a sudden Rhys now possessed these attributes. It was something that now exuded from every pore, and the lad knew it. After his unfortunate bout of drunken sickness at the previous weekend, he had suddenly changed. He had grown up. The man sitting in front of Simon was the same Rhys he had known, and had a terrific sexual encounter with, but was now also different. And Simon liked it a lot.

The mental picture of Rhys standing over him with his cock out and hard flitted across Simon's vision and he shook his head to make it vanish. But the damage had been done and he felt a surge towards his groin. Curling up to cover his embarrassing semi-erection, Simon decided to change the subject.

'So, what would you do if you won the money?'

'That's easy. I'd travel. I used to have other plans, but now I just want to see the world. To go to all those fabulous places I've seen in books and films.'

'Like where?'

Names of places tumbled out of Rhys in a gushing torrent. 'San Francisco, Amsterdam, Paris, India, Australia…I just want to see them all. And while I'm young enough to enjoy and appreciate them. I've realised that I don't want to end up an old man in a wheelchair, saying 'I wish I had...' That would be too awful.'

Sighing, Simon had to agree. This young guy was talking sense. 'Yes, it would.'

With a quizzical lift of the eyebrow, Rhys turned to face Simon. 'So, what would you do?'

'I don't know, really. I might use the money as a down-payment on a property. Open my own gay club. That'd be good. I could decorate it as I want, and it would be filled with the most gorgeous men, and I'd have my pick of the best, and I'd be able to fuck my way through the years!'

'That sounds great!' Rhys lay down beside Simon, snuggling against his body. 'Do you mind?'

'Not at all. I like cuddles.' Simon held Rhys to him, thoroughly loving the warm contact. The idea of more sex with Rhys was very appealing, but he didn't want to force things. Neither of them had spoken of their liaison after it happened, as if they wanted it to be forgotten. Although this was not quite true on Simon's part. He had usually taken the initiative over his previous short relationships, and they had not been as fulfilling as he'd hoped. Here was a chance to let things develop slowly and with more surety and with a smashing and sensual guy. He still couldn't help wanting to ease the situation along, though. Simon ran his tongue around his lips and spoke softly.

'So of all the people in the house, past and present, who have you fancied the most?'

It was a good question, and one that Rhys was in no hurry to answer.

'Well?' Simon nudged him playfully, then let his hand explore his side, aiming for that spot which invariably promotes laughter when tickled.

'Stop that!' Crying out with a suppressed giggle and pushing Simon's hand away, Rhys snuggled deeper into Simon's comforting grasp.

'I'm waiting, young man…'

With upturned eyes that seemed to brim with vitality and charisma, Rhys said 'Well, I have to admit that I didn't really like Jost.'

'Same here.'

'But I did like Peter and would have quite enjoyed getting to know him better, but…'

'But what?'

'Well, I didn't want to intrude. You'd made your move and well…taken him.'

Simon shuffled a little uncomfortably.

'Then, if I'm honest, I have to say that I do like William a lot. I can see that he is quite a sensitive man, who takes a lot of getting to know. But when you do, he is lovely. And I really was quite frightened of Skye when I first met him. The thought of sharing a room with a porn actor was just too much. But like the others, once you get to know him…well, he has a soft side, and is quite vulnerable…if he ever chooses to show that side of himself.'

Taking a bit of a gamble on being too provocative, Simon said, 'And what about me?'

'I like you a lot.'

'But…'

Choosing his words with studied casualness, Rhys replied, 'But I don't see you as someone I could get involved with. You are a handsome, kind man, and I like our friendship the way it is.'

Simon gave Rhys an extra-long hug, trying to hide his disappointment. It was a shame that Rhys didn't want to get involved, but he wasn't going to push him into a relationship that he felt was wrong. Simon did have some standards. Still, the week wasn't over yet, and some opportunity might arise that could change the boy's mind. Simon decided to live in hope.

Saturday

The completed erotic stories had been printed out and were now ready to be read aloud to the housemates. Matt had decided that the toga party would go ahead, and all privations had been lifted. Luxury items, including alcohol and cigarettes, were allowed in the house again, and it heralded the promise of a fun evening. Matt had also come on line on Saturday morning to announce that the cabling problems had been sorted and the house was 'live' once more. An air of despondency settled on the four remaining housemates at this news, as they realised that their small amount of free time had meant a lot to them, and they all now longed for the show to be over.

'I, for one, would be happy to go now,' said William as he picked up a chicken leg and began to gnaw at it. The party had just started and all four of them had gathered in the dining room, draped in white sheets and nothing else, to have their fun and to read their stories aloud. 'I think that I've had enough. So if I go, I won't be sorry.'

'Me too.' Simon joined him at the buffet table and picked up a handful of crisps. 'I know that if I were voted out tomorrow, I'd be sad about losing the money, but I'd be so relieved to have a bath without being watched.'

'I know,' chipped in Skye, who was somehow draped in a sheet in a way that emphasised his figure and showed most of his muscular chest. 'I really want to get back to real life again.'

William fell silent.

'Come on William, what's up?' Simon took him by the arm and led him to the table where a large tureen filled to the brim with a purple liquid sat frothing and bubbling with carbonation, full of pieces of fruit and floating ice cubes.

Taking a cup and helping himself to a sizeable draft of the punch, William downed it in one go and smiled at Simon. 'I was just thinking that I've really enjoyed this last week. The four of us have got on really well, and this time tomorrow one of us will be gone. I suppose I felt a momentary pang of regret.'

His words fell upon the others and quieted them also. They too knew what he said was true. It had been a good week. Like four bricks held together by cement, they had felt strong and united, like nothing could break them apart. And, like all the other weeks behind them, one of their number would soon be gone. The game element of the show had vanished and they had become four friends living together in a strange place. The prize money seemed somewhat extraneous.

'Come on now,' said Simon, taking a cup of punch and holding it aloft. 'Let's have a bloody good evening. Let's get pissed and eat loads and have a great time. Plus, we've got each other's stories to listen to.'

Skye grinned and crossed to Simon's side. 'Absolutely. Here's to us.' He raised a glass and waited until the others had joined him in the toast.

'Us.' Simon smiled.

'Here, here,' William chimed in.

'Right. Here's to us. All of us.' Rhys swigged down his punch and immediately began coughing violently. 'Christ, what is *in* that?'

'A little concoction of my own,' laughed William, his toga slipping off his shoulders and falling about his waist. 'Some red wine, some brandy, some vodka, and a few other secret ingredients! Get it down you, it'll put hairs on your chest.'

Joining in with the laughter, Skye said, 'You leave his chest alone. It's nice as it is, thank you.' Slipping a finger beneath the sheet, Skye unhooked it from Rhys' shoulder and let it fall to the ground, revealing the pristine white briefs that the lad wore beneath.

A chorus of wolf-whistles started up, leaving Rhys red-faced, but unashamed.

'So, you like what you see, do you?' His voice was firm and clear.

The whistles stopped. Rhys continued, 'I don't like being the only one like this. If you are all good friends, then you'll drop those sheets too.'

Electricity surged about the room. The three others sensed that something monumental was afoot. But they all knew they were up for whatever happened. Simon and William dropped their sheets, revealing the underwear beneath, whilst Skye dropped his and got an appreciative glance from the others as his cock and balls came into view.

'I thought I'd go "commando". Any problems with that?' His head was tilted to one side, and his face was innocent. No one could argue with him.

'So, what about these stories, then?' Skye led the way through to the living room and curled up in an armchair expectantly. 'Who goes first?'

'I will,' said Simon cheerily. Picking up a sheaf of notes, he stood before the fireplace and cleared his throat.

'Right then. This is my story called "Train Boy"...I hope you like it.'

Skye, William and Rhys settled themselves appreciatively and waited.

Simon began to read aloud. 'Michael was in a hurry. He looked at the train indicator, which showed that he had only one minute to make the express train. If he didn't catch it, he'd be late arriving in Newcastle and would be very late for his job interview. And he didn't want to lose out on the chance of that manager's job. Picking up his bags, he ran, pushing past people, until he reached the carriage door, grasped it and threw himself in.

'As he sank into an available seat, he smiled as he knew he'd made it, and looking up, he saw that he made someone else smile too. His exhausted dash had clearly amused the guy sitting across the aisle facing him. He was young, perhaps in his early twenties, and with light brown hair; his eyes were dark, and his face was open and friendly. Just the sort of guy that Michael was turned on by. The smile was open and it lit up the guy's face. "I made it." Michael gave a sort of casual laugh. "So I see." The guy chuckled back and returned to his newspaper. Michael settled himself in for the journey.

'After about an hour, drowsiness hit Michael and he was unable to stop himself dozing off. His head lolled back on the seat and he was away. He didn't know how long he had been asleep for, when he was brusquely awoken by someone brushing past him. His eyes snapped open immediately when he realised that he had got an embarrassing erection. He hoped that no one had noticed this, especially the guy opposite, who Michael had already mentally christened "Train Boy". The hard-on was very obvious in the soft white cream of his chinos. Michael had a big dick and was proud of it, but not in such public circumstances.'

The other three gave each other a knowing look, then turned back to Simon.

'Michael looked across the aisle, but Train Boy had gone. Raising his eyes, Michael saw that the young man was at the far end of the train compartment, aiming for the toilet. Perhaps it was he who had knocked Michael as he passed. At the toilet door, Train Boy stopped and turned back. His face was smiling, and he looked straight at Michael. He waited at the door for what seemed a very long time. Was he making an invitation? Michael had to find out. He stood and walked up the aisle, trying not to look too eager. An old man's gaze followed him, as if the old man knew what was on Michael's mind.

Michael reached the door and stood for a moment, wondering if he had misread the situation and was about to do something hideously embarrassing. As he stood, the door opened and Train Boy stood there, still smiling. "Are you coming in then?" he asked. Michael didn't need to be asked twice. He slipped inside and bolted the door behind him, hoping that no one in the compartment had noticed.

'Train Boy was beautiful. His eyes sparkled and his smile was wide and welcoming. Michael could not believe that this vision from above was at all interested in him. But he was. Train Boy leant in for a kiss; his tongue was warm and darting. It filled Michael's mouth and he reciprocated, kissing back with force and vigour. Then Train Boy took the lead. Whilst still kissing, his hands began to explore Michael's chest, slowly unbuttoning his shirt, trying not to bang against the confining toilet walls. In a moment he had Michael's shirt open and he was all over his chest, pinching the nipples and running his hand up and down. Then he moved to the belt, unbuckling it and easing the trousers down. The hands squeezed and massaged Michael's manhood through his underpants, feeling the erection that lay there, pushing a finger through the flap at the front and hooking the cock through the opening.'

He flicked his glance from the printed pages to his three attentive listeners. Simon saw that they were all looking at him, fixedly staring back, now engrossed in the story.

'Michael's knees almost buckled at the contact. Train Boy's hand wrapped itself around the now-hard cock that stood up straight from out of Michael's underwear. The hand seemed to be examining every hard inch of it, from the top to the bottom, every so often yanking up and down due to the occasional jolting of the express train. The grip was hard also, but Michael wanted more. He wanted Train Boy to suck his cock.'

He definitely had their attention now, and so he dropped his voice a little, and slowed his delivery, trying to sound more erotic. Simon continued.

'And then he did. Kneeling awkwardly in the confined toilet, keeping a tight hand on Michael's cock, Train Boy went down on him. His mouth was wet and he was good at what he did. He was able to take the whole of Michael's cock and swallow it, sucking hard and fast. Michael had to grip the edge of the sink behind him to steady himself from the swaying of the train, and to keep himself from collapsing in a heap. It was a good blow job, at times fast and furious and also slow and teasing. This man knew what he was doing. It didn't take long for Michael to be brought off, and soon Train Boy was drinking down his come. Michael looked up as the muffled voice of the train announcer said something about their arrival at the next station. Train Boy smiled up at Michael and wiped his mouth, then whispered "Thank you" in his ear and slipped out of the toilet. Michael cleaned himself up, put away his cock and followed, but when he got back to his seat Train Boy had gone. It was destined to be a quick fling with a handsome stranger, which Simon would remember for a long time.'

William looked up. 'You said Simon, not Michael.' He gave a hearty laugh. 'So admit it...it was you!'

A scarlet blush grew over Simon's face as he sat down. 'Yes, all right...it was me; it did happen. Mind you, I never got that job.'

Skye muttered jovially, 'But you got the blow job.'

The others joined in with laughter, topping it with a round of appreciative applause.

'Thank you. Who's next?' Simon looked around him.

'I'll go next,' said William, standing up with his papers in hand. He took up his position in front of the fireplace and began to read.

'This is a story which I have called "Tunisian Nights". Here goes...The air was warm and balmy the moment I stepped off the plane, onto Tunisian soil. The several gins that I'd consumed on the plane had rather gone to my head and so, as I descended the stairs, I had to clutch at the rail for support. Thankfully, the coach journey to my hotel wasn't too arduous, and soon I was checked in at my beach view chalet. The sand outside had a white glow to it in the bright moonlight, and the breeze off the sea was refreshing and did help to clear my head. There was a knock at my door, and in came a dark, handsome young man carrying my cases. "Just put them there," I said, noticing how very attractive he was. He smiled back, showing a mouthful of gleaming white teeth. I gave him a tip and instead of instantly leaving my room, he hung about at the door, shifting from one foot to another. 'Yes, what is it?' I asked. He smiled again and said that if I needed anything, anything at all, I was to just ring and ask for Ramzi, and he'd bring it straight away. There was something about his voice that made it immediately apparent he was offering more than just room service. I nodded and thanked him.

'The following day after a good night's sleep, I went for a stroll around the local *souk*, enjoying the hustle and bustle of the market, ignoring the cries of the carpet sellers, all determined to get me to buy their wares. I noticed that a muscular young man was following me around, stopping when I did, and walking at the same pace as me. As I ducked down an alleyway, he walked past the end, and so I was able to jump out and speak to him. 'Why are you following me?' I asked. I appreciated his chest, which was only clad in a tight T-shirt. His jeans were also tight-fitting and clung to the contours of his lovely arse. I saw with a smile that he possessed a packet that was worth exploring. He said he was wondering if I needed a guide around town, someone to show him the sights. His English was impeccable, and his manners the same. I was very taken with this young man, for many reasons. Being a stranger in this part of the world, it would be good to have the company of a handsome young stranger, someone to point out the best places to eat and drink and, if he was of the same persuasion, to show where to meet the best men.

'He told me his name was Kamal, and he was a university student, studying English, hoping to move away from his native land to England someday soon. We talked as we strolled, and I noticed glances from many other such lads as we went, glances of envy, perhaps? I was glad of that, as Kamal was by far the most handsome of the bunch. We sat and drank mint tea at a café, and he asked the waiter to bring something else to our table. He brought a large, exotically shaped bottle with tubes twined about it. I recognised it as a hookah, a Mediterranean smoking pipe. We indulged ourselves, and I soon felt very relaxed, assuming that what we were smoking would be classed as illegal in many countries. But this idyllic situation was bound to change. Very soon after that I began to feel nauseous and needed a lie down. Kamal helped me to my feet and away from the *souk*, towards a small wooded lane, where I could see a hut in a grove, surrounded by orange trees. He led me to this hut, and opened the door, taking me inside. It was obvious that he lived there. He laid me down on the rough mattress, and I immediately fell into a deep sleep.

'When I awoke it was much later; there was no sunlight coming through the slats of the hut. I sat up and saw that I was naked; my clothes had been removed and placed in a tidy, folded pile at my side. Kamal was nowhere to be seen. I checked my pockets and my wallet was still intact and nothing had been taken. I sighed with relief, and pulled on my trousers. Poking my head outside, I could see that it was late; the stars were out and the moon was shining brightly. The air was heavy with the scent of oranges and honeysuckle, the fragrance quite overpowering and lovely. Kamal was sitting under a tree, looking up at the stars, a walkman about his head, nodding to the beat of some music. He looked up, smiled and turned the sounds off. 'Are you feeling better?' he asked me. I nodded and sat down next to him. I could feel his hard body pressing against mine and I liked it. Then without warning or invitation, he kissed me. It was passionate and tender at the same time, his tongue working in and out of my mouth. I responded in the only way I knew how. And soon we were embracing, holding each other tight, our hands moving up and down each other's body. He quickly stood and entered the hut, emerging moments later naked and with a blanket. I asked if we should be doing this in the open, but he told me the lane we were on led nowhere and we'd be undisturbed.

'I saw with wide eyes that his cock was big; it slapped between his thighs as he moved, and his balls too were not small. All this and a muscular body. I mused that he would do well in the world of modelling or porn. He spread out the blanket and waited for me to sit upon it. He towered above me, his cock just inches from my face. By now it all seemed totally unreal, and I felt as if I were in a dream. I lifted my head until I could reach the long, thick, semi-hard dick with my tongue. Eagerly responding, Kamal moved forward a little. My tongue licked and teased at the head. I couldn't wait to get a taste of that thing. The massive rod began to part my lips and I let it slide in. I could taste the juice that had seeped from the tip. Kamal spread his legs a little wider and moaned, as inch by inch I took him in my mouth, the shaft growing wider as it got down to the base. Finally I did it, took the whole cock in my mouth, stretching my lips wide, my jaw as open as it had ever been. Then I started to suck him off, working him back and forth, getting faster and faster, sliding my mouth along the rigid shaft.

He grabbed the back of my head and twisted his fingers in my hair with such energy that I wanted to cry out with pain. But somehow I didn't. It was as if I wasn't myself…I was in a vacuum; nothing else existed but me and that cock, and all there was to do was give as much pleasure as I could. My head reeled; my heart banged in my chest, and my own cock had grown hard and was aching for some action, too. My eyes were wide open and I watched that broad slab of flesh slamming in and out of my mouth; it was the most exciting, thrilling, erotic sight that I'd ever seen. My balls needed release and soon. Kamal was now moaning louder as he fucked my face, driving himself deeper into me with each stroke. I could hardly breathe, and had to tell myself to do so several times, but as the lube from his cock and my spit mingled, it became easier and easier to suck. His hands were like a vice, holding me in position. If I'd wanted to stop, I doubt he'd have let me. Then all of a sudden, he gave a deeper groan than before and I felt a trickle of hot juice; then the rest came spurting out in a torrent, hitting the back of my throat. I don't usually swallow, but here there was no choice; it gushed down me, and I took each drop, pouring down, past my tonsils and down. With the vigour of youth, as soon as he'd finished shooting, he pulled out of my mouth and dropped to his knees, his own mouth making contact with my tumescence. In a few short strokes, he had brought me to the edge and I came also, jerking off across his face. I watched as the come dripped down his beautiful features, and his tongue lapped it up voraciously.

'Kamal and I became good friends that holiday, and we spent many happy hours together. I have been back since, but found his hut empty. I hope he is well; he deserves to be, for the pleasure he gave on that wonderful Tunisian night.'

William put down his papers and saw that everyone had some degree of hard-on. Skye's was the most obvious, lolling across his thigh, his hand thoughtfully stroking it. Rhys and Simon also were semi-hard, small tent-poles of slowly growing flesh appearing in their underwear. William grinned. He knew he had aroused them all, and he sat down with a satisfied smirk.

A burst of applause greeted him, as the others showed their appreciation. They had enjoyed the story, and had been able to visualise it all perfectly. Reaching across from his chair, William laid a hand on Skye's cock, and looked into his eyes. 'I hope you liked that...and every word is true.'

Skye put his hand on top of William's and squeezed. 'Oh, I did...I did.'

Simon cocked his head to one side and spoke to William. 'So, you never found him again?'

'No. The hut was there, but he had gone. I just hope that he's all right, and doing well.'

Simon said, 'If he is an intelligent lad, then I'm sure he's fine.'

Rhys stood and addressed his housemates. 'I want to go next.'

'Fire away. I'm in no rush.' Skye gave Rhys a penetrating stare, encouraging him to do his very best. William's hand was still resting on his cock, and he made no effort to move it.

Rhys cleared his throat, and shuffled a little from foot to foot; his recent erection had quickly subsided. He began his story without preamble.

'Rory was a young man who was generally happy with his life. He was clever and bright and had friends and family who thought the world of him. But he was gay. He knew it from an early age, and tried to live with that fact. He had told everyone who mattered to him, and although there were a few raised eyebrows, people were accepting and treated him no differently. The boys at school were different. He was sixteen when he'd announced he was gay, and soon this news had begun to filter about the class and then the school. Being a strong boy, he could cope with the looks and giggles, and rebuffs that frequently came his way. Soon the graffiti started, with a big colourful pattern on the back wall of the sports hall saying "Rory is a cock sucker." He ignored the jibes and went on with his life. His gang of friends – Stuart, David and Col – all seemed OK about things and stayed mates. They even beat up one of the other boys who pretended that he'd caught AIDS from Rory in the school changing rooms. All this was bearable in a strange way, until one afternoon on the way home from school, something happened.

'Rory was walking back from his last lesson which had been sports, carrying his bag full of football boots and kit and towels. He had taken the long detour home through the woods at the back of the school, as the day was bright and sunny. "Watch your arse, boys. Here's the school bum-boy." A voice called out from nowhere. Rory looked up but could see no one about. Deciding to brave it out, he carried on straight ahead. A hand reached out and grabbed his shoulder bag, making him jump. He looked about him and saw a small gang of four or five boys suddenly appear around him. Roger Whipley, the leader of this gang, stood before him, waving the bag provocatively back and forth like a pendulum. "Look, we've got her handbag, boys. Let's see if she's got any make-up." Quickly, before Rory could stop him, he unzipped the bag and threw all the contents about him. Rory knew that in such large numbers there was nothing he could do but wait until they'd had their fun and then collect his things and go. But this was going to be a very different day. Roger was taller than Rory, in fact, taller than everyone else in the gang; he was broad shouldered and muscular, the perfect type for a school bully. His hair was black and curly and his looks dark and brooding. Out of the corner of his eye, Rory had admired his body in the school showers many times, careful not to let Roger see him looking. For a sixteen-year-old boy, Roger had matured very quickly and had a cock that was the envy of most of the school. It was rumoured that Roger had three girlfriends already and that he'd made one pregnant. The others in the gang were just hangers-on, boys wanting to be men, basking in the glow of Roger's glory. Now Roger was still in his tracksuit bottoms, which were baggy and grey, and he was in a T-shirt, which was clinging to his chest.

'Roger addressed the others, who began to close in on Rory menacingly. "Look out, boys. He'll be after your knobs." Rory sighed and tried to push past, but Roger put up a hand and poked him savagely in the chest. "Where you going, faggot?" It was clear that this was going to be hard fight to win. "I'd like to go home, please." Rory knew that sometimes being polite worked with these thugs. This time it didn't. "You are not going anywhere. You are going to tell us what you faggots do to each other. Now…"

'There was no arguing with Roger, and so Rory tried to take the lead in this stand-off. "All right, if you really want to know…gay men love each other." Roger snorted and grabbed Rory by the collar. "Fuck love… what do they do?" Rory stood his ground. "They suck each other's cocks, opening their mouths and licking the end of the cock, then slowly swallowing it, right down until it touches the back of their throats. Then they might suck on each other's bollocks, first one and then the other and then both if their mouths can stretch wide enough to take both in. Of course, if they don't have very big bollocks, then there's no problem." Rory looked at the other guys, who stood about slightly embarrassed and slightly sheepish. He stared in amazement as he recognised his friend Stuart at the back of the group. This was becoming a nightmare. "Then what?" Roger's voice had dropped a little, although his grip on Rory's collar was just as strong. "Then, if they really want to, they will fuck. One will push his cock up the other's arse until he screams because it feels so good, and then the other one'll fuck him like a pig. Is that what you want to hear? Is that what you want to do?"

'This was unwise. It angered Roger, who let go of Rory and threw him violently to the ground. "Is this what you want, faggot?" said Roger, who untied the string of his tracksuit bottoms and hoiked them down, pulling out his cock, which Rory was surprised to see was already slightly hard. It was long and uncut, the foreskin pulled back slightly, showing a small area of purple head poking out. Roger moved in a bit closer, and soon he was standing right by Rory's head. The cock was about an inch from his nose. From the corner of Rory's eye, he could see that another of the boys, a thick-set lad called Mark, had also got his cock out, not that big but quite thick and stubby. Rory realised that he was beginning to get turned on by this show, and felt his own cock starting to get hard. Roger made the move. "So, if you are a cocksucker, then suck some cock." He grabbed the back of Rory's head. Rory, although desperate to taste that dick, had held back as he didn't want to seem eager. But he could hold back no longer. He opened his mouth and took the swollen head in his mouth, sliding the foreskin back as he did so, until it was folded back behind the large head. Roger gave a moan of excited pleasure and his knees sagged for a moment. Then pulling himself together, he began to fuck Rory's mouth. Roger's cock was big; bigger than Rory expected and soon it was making his jaws ache, stretching his mouth wide, as it pushed in and out. The other boys were all now with their cocks out, including Stuart, who barged closer and stood next to Rory. It was clear what he wanted, and so Rory obliged, sliding away from Roger and going down on Stuart. His friend's cock was not so big, but it was just as hard and Rory tried to give as much satisfaction as he could. Soon, all the others were gathered around Rory in a circle, cocks hard and free, waiting for him to suck them off. At times the boys were fucking his face so hard that they seem to be losing control. When Rory got back to Roger, the bully was slamming his cock in Rory's mouth so angrily that the balls began to slap him on the chin. Rory desperately wanted to pull his own cock out and start to whack it up and down, but he didn't dare. That might look as if he were enjoying himself too much. Which he was.

'Soon it came to an end. One by one the boys started to feel a climax coming on and their cocks were jerked away from Rory's drooling mouth and they wanked off. Soon the small wooded glade was filled by the shouts of ejaculation that poured from the gang as their fists beat the come out of their cocks and over Rory's face and hair. Roger was the last to come, as if he expected no less by his superior position in the gang. With a yell and a grunt he came, shooting his cum over Rory, leaving the boy's face dripping with spunk.

'No one said a word. The boys stuffed their depleted cocks back in their trousers and quickly scarpered. Roger took his time. As he hoisted his tracksuit up over his knees and retied it, he looked down at Rory's come-splattered face. "Not bad," he said and disappeared.'

Rhys sat down, his face a deep scarlet hue, his cheeks burning. He had hoped he'd written a story that would turn the others on, and glancing at the three housemates, saw that he had. Skye was hard, and was stroking himself dreamily, his eyes tight shut, and both William and

Simon were feeling themselves through their briefs, both sporting hard-ons. Rhys grinned inwardly. He knew he could turn them on and he had.

'Wow.' Skye was the first to speak. 'What a fucking horny story. I can just picture all those guys fucking Rory's face in the woods. Believe me there's a lot of latent homosexuality at boys' schools. Isn't there, William?'

'Too right, my old love. At school and university. The tales I could tell you. Did I ever tell you about Rogerson the prefect?'

'Some other time, perhaps?' Simon gave William's cock a playful squeeze, momentarily impressed by its size and hardness. Simon too had been aroused by Rhys' tale and had been astounded by how much it had sent signals to his cock, making it grow and twitch. Christ, these stories were getting to him. He needed relief...and soon.

'So was that based on anyone we know?' asked William. 'Rhys...Rory...they sound rather the same.'

Rhys grinned, his face breaking wide with a smile that displayed his white teeth and brought a sparkle to his eyes. 'Sort of. It was a fantasy I had. I really wanted to be set upon by Roger's gang, as they were all attractive, especially Roger.'

'And what about Stuart?' Simon queried.

'He was one of my best friends and I was sure he was gay too, but didn't have the nerve to come out like I had. I'd have enjoyed sex with him, I'm certain.'

Skye chuckled and came out of his reverie. 'Well, that was fantastic. Now finally it's my turn. Get settled in your seats, gentlemen, as I present my story. It doesn't have a title. Here goes...' Standing in front of the fireplace, his cock still jutting out from his crotch, semi-erect, he started to read.

'The porn shoot was not going well. As soon as I arrived, I could tell that it was going to be a tricky day. The director was a screaming queen who was determined to make life difficult, and my co-stars hadn't yet turned up. The location was at a large house in the country, the property of some rich accountant who had a vested interest in gay porn. There were to be several scenes set in different rooms in the house, not linked together at all, with me and these other two guys called Al and Kurt. They arrived in the same car and obviously knew each other. We tried the first scene in the gymnasium, a small room, with a bench and some weights. Neither Al, a Gypsy-like hairy-chested Spaniard, or Kurt, a blue-eyed, Scandinavian-looking guy, could get it up. They seemed listless and uninterested in the whole project. Our director's temper went from bad to worse, and he tried everything to get the guys hard…magazines, videos, even getting the cute young runner to act as a fluffer, which he was happy to do. But even his cute young mouth couldn't get them up.

'I lost my temper, stormed off the set and grabbed a coffee. I noted that the runner was staying quite close to me. His name was Patrick and his big doe eyes were very appealing. I told him he had done well in his fluffing and he blushed. The lighting guy appeared from nowhere and poured a coffee too. We were standing around commiserating with each other, wondering if the day's filming would ever happen, when I noticed that their eyes were both aiming at my lower regions. I'd forgotten that I was standing around in nothing but a jock-strap, and a well-filled one at that.'

Skye stopped and tossed a glance at the others to gauge their reaction to this truism. He happily noted their knowing smiles and continued.

'I took a moment to have a look at the two guys by the side of me. They were rather nice, the lighting guy tall and lean, with close cropped hair, the runner small and perky. Both were wearing jeans that showed they had a useful packet. I suggested we take our coffees and sit down somewhere and they happily agreed. We found a quiet study, where we sat in armchairs, and drank our hot drinks. I could tell that both guys were horny and ready for some sex, so I made the first move. Standing up, I stepped out of my jock and threw it over my shoulder. They were impressed, I could tell, and soon they were also on their feet, getting undressed. In a few minutes we stood there, naked and all with stiffies. I fell to my knees and began to suck their cocks, both nice, not as big as mine, of course. We got into a rhythm, and soon we were lying on the rug, in a sort of circle, each sucking another's cock in a chain. We lost all track of time and were so caught up in the action of taking a cock in our mouths and giving great head, all the time feeling someone else's mouth chowing down on us, that none of us looked up at a small noise by the door, so enraptured were we.

'I wanted some cock up my arse, and said so. I stood up and both of the guys said they wanted to fuck me. Who was I to argue? The runner had a pocketful of condoms, and so both he and the lighting guy rubbered up. I said I wanted to try two cocks at the same time, and they gave each other a look. I don't think it was something any of us had done before. It looked like the lighting guy was the one with the longest, hardest stiffy, the one who'd keep it up longer. I made him lie down on the carpet, and gently eased myself down onto his cock. I hadn't been fucked for a while and so it hurt. I could feel my arsehole opening and closing, as it tried to take each slippery inch up inside of me. Once he was in and I was used to it, I started to lever myself up and down his cock, really loving it filling me. I began to wonder if I could take anymore. But I wasn't given any choice.

'The runner had a finger at my hole and was slipping it in and out, getting himself ready. Then he positioned himself behind me and, with one swift push, he was also inside me. Because of how we were placed, the runner had the ability to thrust more and so he started fucking me hard and fast. I tried to give the lighting guy as much pleasure and so bounced up and down in time with him. I hoped he was having fun, which he should have been because not only was he fucking me, but he had his cock rubbing up against another guy's for extra friction, and their bollocks were slapping against each other's. And for me it was incredible. The sensations were astounding. My hole was really being stretched wide, and it hurt like never before. My cock was hard and bobbing up and down, so I grabbed it and start to wank. A noise made me look up and I saw the director standing at the door, the camera in his hand, shooting our every move. I smiled and continued, knowing that he'd be getting some great footage. And so was I.'

Skye put down his papers and bowed, waiting for the now familiar applause from the housemates, which came hard and fast.

'There you are...I knew you could do it,' said William proudly, his cock standing up in his briefs. He leaned into Skye as he sat down and planted a kiss on his cheek.

'I think we've all done bloody well,' said Simon, standing up, unashamed of his erection. 'The trouble is, all those stories have got my juices flowing and I don't know what to do about it.'

'I do,' said Skye decisively. He beckoned to Simon, who duly approached. With a deft finger, Skye hooked the briefs down, letting Simon's cock spring free. The piercing at the head glistened with pre-cum that had been oozing steadily for a while. Without a hint of hesitation or regret, Skye opened his mouth and took Simon's cock inside. The other two looked on aghast at such brazen behaviour, but did nothing to stop it. Both Rhys and William were also fired up by their stories, and were now really up for some sex. They didn't care about the cameras, and they didn't care about the potential embarrassment factor in the morning. They just wanted to do it.

William looked deep into Rhys' eyes and knew that he badly wanted this young lad. He had for many weeks and now he was going to do it. He reached across and drew the lad closer, and their lips met. Rhys closed his eyes at the gentle touch of their mouths. It all seemed unreal. Shutting his mind to the fact that it was William he was kissing, Rhys let nature take its course. The kiss was long and tender, with William responding magnificently, letting his tongue enter Rhys' mouth slowly and with passion. The Welsh lad let his hand drop and fall to William's crotch, where it squeezed the balls through the soft briefs, rolling them between his thumb and forefinger. A moan started in William's throat; the head of his cock was now sticking up from under the waistband of his briefs and, noticing this, Rhys moved his hand and began to massage the stiff prick. Rhys' own cock was now ready for some action and it pushed out from his body, forming a large tent in the cloth of his underwear. A small patch of moisture had seeped through the material from Rhys' cock-head, and with his other hand he reached down and gave himself a reassuring squeeze. William could hold off no longer. He leant in and put his hand on Rhys', gently easing it away and taking over the genital massage. He ran his fingers along the elastic around one of Rhys' legs, lifting it and making contact with the skin of Rhys' ball sac. The lad shivered. Momentarily, William hooked the finger around the ball sac, easing it out from under the elastic, leaving the hardened cock still encased in the briefs. Rhys gave in and sat back in the chair, his eyes closed. Seeing what was expected of him, William took control. He shuffled out of his armchair and knelt in front of Rhys, his mouth watering with desire for this smooth, beautiful boy. He nuzzled his nose against the hanging balls, letting his tongue flick against them, watching Rhys react as if he'd been electrocuted, gasping and flinching almost at the same time.

Skye continued to suck on Simon's cock with gusto. He bathed the head of the cock in saliva as he went, his tongue lingering over the Prince Albert ring that pierced the slit. The heavy, silver metal swivelled from side to side at his ministrations, and as he swallowed the cock down, it fell against his tongue, eventually hanging past the back of his throat. Skye enjoyed the size of this cock, average but nicely proportioned, the head large and circular. As he sucked and licked, he could see he was driving Simon crazy, his hands unable to stay still, his fists clenching and unclenching. This was too much.

'Oh, I'm going to come…' Simon's voice was plaintive, almost regretful.

Sitting back, and letting the cock pop out from his mouth, Skye eyed the guy before him. 'Not yet, you don't...I want to fuck you.'

Simon had no desire to stop Skye, in fact he was longing for such an event. The thought of that gigantic pole stuffed up inside him made Simon almost come on the spot.

Skye stood and padded across to the mantelpiece over the fireplace and looked in the communal condom dish that sat there. Thankfully, there were still a number of rubbers in it and some sachets of lube. 'Bend over the chair,' barked Skye with an authoritative air. Simon did as he was told. This was no time to argue. Ignoring what Rhys and William were doing, and concentrating on their own activities, Skye snapped a rubber down over his cock.

'Relax now baby, 'cos here I come...' The cold slathering of lube on Simon's hole sent a shiver down his spine, his tight brown ring contracting with anticipation. He knew he had to relax; it would be less painful if he did, but that was easier said than done. The pressure of Skye's cock moving up and down the crack made him more tense. His own cock was still rigid, curling up and slapping against his stomach. This was it. Skye's cock-head had found the hole and was pushing at it, with a sure insistence, pressing and pressing. Simon's head was flooded with doubts, and he was tempted to ask Skye to stop. But a small voice in him muttered that Skye wasn't the kind of guy to stop at this stage of proceedings. Simon gasped as his hole gave way and loosened for a fraction of a second, but this was all Skye needed. The tip slipped inside, causing a cry to leap from Simon's throat. Of all the sexual pleasures in the world, to him this was the hardest and most painful – the first few moments of a really good fuck. If done correctly, the pain soon subsided and the joy and delirium took over. Gritting his teeth, Simon wanted that delirium, and badly.

Skye pushed again, and soon the whole head of his cock was firmly planted inside Simon's arse. He waited briefly for the lad to become accustomed to the hard invader, knowing that very soon he would be ready for more.

'Yes...' The word hissed through Simon's teeth, signalling his need for the rest of the cock inside him. Simon concentrated and tried to relax his sphincter muscles, and again momentarily he did.

Skye realised that he could continue and so he pushed, feeling the shaft inching inside, gripped tightly as he went, higher and higher into the depths of Simon's arse. In a few brief moments he was there, and it felt wonderful. His balls rested against Simon's own hanging sac, and with one hand, he reached under to grab hold of the lad's cock, glad to feel that it was solid. With his fingers, he stroked the silken smoothness of the rigid weapon, bringing fresh moans to Simon's lips. Simon shivered and a spasm rippled through him, sending a wave through his arse, tightening and relaxing about the cock inside, making Skye gasp. The strong muscles were now gripping the whole length of the shaft, urging it higher and deeper, almost sucking him into the very hilt. For Skye this was an amazing fuck; his cock felt longer and bigger than it ever had before, and it seemed as if his bollocks were like cannon balls, heavy and pendulous, waiting for the moment they emptied of their juice. Now it was time to show what he was made of and he began to fuck Simon's arsehole with a vengeance.

Rhys groaned as William opened his mouth and sucked the balls inside. This was something else. He had enjoyed the incredible sensation of a blow job, but never really had time spent on his balls. William's mouth and tongue certainly knew what they were doing, as they pulled and sucked, licked and nipped, taking first one inside, rolling it around, and then the other, pausing for a second before slurping both into his wide mouth. He loved sucking bollocks and Rhys had two of the biggest he'd seen; slightly oversized for the cock that they hung beneath. His tongue flicked back and forth on the underside of the sack, sending an electric frisson through the lad's entire body. He didn't want this to end. But William had other plans. As the balls slipped wet and aching from his mouth, he moved forward slightly and nuzzled against the cock, which was still hard in the briefs. With his teeth, he gently bit the underneath of the shaft, from the tip down to the bottom. This drove Rhys into an ecstatic frenzy. He writhed on the chair, small gasps of elation escaping his throat. William was now in total control; he had this lad in the palm of his hand and the back of his throat. He grasped the elastic waistband and swiftly yanked the briefs down and threw them in the corner. Where they landed was unimportant. What mattered was Rhys' cock. William opened his mouth and spat a gob of saliva onto his fingers, his others pulling back the foreskin with ease and rubbing it around the tender head. This also made Rhys writhe, perhaps more so than the ball sucking. William was undecided. Should he suck Rhys' cock or stand and make the lad suck his? He made his mind up...pleasure Rhys first and then let him have it.

William lowered his head and let his tongue touch the tip; the small drop of pre-come stuck to the end of his tongue and it streamed out in a long strand. He lapped it up, savouring the saltiness. Then he put his lips to the head, kissing it before opening wide and engulfing the head completely.

The warmth of his mouth was more than Rhys could bear. He knew that this guy was able to suck cock, and here he was doing it to him. William was getting into the rhythm, moving at speed down the shaft, taking the whole length in his mouth, his tongue moving around, exploring every inch. His mouth was tightly clamped about the shaft, doing its work, loving it totally. Almost involuntarily, Rhys found himself pushing his cock up into William's mouth, as if he wanted more than he was being given. The cock reached right to the back of William's throat, and his lips were pressing against the soft pubic bush at the bottom. Simon's blow job in the garden had been good, but this was something else entirely. Rhys knew that he could learn much from William's technique, and little did he know that soon he would be able to put that technique into practice.

Skye arched himself backwards, giving him the ability to fuck

Simon even deeper. He pounded away, letting his cock push in and then slide almost out before slamming back with renewed force. This was going to be a fuck that Simon would remember for a long time to come. Pulling out of the guy's arse, he barked 'Change position.' Simon wanted more and so did immediately as he was ordered. He slumped into the armchair, on his back, his head pushed against the cushioned back. Skye grabbed his legs and threw them over his head, exposing the arsehole, which now pulsed, desperate for more. And it got it. Without a moment's pause, Skye plunged in, slamming into Simon's bum with a newly found energy. The cry that burst from Simon's throat made Rhys and William look up, as they focused on what their other two housemates were doing.

For Simon, this new position made it all more exciting. He loved to be fucked like this, his legs over his head, able to see the hot stud doing the fucking, and gaze into his eyes, and if the guy was supple enough, to have him lean forward and kiss. This time the penetration wasn't as bad as the initial one, and although a flash of pain rocketed through him, it was bearable, even enjoyable. This was one of the great fucks of his life. The sides of Skye's cock created a delicious friction, and it seemed as if it would burst out of his stomach, so long and so deep was it pushing. They soon became one person, breathing together, undulating as a single entity, movement regulated by the ramming strokes of Skye's cock. Simon found he could bear it no longer. He grabbed his own swollen prick and began to beat it, his fist becoming a blur in Skye's vision. Skye knew that for him too, a climax was on the cards. He needed to shoot, and so he built up the rhythm more, faster and faster, determined to climax at the same moment as Simon. In a few short strokes they were there. Both letting out groans of release, they came together – Simon's spunk arching out from his cock, flying up in a long stream, landing across his chest and neck. He tried to squeeze his sphincter muscles tight, as he felt Skye erupt within him, the pummelling action continuing unabated as he came.

For a brief, ecstatic moment they clung together, Skye falling forward onto Simon's spunk-splattered chest, his cock still firmly embedded in the guy's tortured hole.

William kept an eye on what the other two were doing as he stood, letting Rhys' cock slip from his oral attentions. He towered over lad, and stepped out of his briefs, allowing his own dick to be free, standing out proudly from his groin. It throbbed and ached, needing some hot mouth to make it feel better. Rhys lay still, his eyes wide with eager expectancy. The world seemed to have slowed down, and everything that was happening was like a slow-motion film sequence. William stood above him, and with a quick, powerful movement, he reached out and grabbed the back of Rhys' head, his fingers entwined in his hair. The cock was pointing straight at his face, moving slowly towards his mouth, and it was clear what William wanted. Rhys had no choice. Besides, he was quite looking forward to it.

Rhys' lips parted slightly and his tongue flitted across them, wetting the skin as it went. William moved ever closer until the head of his cock was brushing the soft lips, insistent on entry. The tongue emerged and licked cautiously at the tip, running around the rim of the helmet and then poking into the slit. The cock reacted as naturally as it could by jerking to the touch, growing, if possible, even harder. Rhys took his time. With his inexperienced tongue, he licked down from the two smooth lobes, following the line of the thick vein that ran along the underside of the shaft, then back again, his lips pressed to that throbbing vein until they butted the lower side of the head again. This was an agony of ecstasy for William, the soft warm teasing of that tongue heralding what was to come. He couldn't wait any longer, and so with one sharp motion he aimed his cock at the willing mouth and forced it inside. Rhys almost gagged, so swift was the entry, as it pushed mercilessly at the beck of his throat. He thought for one ghastly moment that he would throw up. But with an iron will, he fought the urge, squeezing his eyes shut and focussing on the cock, determined not to show himself up as the untested cocksucker that he was. William put his hands round Rhys' head, holding on firmly to his ears and started to fuck the lad's mouth, pulling back and pushing in, harshly and with regular strokes. Rhys tried to remember what had been done to him and emulated those actions. He let his tongue flick under the shaft, licking as it rushed in and out. He put up a hand and held tight to the base of the cock, so as to regulate the blow job and take things at his own pace. William seemed prepared to let him. Rhys licked at the large plum head, swirling it around his mouth, nipping at it with his teeth, before sliding his mouth down it again, swallowing the dick whole.

William was transfixed by the fuck that was going on across the room, unable to tear his eyes away from the fantastic sight. His cock felt fantastic too, as Rhys was proving himself expert at the art of chowing down. The sensations his mouth was giving made him swoon with utter delight. Gripping the ears tighter, he forced the lad's head back, pushing his cock further down the throat than he thought the lad could take, but like a trooper Rhys coped. He seemed to open up his throat and take the lot. William knew he didn't have a monster like Skye, but he was proud of its slightly larger than average size, and its big, symmetrical head. He had had no complaints about it so far. And it looked like Rhys wasn't going to complain either. The boy sucked as if his life depended on it, his head darting back and forth, taking everything in greedy, slurping gulps. It was the most erotic thing he had ever seen, his whole cock being swallowed by this beautiful mouth, Rhys' eyes fixed avidly on his own, the broad solid rod, emerging and disappearing into the maw of this youth's throat. He reached round and grabbed hold of Rhys' cock, which stood straight up, iron-stiff, and began to wank it. Rhys' hand knocked his away and grabbed hold of it himself, jerking himself frantically to climax. As the sounds of Skye and Simon erupting floated around the room, William and Rhys also reached explosion point. William pulled out just in time to see a geyser of hot semen burst out and land haphazardly across Rhys' face. He heard the lad grunt with relief as he felt spatters of spunk hit him on the back. It took a few moments for both of them to subside, and as their breathing returned to normal, so did the colour in their faces.

'Fucking hell...' William sank to his knees, looking up with adoration at the Adonis seated, erect and sated, before him.

'Wow...' Rhys had nothing else to say. He turned his head to see Skye pulling out of Simon, the mammoth cock still hard, the evidence of his ejaculation clear to see in the sagging condom.

Simon was speechless. He had wanted a good fuck, and what he had just received had exceeded all his hopes. In his mind he had wanted Skye to be good, but he hadn't dreamed he would be this good.

'I hope you liked that, because I did...' Skye looked up at the corner of the room, his gaze lighting on the camera that sat silently there. He had had a great fuck, and he had the added thrill of being watched doing it. Life didn't get much better than this.

Sunday

The housemates slept late again, the excitement of the previous evening wiping them out completely. The sex that had happened between them seemed to sap every ounce of energy, and they crawled into bed exhausted but sated.

Sunday morning saw them all up by midday, and all too aware that it was eviction day – one of them would soon be leaving the house.

'I don't want to vote anyone out,' said Rhys morosely over his bowl of corn flakes.

'Me neither,' agreed Simon, who sat at the breakfast bar, a piece of toast in hand. For the four remaining housemates, life had become fun; suddenly things had settled down and they realised that they liked each other. They had got used to having each other around. The balance of the house was perfect, and to have to eject one of their number in an almost arbitrary way would prove impossible.

'Well, whatever happens, it is not personal. I shall miss whoever goes, and if it's me, then I'll bear no grudges. I want you all to know that.' William was remarkably chirpy, his face unable to stop grinning from ear to ear. As he entered the kitchen, he gave each of the others a full, lingering kiss on the lips. As far as he was concerned, this could be his last day in the Boycam house, and he was totally determined to make it a day to remember.

Skye grinned at this obvious happiness. He felt good too. He had enjoyed a wonderful fuck last night, and had slept like a log. As far as he was concerned, the show was almost won and he could already see the ten thousand pounds sitting comfortably in his bank account.

'I'm off to do my exercises. Anyone want to join me?' Skye stood and headed for the door. No answer came so he vanished, whistling a jaunty tune.

'It's going to be a long day, I reckon,' said Rhys finishing his breakfast. 'The hours up to the eviction are going to be so long. What can we do?'

William tutted. 'Dear, oh dear. There's lots we can do...some sunbathing, a chess tournament, snooker, more sex...' He leaned over and gave Rhys a peck on the cheek, provoking a smile from the boy.

'All right. I don't want to be a misery all day. How about...'

He was cut off in mid-sentence by the voice of Skye calling from the hall. 'Hey, you guys, come and look at this. We've got a surprise.'

Inquisitively, the three housemates trooped out to see what Skye was on about. As they stepped down into the garden, their mouths dropped open with amazement and incredulous delight. Sitting against a wall of the house sat a large jacuzzi hot-tub, turned on and bubbling away.

Skye held up a piece of paper that had been attached to it. He read aloud from the note. 'Boycam housemates. This is to thank you for all your hard work and effort over the past few weeks, especially the effort you displayed last night. We at MEN4U TV are delighted with the ratings of the show at present and wished to show our appreciation. Enjoy. Love, Matt.'

William clapped his hands in delight. This was a great way to spend his last day in the house. 'Well, I'm getting in...' In a flash he had shucked his bath-robe and leapt into the frothing water.

'How is it?' Simon sauntered over.

'Gorgeous, just the right temperature, and look...loads of room for all of us. Jump in, my darlings...'

The offer was far too tempting to resist and, after sliding his briefs down and stepping out of them, Simon clambered in, giving small gasps of appreciation as the warm water bathed him.

Skye watched amused as Rhys joined them. 'Are you coming in or taking root?' Rhys giggled childishly.

'Not yet. I want to do my exercises first,' said Skye, his face beaming.

The day passed quickly and happily, with all the housemates now relaxed and content. The jacuzzi had been a masterstroke on the part of the production team, as it made life a little more enjoyable for the four guys. They had something new to think about, pushing the potential gloom of eviction from their minds. A picnic was organised for the afternoon, and the housemates lounged naked on blankets, eating sandwiches and strawberries in between bouts of jacuzzi fun. The day passed so rapidly that Matt's announcement of the impending vote caught them unawares and, disheartened, they shuffled into the house to write down their chosen evictee's name.

As expected, all four found it a difficult task. Rhys wrote the names of the other three on scraps of paper and pulled one out of his tightened fist, that being the only way to decide. William and Simon were equally distraught at having to choose one of their number. Skye made no mention of any problems he was having. With a casual ease he wrote down his nomination, folded it and placed it in the box, ready to be carried down to the gate for collection. Now all the guys had to do was wait out the next couple of hours until the name was announced by Matt.

As that time approached, the guys took their places in the living room, all nervous, all aware that this could be the end of their fun, knowing that whatever happened, they would soon be whisked away by car and back to the routine of their normal lives.

'Hello Boycam house, this is Matt speaking. Well, after a very entertaining week in the house, we have come to the moment where we have to evict another of you. It was obviously a hard task, knowing that you have all become friends. Whoever is chosen will have an hour to pack and be ready to leave. A car will be waiting for you outside the gate to take you home. Now, if you are all ready…the fifth person to leave the Boycam house is…Simon Ho.'

Interview with Simon Ho

'Well, I am sad to be gone from the house, but I did have a bloody good time in there. OK, there were some fights and squabbles, but generally the good times outweighed the bad. I am thrilled that I was given the chance to appear in the show and it has really changed me and my perceptions of life. When I returned to my job at the café, I was given a hero's welcome and I have made so many new friends. I've become like a local celebrity, and been invited to attend functions and host club evenings. It's been brilliant. I've even met a great man. A dot-com millionaire – he got out before the market took a downturn – who I think I've fallen for and he wants to set me up in my own business. I can't believe it's all happened so quickly.

'I suppose I will miss the pace of the house most. It was generally slow, but I liked that, as if you were on an extended holiday, with nothing to do but eat, sleep, do the odd challenge and have sex. And the sex was great! I had some fab times with Jackson, and that Rhys is a real stud muffin, if he did but know it. And that last session on the Saturday night after the erotic story readings – wow!

'I find it difficult to picture life without the others in it; I hope we'll all keep in touch, even Peter, who I've forgiven for being a backstabbing slut…seriously though, I'd like to see them all, and will probably invite them down to Brighton to the grand opening of my new club.

'My most lingering memory of the house was its smell. For some reason it had this strong musky odour of man. Even if we were all clean and showered and smothered in cologne, the place still had the smell of maleness. I guess it's something that happens when loads of men are together, like an army barracks possibly.

'I hope Rhys wins. He deserves to. He needs to win the money and head off into the wide blue yonder to see the world. I know that he'll have fun out there with his looks, and I could tell that he was getting more confident every day. It would be too bad if he just went back to his Welsh roots and vegetated.

'So, yes, in retrospect I am glad I was part of it, and would happily do it all again.'

WEEK SIX

Tuesday

The guys had slept well on Sunday night; the immense relief at not being evicted had flooded through them, and all the tension of the day had vanished, leaving dream-free, heavy slumbers. The night before, Simon had accepted his fate stoically, packing his things and disappearing with no fuss or trouble. He had hugged and kissed the remaining three and left the house with a cheery wave to them all from the gate.

'It's going to feel very odd this week,' said Rhys on Monday morning, as he filled the breakfast cafetière with hot water, and waited for the brown liquid to infuse. He looked tired, his hair spiky and uncombed. Skye appeared looking pristine as usual, having been up early, exercising and showering before the others had awoken.

'It certainly is.' He agreed with Rhys and grabbed a cup from the rack, and stared impatiently at the coffee, eager for its uplifting caffeine shot.

'Morning...' William ambled into the kitchen, his robe flapping open, revealing his nude form beneath. It was clear he didn't care. At this stage in their lives they had seen everything that everyone had to offer and so being coy about such things would be considered very strange. He slumped onto a bar stool, cup in hand.

It was indeed going to be an odd week. The house had been perfectly balanced with four guys in it, but now that it was down to three, the dynamic of the place would be awkward. There would be no one to pair off with, no one to have secret chats with, safe in the knowledge that the others also had a companion. If one went off with a friend, then inevitably someone would be left on his own. And at this stage of the proceedings, no one wanted to hurt the feelings of anyone else. It could prove to be a very traumatic seven days.

'Can I ask you a question?'

'Sure, fire away.'

'Are you still thinking my way?'

'Look, I'd rather not talk about that.'

'But I want to win.'

'We all want to win, but we aren't all being underhand about it.'

'Sometimes people need a little guidance, they need telling what to do. They need a helping hand to see what is the right course of action. That's all I'm doing.'

'I don't think that's fair...'

'Fuck what's fair. There is a large amount of money at stake, and I want to have my chance at winning it. If it means you win and I only get half, then at least I go away with something to show for my time here.'

'I don't like it.'

'I don't care. Look...it all seems to be working out as I'd hoped, so let's forget about all this and just enjoy the week ahead...OK?'

The weekly task duly arrived, in the form of an announcement from Matt. His voice crackled out from the hidden speaker on Monday afternoon, as the boys prepared for a day's sunbathing, standing about the living room, towels and lotion in hand.

'Hello, Boycam house, this is Matt speaking. So now the show hits an interesting stage. As we enter the final week, we have three of you left. This week's voting will happen earlier on Sunday at four o'clock, with the sixth eviction announcement at five. That person will have an hour to pack and he will leave the house at six. Then out of the remaining two housemates the winner will be announced at seven o'clock. The winner will be decided by the amount of points you have accrued for your weekly tasks throughout your stay in the Boycam house. But first things first; there is this week's challenge. It should prove quite fun and is in two parts, for which I hope you'll all rise to the occasion. At first this may seem a peculiar challenge, but I am sure you'll see the wisdom in such a task. This week we want you to find out as much as you can about your remaining housemates. Quiz them on their likes and dislikes, fears and fantasies, because on Saturday each one of you will be asked ten questions about the others. You will collectively be allowed three mistakes, and after that points will be deducted from your total score. This is not all though; we challenge you to spend the week naked. Anyone who even thinks about putting on clothes will forfeit points. If you don't believe you can do this, speak now...good. Then have a good week. Enjoy!'

Then the room fell silent.

'Right then. Let's get these off...' William keenly stepped out of his bathing trunks, and tossed them casually away. 'Could be interesting this, you know. A week naked. I've always wondered about the joys of naturism.'

'You are a bit of a pervert really, aren't you, William?' joked Rhys, standing up and taking off his trunks.

'At your service.' William laughed heartily, and led the others out into the garden, all of them naked and unashamed.

Naturally, the day's conversation turned to finding out those more intimate details which Matt required. Up until the moment they all went to bed, an occasional question would occur to one of the housemates and they would ask away, mentally storing the information in case it might prove useful. Did you ever have a pet? Who was your first kiss? What was the first movie you ever saw? What is your favourite sexual position? What is your most secret fantasy? Which film star would you most like to have sex with? The probing questions were fired off through out the day, with all the guys deciding to keep a notebook of the facts they discovered about each other. They were determined not to let themselves down this close to winning the money, and just one slip could jeopardise their chances irrevocably. Their dreams that night were full of strange and distorted images, of film stars and weird sex, of barking dogs and stolen kisses.

Tuesday was bright and warm, and after breakfast there was only one thing on the guys' minds. Sunbathing.

'Which one of the eight guys in the house did you fancy the most?' The question that William posed took Rhys by surprise, as they smoothed suntan lotion on each other's back.

'Now that's a rotten question.'

'I know. So what is your answer, luscious one?' William lay on his stomach, his chin cradled in his hands, grinning like a proverbial Cheshire cat.

Rhys didn't answer, weighing the question in his mind. It was a rotten question. That first day, he had been so overawed by the whole Boycam experience that he hadn't really thought about who he had fancied. It had taken him a few days to settle in and get used to the extreme circumstances, and in that time he had been constantly bothered by Skye. He wasn't used to being in the company of such an individual. Coming from the sheltered background of the Welsh valleys, the notion of a male stripper and porn actor had scared him. He had grown to care a lot about Skye in recent weeks and even felt himself falling for the guy in a deeper way. But he wasn't the one he first fancied. Mulling it over, he came to his conclusion.

'Colin. I think I fancied Colin.' His answer was brief and to the point.

'Why Colin?' William was intrigued. He had watched Rhys grow in confidence and stature, seeing a handsome young man finding himself, and he liked what he saw. Secretly he hoped that he had been the one that figured in Rhys' fantasies.

'I liked the look of him, and he seemed a nice guy. What I wanted from a boyfriend was someone who I could take home to meet the family.'

'So you thought of him as boyfriend material, did you?'

'No. Just that he seemed the nicest of the bunch...at first sight, of course. Once I'd got to know everyone better, then I realised that my fancies had changed.'

This was absorbing news. 'So, who heads your fantasy list now then?' William was desperate to know. Rhys was the kind of young man that he had been longing to get involved with for years and here he was before him, friendly, handsome, sexually exciting, and naked. What more could any self-respecting shirtlifter want?

'I don't think it'd be appropriate to say. Not now that we are down to the three of us.'

'Spoilsport.' He turned to the third housemate. 'What about you Skye? Who did you fancy?'

Stretching his muscular arms behind him and without opening his eyes, Skye said 'Hmmm, not sure. I was rather taken with Jackson. He had a great body. And if I have to be honest, I was intrigued by Jost. He was a bit lacking in the personality department, but I think he knew a thing or two about great sex.'

'Interesting choice.' A slight note of mischief crept into William's voice. 'So, did you ever do anything with Jost?'

'No, sadly. I was tempted. But as we didn't know each other so well in those early days, I didn't have the courage to ask. I bet he was a good fuck though, especially with all that Tantric stuff.'

'Was Simon a good fuck?' Rhys surprised the other two with his question. But it was something he wanted to know.

'Yes, actually. He had a way of gripping me deep inside; it was incredible. Like waves of muscle action all over my cock. It was amazing.'

Wriggling uncomfortably on the blanket, William gave a cough. 'Careful now, you'll be giving me a pan-handle...'

'Really? Perhaps you should cover yourself up.' Skye's tone was light, and he sat up to see William's reaction.

'Not bloody likely, old boy. I'm quite getting used to being starkers; it's quite refreshing. Letting the air get to the bits and pieces. Don't you think so, sweetheart?' He patted Rhys' bottom, letting his hand lie there, gently squeezing the buttocks fondly.

'I do. And if you don't stop that, I'll...' Rhys tailed off, unsure of what to say or do next. The warmth of the day had permeated every part of his body, and talk of sex had begun to arouse him. The contact of William's hand of his tanned arse was rather nice. Sobriety told him to stop, but then again he was in a house with two other naked gay men, why should he stop?

'You'll what?' William's mouth creased up into a lopsided grin. 'You'll begin to enjoy it?'

'Absolutely, so stop it!' Rhys sat up, cross-legged, the evidence of his semi-arousal quite clear to the other two. 'Let's not be stupid about this. We are three healthy, attractive gay men, living together in this bizarre place. We are spending the whole time without any clothes on. There are bound to be temptations. There are going to be moments when we really want to have sex; it's only natural. But I think we should try to control ourselves. Show some restraint. Otherwise the sex just becomes part of the everyday, mundane life we have. If we wait and hold back from doing it whenever we want, then it'll be more special. Won't it?'

Skye and William looked at the lad with wonder.

'Since when did you become so grown up?' Skye asked with a puzzled frown.

'Since I came in here and learned a few things about myself. I'm not the innocent youngster I was five weeks ago. I've done a lot of thinking and wondering, and I've reached quite a few conclusions. And there are certain things that I'm not going to put up with.'

This was a peculiar thing to say and William wanted to know what he meant. 'Like what?'

'Things. That's all I'm going to say for the moment. Now are you going to rub some more of that gunk on my back or are you going to sit there like a frog with your mouth open?'

Friday

The week continued as it had started. Rhys, Skye and William made the most of their company, revelling in the sunshine, and in the effervescent water of the bubbling jacuzzi. No mention had been made of the forthcoming vote and the fact that one of them would soon emerge the winner with ten thousand pounds in his pocket.

The household chores had been equally shared out by Rhys, who had taken the lead in most of the household activities. Skye and William were happy for him to do so, as it took the onus off of them, and they had nothing dull to think about. Cooking, cleaning and other boring tasks were allocated by the Welsh lad, and the house was running smoothly and harmoniously. The only note of animosity was on Thursday evening when Rhys threw a sopping wet towel at Skye, threatening him with no dinner if he didn't go upstairs and clean the mess he'd just left in the bathroom. Not wanting an argument, Skye complied, and was back downstairs in time for Rhys to serve up the casserole he'd finished creating.

The enforced nudity had also ceased to be anything of note. After just a couple of days, the sight of the other housemates with their equipment on display failed to have any erotic effect whatsoever, and all thoughts of constant, steamy sex evaporated. Whenever Skye,

William or Rhys saw each other they saw a friend, not a naked man.

By Friday evening, the house was quiet. William was reading on his bed, wanting some peace and quiet after their filling dinner, and Skye was having a doze in an armchair.

'I think it's time we quizzed each other, to see what we know. We want to be ready for the test tomorrow.' Rhys was in an ebullient mood, and was determined to do the best he could. Gathering the guys in the kitchen, he opened a bottle of cider, grabbed three glasses and led them out to the garden, switching on the jacuzzi, and clambering into it.

'Here's to a successful test,' he smiled raising a glass and downing it in one.

'Cheers.' William and Skye chorused. They had absorbed as much as they could about each other's lives, and were ready to see what they knew. Sitting in the hot-tub with a bottle of cider was as good a place as any to try out their knowledge.

The evening air was balmy and played across their exposed torsos while the water burbled and caressed their lower halves.

'This is the life...' William looked at Rhys through his empty glass. 'I can honestly say I am totally content.'

With one eyebrow raised quizzically, Rhys said 'Don't get too settled. Let's have a try at the challenge first.'

'OK, ask me a question.' Skye swished the water between his legs and waited.

After a moment's pause, Rhys asked, 'Where was William born?'

'Easy. Cambridge. Next question.' Skye looked smug, crossed his arms and waited.

'What are William's cats called?'

'Easy. Patsy, Edina and Saffy. Next question.'

'What is William's favourite wine?'

'Easy. Crozes-Hermitage. Next question.'

This smug attitude was beginning to bug Rhys greatly. He turned to William. 'Ask him a question then.'

Thinking for a moment, William asked 'What are Rhys' brothers called?'

'Now that's a good question, give me a minute...' Pressing his fingers against his forehead, Skye was lost in thought for a moment. 'Er... there's a Robert, er... Hugh... and I can't remember the others... fuck.' He spat out the curse and punched his fist into the water.

'Lloyd and Aldwyn. Ha...that's one point down. Now ask me one.' A triumphant gleam shone in Rhys' eye. He grinned maliciously at Skye and waited for a question.

'Right, this'll fix him,' said Skye, sitting forward, staring at Rhys, eyes wide. 'What was the name of my first porno movie?'

Rhys grinned. 'Oh, too easy, *A Back Passage to India*. You are the weakest link...goodbye.' Crowing with satisfaction, Rhys ducked beneath the surface of the frothing water and emerged a moment later, smoothing down his hair.

'Hang on smart arse, we've only just started. Where did I get my first blow job?'

Rhys whistled through his teeth. 'Hmm, that's a tough one. It could be anywhere. I mean, you've probably dropped your trousers all over the globe.'

'Cheeky sod.' Skye gave Rhys a mock punch on the jaw, then dropped his hand into the water feeling for the lad's thigh, which he gave a good squeeze. 'Well?'

'I think it was in the toilets near your house. Am I right?'

'Damn. Yes, you are. And who was it?'

'An older guy, I seem to recall. Was he a trucker?'

Skye had to admit defeat. 'Yes. All right, this'll floor you. What is my real name?'

Rhys was taken aback. He had only ever known this muscular blond hunk as Skye. The thought of his real name had never entered his head. 'I have to say that I don't know. Have you ever told us?'

'No, I haven't. It's a secret between me and my maker.'

'So why bring it up now?'

Skye pondered for a second and then said 'To shut you up, I suppose.'

William couldn't hold back any longer. Curiosity was pouring out from every pore. 'So, what is your real name? Go on, you can tell us.'

Skye dropped his voice and moved closer to his housemates. He didn't want the eavesdropping microphones to catch what he was about to say. 'Martin...Martin Greaves. Dull, isn't it? Not the right kind of name for a celebrated porno star. But don't you ever call me that or I will kill you...understand?'

His intentions were clear, and the steely tone in the voice meant that neither Rhys or William were about to argue.

'No problem...Marty-babes.' William ducked out of the way from Skye's fist, which made a peremptory pass at him. There was a dangerous look on Skye's face. William knew not to push that particular joke any further. But for the first time he registered that expression on Skye's face. It was quite hard and unforgiving, the look of someone you'd not want to cross. Perhaps there were darker depths to Skye, depths that William had no intention of exploring.

'Right then, I've got a question for William,' said Skye, the menacing frown gone from his face. 'What is Rhys' sexual fantasy?'

Taking a few seconds to ponder this, William chewed on the end of a finger. His skin was beginning to pucker and shrivel; a sure sign he'd been in the water for too long.

'I'm not actually sure about that. This lad tends not to tell people about that side of his mind.' He turned to Rhys and stroked the side of his face, feeling the rough stubble that had begun to poke through. 'What does really turn you on?'

Rhys said nothing. William was right about one thing – he didn't like talking about sex; it seemed wrong. Up until he entered the Boycam house, Rhys thought sex was something private and personal, not to be talked about or shared with other people. But his attitude had changed, and now he was fully prepared to share his fantasies. He had nothing to lose. He would probably never see these two guys again after the weekend. And as for the cameras and the public watching the show – well, they might as well be party to his thoughts too. They might even love him for them.

'Well...if you must know...I have quite a few fantasy ideas in my head.'

'Marvellous,' countered William. 'What's the first?'

'I'd like to be tied down to the bed, with my hands and feet spread apart, and have a guy explore every inch of my body with his tongue, licking and biting from my ears all the way down to my toes, going nowhere near my cock and balls, saving them until last, then taking his time; he'll begin to lick my cock, starting at the top, and inching down, not sucking it yet, just licking, and when he's got it nice and hard, he'll blow me and all the time I'm unable to move or resist or anything.'

'Jeez, that's hot.' Skye had let his head fall back onto the side of the hot-tub, and his eyes were closed, picturing the scene. Under the surface of the water he was fondling his cock.

Continuing unabashed, Rhys said, 'Then when I'm about to come, he'll stop and untie me. Then I'll tie him to the bed, face down, legs spread, and I'll get my cock rubbered and ready and I'll slowly fuck him. I've never fucked anyone before, and think this would be the horniest way to try it.'

'Me first...' William's mouth was open and his eyes wide with desire. The images conjured up had aroused him totally, his cock sticking straight up through the swirling surface of the water.

'But then,' continued Rhys, 'I also want to be held down over a chair, and have some hunky guy smack my arse. Just gently, enough to get the skin tingling a little. I'm not into pain; I just like the idea of being slightly subjugated...I've never told anyone this before.'

Skye squeezed his thigh again in an encouraging fashion. 'You are doing brilliantly. Then what?' He wanted to know more. This young innocent lad was really turning him on with the pictures in his mind, and he needed them to continue.

'Then when my arse is pink and glowing, he'll keep me bent over the chair, and he'll start to lick my arse, poking his tongue in; then he'll fuck me, long and slow.'

This was too much for the other two. The words and images pouring from Rhys' inexperienced mouth had provoked an intense reaction. Their cocks had swollen and stiffened, and they needed relief. If they were both honest, they wanted sex. And now seemed a perfect opportunity.

Rhys had turned himself on with his verbalisation of his hidden dreams, the fantasies he had never told anyone before. They were thoughts that he kept locked away in his inner self, and tried to deny, knowing that life in a small Welsh town was not compatible with such notions. But here and now, sitting immersed in a hot-tub, shared with two other attractive gay men, it was the right thing to do, to share his soul. And strangely, he was ready for what Skye did next.

Sliding across the tub, Skye leaned in and put his hand around Rhys neck, pulling him in for a kiss. Tongues and lips met, hard and fast, pushing deep, as William looked on enthralled. He stood up in the tub and began to stroke his cock, encouraging it to its maximum rigidity.

The kiss between Skye and Rhys came to a natural conclusion, and the two guys stood knee deep in the bubbling water, eye to eye, drinking each other in, seeing what they could see deep in the other's face. What they saw was lust. But it was Rhys who made the next move. With both his hands planted squarely on Skye's shoulders, he pushed him down to his knees, until his eye line was level with the lad's stiff cock. Looking down into Skye's open face, Rhys spoke slowly and clearly, his voice unwavering and determined.

'If you want my cock, you are going to have to beg for it.

Understand?' No reply came. 'Understand?' he said again with a slightly fierce intonation.

'Yes.' Skye nodded.

'So beg me…'

Swallowing hard, Skye realised he was lost for words. He wasn't used to being in the supplicant position. This was a wholly new experience, and he wasn't sure if he liked it. For the moment, though, he knew he had to go along with it.

'I want to suck your cock, Rhys.'

'Make me believe that…' The lad had grown harder, meaner and was now relishing the reversal of character.

'I want to suck your cock. Please, please let me.' The words almost choked in Skye's throat.

'I don't believe you.'

'Please, I want to take your cock in my mouth and suck it.' Skye realised that he actually meant what he was saying. Rhys' meat stood gloriously in front of him and he longed to taste it.

'Open your mouth.' The command was clear and Skye did what he was told, licking his lips to wet them, and letting his mouth fall open.

'Show me your tongue.'

He did, letting it unfold until his mouth was wide. Rhys moved closer, and let the head of his cock just rest lightly on the tongue 'Don't do anything.' His tone was firm. He rested the cock-head on the warm, quivering tongue, eyes locked on Skye, brow furrowed.

For Skye the temptation was to take that cock deep inside his mouth and suck, but he knew he was forbidden. It was like eating a jam doughnut and not licking your lips. The natural reflex was to suck. Squatting in the water, with this hard dick resting teasingly on his tongue was torture.

'Good. Now keep your mouth open. I don't want you to close your mouth…understand?' Rhys was clearly in control and loving every second. Here was the real Rhys finally emerging from his shell, the highly sexual being with desires and feelings. This was the start of his new life.

Skye nodded. With studied slowness, Rhys slid his cock into Skye's open mouth, feeling the gentle frisson as it passed the teeth and made contact with the furry surface of his tongue and the pulsing walls of the oral cavity.

His reflexes took over and Skye closed his mouth, exerting suction on the solid pole. But the stinging blow that Rhys smacked across his cheek made him stop. He sat back in astonishment.

'What the fuck?' He had never had anyone discipline him before, and he was damned if he was going to let this Welsh upstart be the first.

'Shut up.' Rhys' tone silenced him, and he sat back in the water. 'Come here.' Rhys pointed at William, who had watched this scenario with amazement. Rhys had become someone else in front of his eyes; a hard dominating character who was leading the situation, and William found it incredibly horny to watch. His cock was stiffer than it had been for ages. He obeyed the instruction and squatted before Rhys.

'Do you want to suck my cock?' asked Rhys commandingly.

'Yes please, Rhys. I really want to suck your cock.'

Placing a hand behind William's head, Rhys guided him towards the object of his desire, watching entranced as William closed his mouth about the shaft and began to suck, sliding inch after inch of rock-hard meat between his moist lips. Rhys sat back on the tub wall and stared down at the man before him, watching his mouth being engulfed by that willing mouth. He was a good cocksucker, working his tongue around the head, lapping up the pre-come. Skye was watching every move, and it was clear he wanted some of the action. With a gesture of his head, Rhys invited Skye closer, and so in a few seconds both of the guys were at Rhys' feet, fighting over his cock. Taking it in turns, first one and then the other slurped on the lad's weapon, as if they were competing in some kind of erotic competition – the 'who was the best at giving head' contest, each determined to pleasure Rhys more. They settled themselves either side of Rhys' cock and clamped their lips to the shaft, sliding up and down in unison, increasing the speed, and then one after the other let the head pop into their mouths for a sucking, before resuming the previous sliding attentions.

For Rhys, he was in heaven, for both Skye and William were treating his cock to the best blow job he'd ever had, and knew he probably would ever have in the rest of his life. He was going to enjoy this. Standing up, he grabbed both the guys by the hair and fucked their faces, pounding one mouth and then swivelling and filling the other. Skye's tongue worked along the shaft as it plunged into his mouth, slathering it and swishing about its length. William just took the cock deep, right up to the back of his throat, feeling the entirety of it pull out and plunge back with every stroke.

'Suck my cock, yeah...' Rhys found himself crying out, unembarrassed by the corny nature of the words, so overwhelmed by the hot action he was receiving. Both guys before him were now gasping for breath. They had never been in such a hot situation before and for Skye, who had had his share of erotic scenes, this beat anything he'd ever done.

'Stand up.' Rhys was still in charge, and his two housemates obeyed without question. He turned to William, whose mouth was ringed with spit. 'Fetch some condoms and lube. Go on.' His tone was clear, and his intention obvious. William hopped out of the tub and obeyed, dashing into the house, his cock still rigid. Skye stared at Rhys wondering where this evening was heading. It had already taken a few unexpected turns and he knew it wasn't over yet. He grabbed his dick and gave it a squeeze, satisfied at its hardness, and more than pleased with its size. He knew that no man could choose a dick size and most had to make do with what they'd been born with, but he also knew he had been one of the lucky ones. Most guys who saw it wanted it, and he was usually more than happy to oblige. And if the sight of his cock in some porno flick helped guys to whack themselves off, then he was equally delighted. Something told him, though, that tonight he'd need to call on all his stamina and sexual reserves. Don't let me down now, he silently said, gripping and releasing his throbbing meat.

'Here you are,' said William breathlessly, as he charged back into the garden, his fingers clutching a handful of metallic packets.

'Good. Now come here.' Rhys motioned to William, who hopped back in the tub and moved to Rhys' side. He let himself be bent over the wall of the tub, holding his breath, knowing what the lad had in mind. 'Now eat his arse.' The command was aimed at Skye, who knew better than to ignore the order. Swiftly, he knelt down and spread wide the cheeks, noting that William had eased his thighs as wide as he could. He saw the bollocks hanging between them, swinging and trembling, dripping with foamy water. This was going to be a pleasure. His tongue dabbed at the hole, which flinched at the touch, snapping tight, then relaxing after a few seconds. It was clean and smelt of soap, and with his eager tongue Skye went to work, licking up and down the puckered skin, then darting the tip inside the knot of muscle, feeling it relax enough to let the tongue's end penetrate. He spat onto the hole and watched the gob roll down the skin, before he licked a finger and pushed it at the ring, feeling the muscle give way, and hearing a small gasp escape from William's lips. The sound of a condom packet being ripped made Skye look up, and then he saw Rhys rolling it down his hard prick. He raised an eyebrow as Rhys handed him a condom and sachet of opaque lubricant. In a flash he understood. And as the realisation hit him his cock swelled again, ready for the task in hand. Quickly and surely he slipped the condom on and slathered it in lube, mimicking Rhys' recent actions, and they stood side by side, hard and prepared.

William had stood to watch proceedings and gasped as Rhys

pushed him forward again over the tub wall and positioned the head of his cock at William's waiting hole.

This was Rhys' first time at fucking a man, and so he momentarily wondered if he'd be able to do it. He kept the picture in his mind of Skye fucking Simon the other evening, and knew it couldn't be that difficult. William's hole wanted that cock inside and so it relaxed momentarily, enough to let the head of Rhys' cock slide in. William grunted, but it was a grunt of pleasure, and so with renewed enthusiasm Rhys pushed on. He was unprepared for the sensation that followed as his dick was swallowed by William's sphincter; the muscles seemed to grip him tightly, drawing it down in pulsing ripples until he knew he could go no further. Rhys realised he had been holding his breath and he let it out in a hissing stream, inhaling through his nose and grasping what he'd achieved. His cock was buried in William's arse right up to the base, and that ring of tight muscles held him firm. Gritting his teeth, he pulled the cock back, watching the brown opening contract around the sliding shaft. Then without warning he shoved it back inside with such force that William screamed with pleasure. This was it. This was fucking a man, pounding your cock inside him until he screams.

Bending William over the side of the tub meant that Rhys' arse was also exposed and, as he was caught up in his current position, he had forgotten about Skye. The touch of Skye's hand on his arse made Rhys jump. Of course, there was more to come. He moaned as the head of Skye's cock butted at his own hole. His mind raced, could this actually be happening? Were they going to do a double-fuck? Could Skye manage to get his cock up inside Rhys' hole at the same time? Rhys desperately hoped so. This would be an evening to remember all his life.

The massive cock-head pushed insistently at Rhys' arsehole, and for a moment fear flooded him. It was too big, and it would hurt, and he wanted Skye to stop. But the blond didn't. Rhys was subjected to the most amazing sensation ever. With a grunt of delight, Skye penetrated him, and the pain sizzled through Rhys, blinding him, searing and stretching. He cried out, his body tensing up, feeling his sphincter squeeze tight about the cock inside him. William cried out too, a groaning, lust-filled cry, as Rhys' reaction had forced his cock deeper inside William's arse. He didn't want to appear unable to take it, and so he bit his lip, and accepted his fate. For what seemed an age he wanted the pain to stop, for the monster in him to go, but it didn't; it kept sliding up, deeper and deeper into him, until incredibly it became easier, and Rhys was full of the astounding wonder of having another man's cock up inside him. It felt like no other feeling. He had experienced nothing like it, but silently hoped he would again. The sensation of fullness took his breath away, the sweet pain flooding his mind and body. Then Skye took command. Grabbing Rhys' hips he began to fuck, slamming away hard and with a vicious energy that drove the breath from Rhys' lungs. He knew he had to give as good as he was getting, so after a few moments of gauging the rhythm, Rhys started to fuck William, until all three of them were a solid pumping machine, all living for the moment, all intent on each other's pleasure and nothing more. Cries of satisfaction and lust filled the garden, the sounds of the bubbling water and the slapping of sweaty thigh against sweaty thigh.

The pace grew faster and more furious, both Rhys and Skye able to pull himself out from the hole he was fucking and plunge back in unison, filling each aching passage with their pounding. Each one of them was utterly engrossed. The world and the Boycam house had ceased to exist, and the only thing in their universe was the slamming of these rigid cocks. By the laws of nature, this constant action had to come to a close soon. Both Rhys and Skye could feel the come boiling up inside their balls, and knew that a climax was inevitable. Skye pulled out from Rhys' arse and quickly snapped the condom from his cock, wrapping his fist about its hardened length. He watched as Rhys' hole slowly squeezed itself shut, and then the lad pulled free from

William, also yanking the rubber off. With his other hand, Rhys grabbed William by the shoulder and spun him round onto his knees. With eyes glistening, William positioned himself between Rhys and Skye, mouth open, tongue extended, moaning as Rhys' prick moved closer, and pushed between his lips. He had been sucking for only a couple of seconds when the lad came, crying out as a huge stream of come was released, flowing down William's throat, disappearing in triumphant gulps. Skye was also there, his hand flying up and down his dick, and in a yell of victory he came too, squirting out a gush of hot spunk which landed over William's face, splattering in irregular blobs.

It took fully ten minutes for all three of them to recover. Breathing finally slowed and their heartbeats eventually got back to normal. They sat, silently in the tub, the water flowing around their satiated bodies, washing the spunk and sweat from their exhausted forms. Rhys opened his arms wide, an invitation to the others, who duly moved closer and joined him in a hug, revelling in the warmth and the swooshing water around them. They had reached Nirvana. A place of utter contentment, that made this whole Boycam thing worthwhile. Whether they lost or won, they didn't care anymore. This was what being gay was all about. Enjoying the marvel of another man, and becoming one with him – or with them, in this case. They had known true ecstasy, and they would be better people for it.

Sunday

The three guys had never been closer to any other person in their lives than they were with each other. That final day they knew that something special was coming to an end and an air of total depression fell upon the house. A week before they had all been miserable about voting out one of them, but somehow today was even worse. Today they would leave the house, one of them a winner, and it was possible that they might never see each other again.

Lunch was a quiet affair, with only the barest small-talk peppering the conversation, and their chicken salads were hardly touched. They hardly talked about the test they'd been given the previous day, when Matt's questions had not foxed them. In fact, they knew the answers to everything he asked them. As his voice posed a question, each individual contestant fired off the correct answer, and at the conclusion to the test he immediately announced that they had all passed with flying colours and had got nothing wrong.

But now, after they'd eaten as much lunch as their desultory appetites would let them, they sloped off to different parts of the house for an afternoon siesta. Rhys lay on his bed, with the curtains drawn, the cool shade necessary for him, as he needed to think. He had dreaded this day coming, for many reasons. He would miss the camaraderie of the house, the friendly companionship that the other guys had provided. Growing up in a house full of four other brothers, Rhys enjoyed the rigours of constant male company, and being gay he somehow needed to be amongst men as he badly as needed air. Only in the last few weeks had he realised that it had to be gay company, as he finally knew that he was happy with his sexuality and it wasn't something to hide or to be ashamed of. He knew that when he returned to Tredegar, and saw again the bustling Welsh town that he would be a different person – a stronger man with a fresh outlook on life and a determination to enjoy living it. Here in the Boycam house he had grown, like a plant nurtured by its environment, watered by the people within, and was now tall and independent, able to cope on his own. He knew that life would seem a little dull after this, and that it was up to him to make the most of it. But there was something niggling at the back of his mind, a situation that needed resolving and he made up his mind to do something about it before the day was over.

The garden was quiet and radiating in the sun's warmth. Skye spread out a blanket for a last few hours' sunbathing. He was also deep in thought. There were things he'd done in the house which he regretted. At the time they seemed like the right thing to do, but know he wondered if he'd gone too far. Like Rhys, he also knew that he would miss the Boycam house, and everything about it. In his life he was the one who made all the decisions, who drove himself forward, taking himself from place to place, from job to job, usually enjoying himself and all that came his way. Here in the house, all that had been taken from him. All he had to do was get up, and do what the housemates and the production team expected him to do. He had no worries, no problems and he liked it. As if his real life was on hold and this unreal fantasy life could be lived. When he left the house this evening he would be back to normalcy and he wasn't sure if he wanted that anymore. Living like a vagabond, hiring out his body to anyone who wanted it. Surely he was worth more than that. He had done many things that he was ashamed of and he wanted to live a better life from now on. But he had recently reached the conclusion that there was a nagging emptiness in his life. He needed someone. He was lonely. The time spent with the other guys had shown him the fun that could be had sharing your life with others. And he now wanted to share his life with someone wonderful. A young lad from Wales. But he knew that he was not the sort of guy that Rhys would want. He closed his eyes and tried to snooze.

William pottered about the kitchen, tidying up, washing the lunch dishes, in a meditative mood. He had entered himself for the show as a bit of a laugh, for something to do, a way of escaping from the mundanity of his stockbroker life. All of his friends knew that William was a bit of a joker, always ready with a lewd quip or a dirty story; someone who could be relied upon to help a party get going and who enjoyed the finer things in life. They didn't see the morose loner, the guy who put on an act, afraid that, if he didn't laugh and fool around, no one would like him. In the Boycam house the other guys had quickly grown tired of his act and he had begun to drop his defences. He had let Rhys get to know what he was really like and soon the others saw that he was a nice bloke. He had soon been drawn into their lives and they had seen the real William. And he hoped they had liked what they had seen. When the show was over and they went their separate ways, he desperately wished that they would keep in touch, as a means of him keeping in touch with his true self. Looking up at the clock he saw that it was nearly three-thirty. Wiping his hands, he went in search of the others. The Boycam experience was drawing to a close.

'It's nearly voting time, you know...' William called out from the front door at Skye's comatose form.

'Coming,' yawned Skye with a stretch. He jumped to his feet and moved with panther-like smoothness into the house.

I shall definitely miss looking at you, my love, thought William, patting Skye's bare arse as he passed.

'Make the most of it,' Skye muttered as he strode into the hall, making William stop in his tracks. Had he read his mind? William decided not.

Seated around the living room with their nomination papers in hand, the three remaining contestants looked wistfully at each other. They hoped that the one they voted out wouldn't take it personally, and would accept eviction in the true spirit of the game.

The votes were duly cast and the voting box carried to the gate, then they settled again in the living room. As they sat, the lilting strains of a Frank Sinatra song poured into the room through the hidden speakers and, as if a cloud had been lifted, they all smiled.

'God, this is so nerve-wracking.' William stood and headed into the kitchen, returning quickly with a bottle of white wine that he'd been chilling in the fridge. 'I shall need some help to get through the next hour.'

'Pour me one of those,' said Skye, throwing his legs over the arm of his chair, comfortably rearranging his genitals. 'I'll need something to help the time pass.'

'I can think of something we could do,' piped up Rhys, a sly grin on his boyish features.

'I couldn't possibly... I'm too nervous to think about sex. You wouldn't be able to, would you?' Skye poked at his slumbering cock, and smiled up at Rhys. 'Sorry... he's taking a nap.'

The hour quickly passed, filled up by light conversation and Sinatra, and when Matt's voice crackled into life and the music faded, they were brought up sharp. The moment for the next eviction had come.

'Hello, Boycam house. This Matt speaking. Thank you for all your efforts this last week, especially over the challenge. We were very impressed by your knowledge of each other, and were delighted that you took to naturism so readily. You are now all free to dress again. But to more important matters. I have the result of the sixth vote in front of me, and that person will have one hour to pack and be ready to leave. A car will be waiting at the front gate to take them home. Then at seven o'clock we will announce the winner. So...the sixth person to leave the Boycam house will be... William Blake-Harper.

Interview with William Blake-Harper

'Of course, I am absolutely devastated. I really thought that getting down to the last three meant I was in with a chance of winning, and I really believed I had that money in my grasp. Not that I needed it, of course, it just would have been nice to be declared the winner.

'The whole Boycam thing has changed me a lot; I think you can see that. I went in a rather loud chap, boorish and jokey, and I came out a different person. It was Rhys who helped me to see what I was like. And he helped me to change. I owe him a lot, and since I came out I've been more relaxed and mature, less hyped up and over the top in my behaviour. I think a more attractive person. Don't you? He was definitely the one man in there that I could have lost my heart over, in fact I nearly did. Although Skye came a very close second. It's hard talking about it, actually, because those two became such close friends that picturing them as lovers is odd.

'I did get on with all the chaps in the house, I think, although it did take a couple of weeks for us all to settle down and find our feet. I felt sorry for the two evicted early on, as they didn't get to experience the real joy of the place. I'm not saying it wasn't hard...it was, but it became our lives, and all we had to think about every day was what to eat, and what we'd do to pass the time and who we'd have sex with...if possible!

'I shall definitely say that it was the most wonderful experience of my life. It does mean that I won't be able to go back to being a stock-broker. Life is too precious to live in a dull way. I have got a book deal about my time in the house, and I've a book of poetry up my sleeve that I want to try to get published.

'I can't say who should have been the winner. Both Skye and Rhys are smashing blokes and I think at that stage of the show everyone was a winner.'

The Result

The hugs and kisses as William left were real and heartfelt. Both Skye and Rhys were sorry to see him go. William was relieved and saddened at the same time, waving at them as the car drove away and the garden gate shut, imprisoning the two remaining contestants for only a short time more.

Skye led the way, slowly and wearily back into the house, heading straight to the kitchen, searching for more alcohol.

Rhys followed behind, at a distance, certain that now was the time to raise a subject that had been on his mind for a while.

'Skye...?'

The blond turned from the fridge, a victorious grin on his face and a bottle of wine in his hand. 'What?'

'Why did you do it?'

'Do what?'

Rhys took his time. 'Do all that secret stuff...I mean talk to the guys and try to influence their voting.'

Skye put down the bottle and crossed the room, taking Rhys by the arm and whispering in his ear.

'Keep your voice down.' He led Rhys into the garden, away from where he thought any microphones could pick up their illicit conversation.

'I only did what I thought was right.'

'Really? Making people vote the way you want? That can't be right.'

Skye's voice was more urgent now. 'It worked though, didn't it? We are both still here…look…' he paused, suddenly deflated, all the previous bravado suddenly evaporated. 'At the time I thought it was the right thing to do. I thought if I didn't help things along, then I'd be evicted. I never dreamed that I would really end up in the last two. And with you of all people. I am sorry about what I did, but it can't be undone. Do you forgive me?'

A million thoughts crashed around Rhys' head and he needed to think. 'I don't know. Just go away, will you?' He crossed the garden and re-entered the house; slowly padded upstairs and sat on his bed, contemplatively.

Five minutes later came Skye's knock on the door. 'Can I talk to you?' His voice was plaintive and uneasy, and Rhys nodded, watching him nervously sit on the edge of his bed.

'Well…?'

'Look Rhys, it didn't really worry me before, not when the house was full of other people; I thought what I was doing was the only course of action. I wanted to win and thought that a little cheating wouldn't hurt. But now that it's just the two of us left, I feel like I am here under false pretences.'

'I think you did a bad thing, and I think that because of your swaying of the votes, and influencing people, I shouldn't be here at all, and I'm having trouble coming to terms with it. I reckon I'd have been out of here a lot earlier if you'd have let things work out naturally. It feels wrong.'

'But you do like me, don't you? And we've had some great fun here, haven't we?' Skye almost pleaded with Rhys. He knew that he had gone too far. Had broken the rules of the Boycam house. But he hoped that his machinations had been sly and devious enough not to be noticed by the production team. He assumed that they hadn't.

'Yes, we have had fun, and I have feelings for you; I can't deny it.'

'So...'

'So nothing. I will be honest and say that I had high hopes of seeing you on the outside.'

Skye lowered his eyes. 'Me too.'

'But I don't know if I can actually trust you. Sure, I have fancied you something rotten, and had some fantastic sex, but in the back of my mind now is the fact that you cheated. I don't know if I can accept that.'

Skye nodded and stood. With one last glance at Rhys, he left the bedroom and made his way downstairs.

Both Skye and Rhys were seated in the living room, both now fully dressed, with their cases packed, ready for the climax of the show. Even though there were only two of them now left, the atmosphere was tense, and they both longed for the hour to arrive and for Matt to get on with it.

They had hardly spoken another word to each other since their conversation in the bedroom earlier. Rhys' mind was still whirling with many thoughts. Skye had sunk into a deep silence too, brought on by a mixture of guilt and anxiety.

The loudspeaker crackled into life for the last time as Matt's voice resonated.

'Hello to the two remaining Boycam housemates. Skye and Rhys. Well, from our point of view, it has been a wonderful experience. The people who made up the house proved worthy contestants, but it has now come down to you two and a winner has to be announced. We do have a winner, a clear winner in fact. And I want to make it clear that this person has won because of the amount of points he has earned during his stay in the house and for no other reason. Please do not take losing personally, as it is no such thing.

'There has to be a victor and a vanquished and at last I can announce the winner of Boycam. The person who will go home with ten thousand pounds and be declared the winner is...Skye Blue.'

Interview with Rhys Llewellyn

'I was completely stunned. After all that had happened, I could not believe that Skye had actually won. It wasn't just the money, but the fact that I'd spent so much time in that place and come out with nothing. On reflection, though, that is not strictly true. I have come out of there with a different attitude. I have become a man, if you like.

'When the winner was announced, I just sat there open-mouthed. I guess I should have congratulated Skye, given him a kiss or something, but I didn't have the heart. He stared at me, also unable to believe he'd done it. I suppose in my naïve way I thought that dishonesty never pays, and I was wrong.

'We made our way down to the gate where Matt came to meet us and to show us to our chauffeur-driven limousines, which drove us to the production office for a big party to celebrate the end of the show. Matt drove with Skye in his car and I went on alone, utterly miserable. Not just because I'd lost, but because of the way in which Skye had won.

'When we arrived at the head office in Soho, I saw the first car had drawn up and Matt had gone in, although oddly Skye was still sitting in it. I didn't even look at him as I went inside the building. The office boardroom was full of people, mostly production company bods, a few from the gay press and, surprisingly, the other Boycam guys. William was there, and Simon and Jost, Peter and Colin, and Jackson. It was lovely seeing them. But as I went in, everyone was quiet. Matt took me to one side and said that in the car he'd had a conversation with Skye, who told him what he'd done. All about the vote rigging. Skye had told him he didn't want to win under false pretences and so he pulled out of the programme. This meant that I was actually now the winner! Everyone hugged me and we celebrated like it was going out of fashion. No one spoke of Skye that night, and he seemed to have been wiped from everyone's memory. I got everyone's phone number, promising to keep in touch. I also got Skye's from Matt, because we have a lot to talk about. I am hoping to meet up with him next week, as in spite of what he did…no…because of what he did at the end, I think I want to be his friend still. To be honest, I still have feelings for him, and if he has them for me, then I want to see if we can't give it a go. Well…it's a short life and you only have one chance to live it. I reckon that given the opportunity and a little work on his character, Skye and me can be very happy together. And we have Boycam to thank!'

Interview with Skye Blue

'I was so ashamed. All through the six weeks I spent in the house, I was trying to sway the voting. I had to win at all costs. I don't know why I felt like that. Even if I'd lost, the attendant fame from doing the show would have been good for me. It was so stupid, but I just had to do it. As the weeks went on, I kept on trying to influence the other guys, and it seemed to work. I just knew that if I were one of the last two, I would be in with a chance of the money, and if the other guy won then he might even split it.

'In retrospect, it was a damn foolish thing to do, and now I wish I had never done it. I will never know if I could have won on my own merits, and now my name will probably be on everyone's blacklist.

'All I hope is that the guys forgive me when they hear that I told Matt everything, and that Rhys finally was declared the winner. He truly deserved to win, and I hope that he makes good use of the money. He needs to travel the world, to open his eyes to new experiences and new men. He will be a real hit, I just know it. I sincerely hope from the bottom of my heart that he will also forgive me…I can't explain the feelings I have for him. I just want to know that he bears me no malice and that perhaps we can still be friends. I assume that there can be nothing more, as who would want to settle down with a loathsome, lying, despicable toad? Not me.

'I am glad I did the show, and in a way am happy at the outcome. The best man won and the world's biggest arsehole got his come-uppance. I am certain that whatever comes my way in life, I'll never be so stupid again. I have changed, and I'm a different man to the arrogant shithead that went into the Boycam house. I raise my glass to such shows and also to Rhys, a wonderful man with a wonderful character, who has, if he but knows it, a wonderful friend in me.'

More from Sam Stevens:

The Captain's Boy

This tale of homosexual lust centres on Robert, long-limbed lusty son and heir of Lord Marchant. Robert has had a priveleged childhood at Marchant Hall, during which he has only scratched the surface of his sexual capabilities. Now a fine, handsome young man, his sexuality begins to fully awaken. When his father discovers him with the gamekeeper's boy, his horror knows no bounds. He insists that Robert join the Navy forthwith or be disinherited. Unwilling to comply, Robert runs away, only to fall foul of the ruthless press-gangs who roam the ports seeking just such unwary victims and forcing them into the service of His Majesty. At sea, Robert finds he has much to learn about the sexual tastes of seafaring men – and when he and his crewmates are captured by pirates intent on regular man-on-man orgies, he discovers just how far men will happily go in order to satiate their carnal desires.

UK £7.95 US $11.95 (when ordering direct, quote FIC20)
ISBN 1 902644 23 9

Boy Banned

Four young men are about to get the biggest break of their lives. In a hot new boyband, they ride into the pop charts on a wave of sex and success. But they're not like every other clean-cut bunch of cuties: they're gay, they're out, and they're horny as hell.

In this fresh new erotic novel from the author of *The Captain's Boy*, fame is the biggest turn-on of them all.

'You certainly have high opinions of yourselves, I will say that. Now what is your band called?'

Joe crossed his arms and grinned sheepishly at the older man. 'The Big Boys.'

'Interesting name. What's the reason behind that?' Nick gazed unblinkingly at Joe, who returned the stare. 'Well... we liked the name, and it sounds good and er...'

'I hope you live up to your stage soubriquet.'

Paul looked puzzled. 'Our what?'

'Your band name. If you call yourselves big boys, it seems only right and fair that you should be.' A palpable tension seemed to be hovering in the air about the three men.

Joe broke the silence, shifting a little in his seat and spreading his legs slightly, easing himself forward an inch or two, his tight trousers emphasising the bulge within them.

'I've had no complaints so far.'

UK £7.95 US $12.95 (when ordering direct, quote BOY360)
ISBN 1 902644 36 0